Praise for Cynth...

Fall into the historic cadence of Cynthia Roemer's masterful storytelling as she takes you back to the 1800s prairie. Chad and Charlotte will win you over from page one in this heartwarming story of second chances!

— MISTY M. BELLER, BESTSELLING
AUTHOR OF THIS TREACHEROUS JOURNEY

Roemer's spunky heroine, slow-burn romance, and twist of plot left me smiling long after I turned the last page.

— AUTHOR, CARA GRANDLE

With endearing characters and a charming romance, Under Prairie Skies will sweep you away to the 1850's and leave you inspired by God's beautiful redemption.

— AUTHOR, SAVANNA KAISER

Under PRAIRIE SKIES

Prairie Skies Series ~ Book Two

CYNTHIA ROEMER

Scrivenings
PRESS
Quench your thirst for story.
www.ScriveningsPress.com

2020© Cynthia Roemer

Published by Scrivenings Press LLC
15 Lucky Lane
Morrilton, Arkansas 72110
https://ScriveningsPress.com

Printed in the United States of America

Paperback ISBN 978-1-64917-038-5
eBook ISBN 978-1-64917-039-2

Library of Congress Control Number: 2020940041

Cover by Diane Turpin, www.dianeturpindesigns.com

(Note: This book was previously published by Mantle Rock Publishing LLC and was re-published when MRP was acquired by Scrivenings Press LLC in 2020.)

All characters are fictional, and any resemblance to real people, either factional or historical, is purely coincidental.

All scripture is quoted from the King James Version of the Bible.

To my parents,
who taught me how to love the Lord
with all my heart and soul.

Acknowledgments

There are a number of special people I wish to thank who've helped to shape this novel. First and foremost, I thank the Lord for allowing my dream of being a published novelist to become a reality. He is the guiding force behind what I write, and I'm so grateful for His love and mercies. His name be praised!

I wish to thank my husband, Marvin, for his patience and understanding as I spent countless hours at the computer writing, editing, and figuring out this whole book publishing process. I'm so grateful for your love and support.

Thanks to my sons, Glenn and Evan, for all your help in navigating me through unknown technical areas. Thanks for making me laugh and teasing me about being a #1 best-selling mom. I love you both dearly!

I'm so grateful for a loving, Christian family. Thanks for cheering me on and for your love and support as I pursued my dream!

Special thanks to author, Misty Beller, for your wonderful endorsement and to my sweet Skype partners and beta-readers, Savanna Kaiser and Cara Grandle, for your wise counsel, support, and much needed pep-talks. Your friendship is truly a gift from the Lord.

Thanks to my big sis, Lisa Cannon, and friend, Tish Martin, for taking time to advance read the manuscript and share your input. Thanks to my critique partner, Pamela Meyers, for helping to refine my writing skills, for your honesty, your candor, and your encouragement.

Lastly, thanks to the staff at Mantle Rock Publishing: Jerry and Kathy Cretsinger for giving me this opportunity to fulfill a life-long dream, Diane Cretsinger Turpin for her beautiful cover art and typesetting, and editors, Erin Howard and Pam Harris for helping fine-tune my writing and weed out unnecessary words.

Chapter One
PART ONE · THE RETURN

April 14, 1855, Hollister homestead, Illinois

THE SOUND of a spry whistle froze Charlotte Stanton in her tracks. She tightened her hold on her bucket of creek water, eyes narrowing. Her uncle's cabin and property had been vacant for nearly a year. Odd someone would be about.

The whistling grew louder, and Charlotte ducked behind a hickory tree, her heart at her throat. She set her bucket on the ground and peered through the timber in the direction of the sound. Something resembling a deer moved along the timberline.

She swallowed. But, deer didn't whistle.

Craning her neck for a better look, her stomach clenched as the "whistling deer" transformed into the fringed buckskin jacket of a broad-shouldered man. He emerged onto the open prairie, a string of quail draped over one shoulder and a rifle leaning on the other. Long, easy strides carried him closer to her uncle's cabin.

Charlotte whirled around and pressed her back to the hickory tree, heart pounding.

A squatter. Sure as winter gives birth to spring.

She smacked her fist against the rough bark of the tree. Why hadn't she thought to bring her uncle's muzzleloader? Then again, would she have had the gumption to use it? Though Pa had made certain she knew how to shoot a gun, the thought of pulling the trigger, or even pointing the barrel at someone, turned her stomach.

Still, she had to do something. The man was squatting on her uncle's land.

Another glance at the buckskin-clad stranger assured Charlotte she couldn't outrun him. He was as close to the cabin now as she was. She scoured the ground for some sort of defense and spied a good-sized rock wedged in the soil.

She arched a brow. A blow to the head should do it.

Stooping, she pried at the rock, and then paused. She meant to drive the man off, not bludgeon him. Besides, it looked far too heavy to lug all that way.

To her left, lay a blunt shaft of wood about the width of a rifle barrel. Perhaps she could fool the stranger into thinking she had the upper hand. The risky notion seemed her only hope. Snatching up the stick, she lifted her eyes heavenward. *Lord, help me.*

She crouched low and maneuvered her way along the timberline until she'd positioned herself at the man's back. With soft steps, she emerged from the undergrowth, narrowing the gap between herself and the stranger. His steady whistle worked to her advantage, helping to drown out the faint rustle of grass in her approach.

Hands quivering, Charlotte raised the stick then lowered it. Who was she kidding? With those firm muscles, if the man turned, he could easily overpower her.

A few more paces and he'd reach her uncle's cabin. Then there'd be no stopping him.

She lifted her chin and wedged the makeshift gun into the

small of the stranger's back. "Drop the rifle," she ordered, in as gruff and masculine of voice as she could muster.

The young man whipped his face to the side, revealing a square, clean-shaven jaw and a handsome profile. "Hey now, listen boy..."

"Turn around." With a hard swallow, Charlotte jabbed the stick in deeper. "I said drop it."

The man faced forward and stooped to lower his rifle.

Charlotte threw back her shoulders. So far, so good. He'd not seen through her guise. She bent to reach for the gun, only to feel strong hands grip her arm and hurl her through the air in one smooth motion. The sky was still spinning as her back hit the ground with a thud. She cringed, the air expelling from her lungs in a soft moan. With a slow blink, she shook her head, struggling to regain her senses. She squinted into the mid-morning sun, and tried to push herself to a sitting position. The man's shadowed image stared down at her, his firm hold pinning her arms to the ground.

With a frustrated sigh, she lay back, jaw clenched. He'd bested her.

What now?

CHAD AVERY STARED down into the greenest eyes he'd ever seen. Was it fear he sensed in them, or contempt? The young woman in his clutches squirmed for freedom, her crimson red hair accenting the fairness of her skin. Instinctively, he loosened his hold. "Sorry, I thought . . ."

In the same instant, his assailant grabbed for his rifle. He snatched it away, and then stood, holding the gun out of reach. "Now miss, I'm not sure how I got on your bad side, but I've no quarrel with you, so let's not get hostile."

The woman sat up in a huff, brushing dirt from her calico

dress. "You may have no quarrel with me, sir, but I have one with you."

Chad bent to retrieve the string of quail that had fallen to the ground in a heap. "And what might that be?"

"You're trespassing on my uncle's land."

With a nod, he managed a slight grin. Things were starting to make sense. Jed Stanton had mentioned having two daughters, the younger one, Esther, timid and fair-haired, the older a red-headed spitfire. What was her name?

He widened his stance. "You must be Charlotte."

Her emerald eyes flinched, then narrowed. "How do you know my name?"

"Your pa said you had hair to match your fiery spirit."

His words produced a rush of crimson in her cheeks. He tipped his hat then offered her a hand up. "Name's Chad Avery."

Ignoring his outstretched palm, she pushed herself to her feet, her steady glare demanding more.

Chad drew his arm back and cleared his throat. Too bad the young lady's manners didn't match her striking looks. "I bought the old Randall place a few weeks back. House isn't fit to live in just yet. I met your pa in town, and he offered for me to stay here and keep an eye on things till your kinfolk returned."

She rested her hands on her hips. "Funny, he never mentioned such an arrangement to me."

"Never mentioned you comin' round neither, so I reckon that makes us even."

An awkward silence fell between them. It seemed he'd made his point. Glancing at her feet, he spied the stick she'd used to waylay him. He picked it up and shook his head, his gaze shifting from the shaft of wood to the young woman. Taken in by a gal with a stick. A gutsy move on her part. And a careless one for him.

A slight grin touched her lips, and then her expression sobered. "Well, if what you say is true, your time here is short-lived. My uncle is due back in a few days. I've come to ready the cabin."

She crossed her arms, her steady gaze daring him to defy her. No doubt, the spirited beauty meant to boot him out at once. He'd give no argument. Tossing the stick aside, he nodded toward the cabin. "Then I best collect my things and lit on out of here." He looped the string of limp quail over one shoulder and leaned his rifle back on the other, then started toward the cabin.

Soft footsteps trailed to his left, keeping pace, but never nearing. He sensed Miss Stanton's gaze upon him, but when he glanced back, she quickly turned away.

At last, her much more feminine tone cut through the silence. "What brings you to the area, Mr. Avery?" There was an air of distrust in her voice. The young lady was the suspicious sort. He couldn't blame her. She had every right not to trust him.

"Needed a change of scenery, I reckon." He'd no intention of divulging too much and squelching her curious nature. Somehow it humored him to keep the feisty young woman guessing.

Hadn't he a right, after the trick she'd played on him?

As they neared the porch steps, she darted ahead of him then turned to face him, her back to the cabin door. She pointed to his rifle, her wary eyes never leaving his. "The gun stays here. Along with the knife."

One corner of his mouth lifted. She wasn't taking any chances. "Whatever you say, miss." He propped his rifle against the porch beam, then unsheathed his knife from around his waist and laid it on the railing.

She tugged on the latchstring and stepped aside as the door swung open. "I'll wait out here while you collect your things." She eased into the rocker, her emerald eyes trained on his face.

With a nod, he met her gaze, a bittersweet thought sweeping through him.

She was spirited all right.

Like Lauren.

IT HADN'T TAKEN Mr. Avery long to clear out. He appeared to travel light. His shrill whistle had produced a buckskin gelding from the direction of the creek. How had such a fine animal escaped her notice? Mr. Avery saddled the horse and mounted. With a polite tip of his hat and a soft-spoken "Good day miss," he knocked his heels against his horse's flanks and trotted westward.

Charlotte held her post outside her uncle's cabin until he'd ridden some distance away. She stared after him, nearly tripping as she backed her way inside the cabin. What sort of man was this Mr. Avery? A trapper? A drifter? If so, what did he want with the Randall place?

Turning, she heaved a quiet sigh. Long as he was off the premises, it was no concern of hers. She shifted her attention to the trail of boot prints tracking across the dust-coated floor, ones which earlier she'd suspected were her father's. She knit her brow. It appeared Mr. Avery wasn't much on housekeeping. How could a man abide to live in such filth?

She snatched the broom from the corner and gave it a swish back and forth. Why Ma had commissioned her to ready the cabin for her uncle's return she couldn't say. Perhaps it was her penance for not getting along better with her cousin, Becky. In a matter of days, she and Uncle Joseph would return.

Would hard feelings return with them?

She paused and leaned on the broom handle. Such a cozy cabin. What would it be like to marry and tend her own home? At eighteen, she was certainly capable enough to run a household, but other than Norris Pickford, she'd had no willing suitor come to call.

Poor Norris. For months now he'd been set on courting her. Thus far, she'd had a ready excuse not to accept his advances. But, how much longer could she hold him off? There was nothing particularly wrong with him. But then there was nothing all that right either. His timid nature and expanding waistline weren't what she'd envisioned for the man of her dreams.

A hint of a smile touched her lips as she resumed sweeping. What a conspicuous couple they'd make, him with his bright orange hair, alongside her red. Why, any offspring would be destined for some similar hue.

She breathed a low sigh and snapped her broom harder against the floorboards, smearing Mr. Avery's boot prints beyond recognition. Was she too high-spirited and headstrong to warrant any worthy suitors? Would she be forced to settle for less of a love than she hoped for?

The stir of dust began to choke her. She swatted at it with her hand and rushed to open the window. Bending for a breath of fresh air, she caught a glimpse of Mr. Avery just before he topped the ridge and disappeared from view.

She leaned against the windowsill. If not Norris, what sort of man would catch her eye? Someone handsome and strong, yet gentle. A man of faith, with an undying love for her alone. Her eyes moved to the spot on the horizon where the sandy-haired stranger had disappeared, and her heart sped up a notch. He was strong and handsome to be sure. But gentle?

She rubbed her elbow, noting the smudge on her dress from the fall she'd taken. A trace of blood stained her sleeve above a tender spot on her arm. She heaved a soft sigh. The man was much too abrasive for her liking.

And as for a man of faith and undying love? He seemed too much a loner set in his ways to consider a worthy suitor.

Drawing herself from the window, she turned and brushed her hands together. Enough woolgathering. The sooner she got this place in order, the quicker she could leave.

Chapter Two

CHAD RAN his finger over the faces of the woman and young child in the copper-plated photograph. The raven-haired woman smiled back at him, bringing tears to his eyes. A raw ache churned inside him. Had it only been a little over a year? It seemed decades since he'd held her in his arms or heard her lilting laughter.

He rubbed his sleeve over the dusty mantelpiece and set the picture atop it. Leaning against the rough, stone mantel, he pressed his forehead to his arm and stared down at the gray ashes strewn about the fireplace. If he'd only been home that night, they might have been saved.

Squeezing the bridge of his nose, he forced back the moisture burning his eyes. Three short years were all they'd had. Their young son's life had been snuffed out before it'd barely begun. The sound of his giggle still played in Chad's ears, as well as Lauren's sweet lullabies. His kinfolk had urged him to put his loss behind him and start anew. But how could he, when all he'd ever loved had been lost?

Unable to bear the emptiness of their cabin, months of wandering brought him to this place. Here he would build their dream — a cattle farm, with a large garden beside the cabin, and a well for drinking water — like he and Lauren had planned.

He glanced around the broken-down shack, cluttered by splintered timbers and dirt. By summer's end, he'd need a sturdy shelter, whether it meant fixing up this run-down cabin or building a new one. In the meantime, he would bed under the stars, alone with his Creator.

After months of wrestling with God, he'd found solace in the stillness of His presence. And though he ached for companionship, his vow not to love again had burrowed its way deep inside him, sealing off his heart. There were worse things than being alone.

Like suffering another heartbreak.

Heaving a sigh, he took up his rifle. Nothing would get done so long as he moped about feeling sorry for himself. He stepped over a mound of broken mortar, making his way toward the rickety door. The Hollister cabin had been grand while it lasted. Too bad he'd been booted out sooner than he'd hoped. But repairing this cabin could wait. His first order of business would be to replenish his supplies and ready the ranch for his herd.

His stomach rumbled. Last night's quail no longer satisfied. He'd nothing here but a can of beans and a few chunks of venison jerky, neither of which sounded appealing. He needed to stop in at the mercantile and restock. And while he was at it, maybe he could catch a bite at the restaurant in town.

He stepped outside, casting a glance at the lonely horizon. How was Miss Stanton faring after her hard fall? The feisty young lady had done her best to waylay him, and had pert near accomplished her goal. In fact she had accomplished it. She'd sent him packing.

A smile tugged at his lips. She was likely to have a few bruises to show for it.

He pulled Buck's saddle from the porch rail and looped his

arms underneath. The Stanton place was on the way. Maybe he should stop by to check on her.

The question was, would he be welcomed or thrown out on his ear?

CHARLOTTE GROANED and turned on her bed. If there was a place on her that didn't ache, she had yet to find it. And she had that dreadful Mr. Avery to thank. He'd given her quite a tumble. With a soft moan, she stretched out her legs. How could she have been so dim-witted, using a stick to try to outwit a man with a gun? Chad Avery seemed harmless enough, but what if he hadn't been?

A shiver rippled through her. What if he'd been a ruffian, or a thief?

The whole incident had set her on edge, not to mention robbing her of a good night's rest. Or had she lost sleep over the young man besting her? Though quite handsome, it was his cocky grin that had plagued her dreams. She had no wish to cross paths with him again anytime soon.

What irritated her most was that she'd not had the chance to scold Pa for neglecting to tell her about Mr. Avery. Perhaps today she'd get the chance. She vaguely recalled hearing the door open late last night and his and Ma's hushed voices wafting up into the loft. Always a bit bone weary after his logging trips, Pa would likely sleep half the morning. She'd bide her time, then broach the topic of Mr. Avery.

Prying open tired eyes, Charlotte glanced at Esther still asleep beside her. How she envied her sister's golden locks and sweet disposition. Barely fifteen, Esther seemed to catch the eye of every boy her age or older. Nary a social event passed by without her being sought out and doted on by friends, as well as would-be suitors.

Charlotte slipped from the bed and took up the small looking glass on the wash stand. Flashing her best smile, she peered at herself in the mirror. It wasn't that Esther was so much more attractive. Other than the difference in hair and eye color, they shared similar features. Yet, Charlotte seemed to lack the inner draw her sister possessed.

Her smile faded as she slid the mirror back on the wash stand. Perhaps Esther's closeness with their cousin, Becky, had grated at Charlotte too. From the start, she'd disliked the idea of sharing her family with Becky. Especially where Pa was concerned. Charlotte and he had always shared a special bond. Watching him coddle Becky, in the short time she'd stayed with them, had unleashed a fierce possessiveness within Charlotte. Even knowing Becky had lost her own mother and sister hadn't stemmed the jealous tendencies. Somehow the gravity of the loss hadn't fully sunk in . . . until too late. By then, the damage had been done.

She could only pray things would be different once Becky returned.

The white light of morning filtered through the small loft window, displaying more clouds than sunlight. The crackle of kindling below, accompanied by a faint ashy smell, hinted Ma was stoking the fire for breakfast. Charlotte washed her face, then retrieved her calico dress from the dresser drawer. She rubbed a hand over her sore backside. The thought of tackling the extra chores she'd taken on in Pa's absence seemed almost more than she could manage this morning. Yet, after countless hours of work and travel, he was sure to be bone tired.

How she wished he'd give up these logging ventures. Though he made more money each trip than from a season's worth of crops, it wasn't worth the toll it took on him. Or the rest of them, for that matter. Ma fretted something awful from the time he rode out until he returned.

"Did Pa make it back?" Esther stirred and sat up with a yawn, her soft voice slicing through Charlotte's thoughts.

"He made it. And you'd best get moving' if you're gonna get your chores done before he wakes."

Throwing off her linen sheet, Esther swiveled her legs over the side of the bed. "I don't mind the chores, so long as I don't have to go to school."

Miss Prescott's abrupt departure two weeks ago had left the students without an instructor, forcing them to cancel school. Strange she'd left so sudden-like, without a word of explanation. Everyone had such high hopes she and Pastor Brody were headed toward matrimony. Charlotte swirled her braid into a bun and pinned it in place. "You'll have a new teacher soon enough. Pa being on the town board, he'll see to it something's done."

Rubie's spry bark sounded outside the cabin. Through the window, Charlotte spied the red and white Border collie at the edge of the yard, ears tipped forward. The dog had a language all her own — a high-pitched bark to acknowledge a friendly visitor, a sharp yelp to warn something was amiss, and a low growl to alert them of strangers. Oddly, this bark seemed a mixture of all three.

"Who is it?"

"Don't know." Charlotte strained to see what held Rubie's attention. A lone horseman appeared on the far side of the outbuildings. He sat tall in the saddle, his buckskin mount approaching at a lively clip. Recognition washed over Charlotte, and her pulse quickened. "What's he doing here?"

"Who?" Esther scrambled for a look.

"Never mind. Get yourself dressed." Pushing past her, Charlotte snatched up her shawl and started down the loft ladder. Each painful movement gave her more incentive to see Mr. Avery on his way.

Hushed tones sounded in the dim, back corner of the cabin. Ma's frantic whispers reaped only faint baritone grunts from Pa.

Charlotte paused at the bottom rung. No sense disturbing his sleep for the likes of Mr. Avery. She'd ousted him once. She could send him on his way again. "I'll see to the visitor, Ma."

"Charlotte! You wait for your pa." Ma's tone grew sharper, her footsteps edging closer.

Charlotte hesitated. Somehow she'd escaped her mother's cautious, worrisome nature and clung to Pa's bold, voracious ways. "No need to fret, Ma. The man's harmless."

Just a nuisance.

Ignoring Ma's promptings, Charlotte swung the door open and stepped out onto the porch, the crisp morning air biting at her exposed skin. Rubie's bark intensified at sight of her, a sign of her protectiveness. A light haze lined the creek and low spots, accenting Mr. Avery's broad-shouldered frame. He was indeed handsome, with his sandy hair and chiseled jaw. Charlotte struggled not to stare.

He tipped his hat, his steely gray eyes boring into her. "Miss Stanton."

A shiver ran through her. She clutched her shawl tighter to her chest and stepped from the porch. "What can I do for you, Mr. Avery?"

He leaned forward in his saddle. "My apologies for coming by so early. I have business in town. Thought I'd stop by to see how you were faring after your…fall yesterday."

Charlotte tried to stem the flow of warmth in her cheeks. Did he mean to humiliate her all over again? Her chin lifted. "I'm quite well, thank you, despite your display of brute strength," she lied.

The slightest movement in his features hinted her jab had found its mark. "I'm afraid you left me little choice."

A faint smile pulled at her lips. That she'd fooled him for even a short time gave her great satisfaction. "I simply did what I had to under the circumstances."

"As did I." His tone remained friendly, though the tension in his jaw seemed to deepen.

Charlotte rubbed her arms against the chill. This conversation was leading nowhere. Best to end it now. "Thank you for stopping by, Mr. Avery. Good day to you."

She pivoted toward the cabin as the door eased open. Pa's large frame flanked the doorway. He raked a hand over his red beard, tired circles lining his eyes. Charlotte tensed inwardly. Why had Ma insisted on rousing him? She'd had no trouble handling the situation. A minute more and Mr. Avery would have been on his way.

Pa stepped out onto the porch, his face parting in a smile. He stared past Charlotte to the man at her back. "Mornin', Avery. What brings you over our way?"

Charlotte slowed her pace, listening for the man's reply. Surely he'd refrain from mentioning their encounter from yesterday. Although it might not hurt Pa to know the disgrace he'd put her through. Not to mention the pain.

"Just passing through on my way into town. When'd you get back?"

"Late last night." With a nod, Pa leaned into the porch beam. "How's that place of yours coming along?"

"Slow. I'm on my way in to pick up more supplies."

Charlotte edged closer to her father, resisting the urge to turn and face Mr. Avery. Perhaps he'd take the hint and leave.

Yet, Pa motioned over his shoulder. "We was about to eat a bite of breakfast. Have time to join us?"

Brief silence blanketed the cool, April morning. Charlotte cringed, her father's eager invitation squelching her hopes. Though he seemed oblivious to her, she kept her eyes trained on his face and waited for the man's response.

"I'd be obliged."

Charlotte shot another glare at her father. Yet it, too, went unnoticed. It was difficult being miffed at someone who continued to ignore her.

The creak of Mr. Avery's saddle hinted he was dismounting. Charlotte strode inside without a backward glance. If she had to endure the man's company, she'd do it with as much grace and poise as she could muster.

And as little talking as necessary.

"Where do you hale from, Mr. Avery?"

Chad swallowed his bite of biscuit, meeting Mrs. Stanton's inquisitive gaze. "Benton County, Tennessee. Just west of the Big Sandy River."

"Sounds beautiful. Whatever caused you to leave?"

He pressed down the hurt and heartache the question resurrected. Did all the Stanton womenfolk require a reason for his coming? Straightening, he pushed his empty earthenware plate aside. "Reckon I needed a fresh start, ma'am."

Jed leaned back in his chair with a grin. "He's bought the ol' Randall place to fix up."

Chad sensed himself relaxing. At least he had the approval of one member of the family.

"The Randall place?" Mrs. Stanton's face pinched. "Why that old shack has set empty ten years or better. Wouldn't be fit for coons."

Chad crossed his arms. It may not be much of a place, but it was all he had. "Needs some repair, but seeing as it's just me, I'll make do."

His gaze flicked to Charlotte, who was busy tracing her finger along a crack in the oak table. She seemed strangely subdued compared to the vivacious personality he'd witnessed earlier. Had he offended her? Or was she still licking her wounds from yesterday?

"Gonna have himself a cattle farm." Jed puffed out his chest like a proud father.

"A cattle farm?" Charlotte's eyes were on Chad now. By the look on her face, the words had escaped before she could stop them. She pursed her lips as if stifling more. Her younger sister leaned in closer, seeming equally intrigued, but saying nothing.

Mrs. Stanton poured him a cup of coffee. "That's quite an undertaking for one person."

"Yes, ma'am." The words caught in his throat. To go it alone had never been his plan. But what choice did he have? He had a promise to keep.

Jed rested his arms on the table, cradling his cup. "How many head you figure on having?"

"Thirty for starters. But in time, I hope to own several hundred."

Charlotte's eyes sparked of interest. "But there are no cattle herds around. Where will you get them?"

"There's a drive pushing through north of here in a few weeks on their way from Sedalia, Missouri to Chicago. I've made plans to meet up with them." Chad finished off his coffee and scooted his chair back. "Got a lot of work to do before then, so I'd best be on my way."

Jed rose along with him. "I'd be happy to help you out when I'm able. Just give me a holler."

"Thanks. I may just take you up on that." Chad reached out his hand, and Jed gave it a shake. Donning his hat, Chad turned to Mrs. Stanton. "Much obliged for the victuals."

She nodded. "You're quite welcome, Mr. Avery. The best to you in your venture."

"Thank you, ma'am." He shifted his gaze to Esther, then Charlotte. "Nice to meet you, Miss Esther, and to see you again, Miss Charlotte."

All eyes trained in Charlotte's direction. Her cheeks pinked, and she flashed him a pointed stare. Obviously she hadn't shared yesterday's encounter with the rest of them. As he turned to leave, Chad couldn't help but think he'd just given her one more reason not to like him.

"WHAT DID he mean 'see you again'? Have you met before?" The heightened tone of Ma's voice hinted of uneasiness.

Charlotte cringed. Mr. Avery was barely out the door. He was certain to have heard the inquiry. She glanced out the window, waiting until he'd mounted before responding. "Wasn't my doing. Pa neglected to tell us he'd given Mr. Avery free rein of Uncle Joseph's land. Found him traipsing his way to the cabin with a line of quail yesterday."

Dare she tell how he'd thrown her to the ground and nearly knocked the wind out of her?

Ma's eyes widened as she turned her gaze on Pa. "What's this? You gave a stranger permission to stay on Joseph's property?"

Looping her arms together, Charlotte smiled a knowing grin. This was exactly why she hadn't broached the issue while Mr. Avery was here. She'd wanted to see Pa scolded, but not in the presence of strangers.

Her father's brow furrowed, and he slapped his palm to his forehead. "I plumb forgot to mention about the lad."

Ma's hands flew to her hips. "He could have been a thief for all you knew."

Pa shrugged. "Seemed a right nice fella to me. Took to him like a fly to sorghum when I met him in town. He had no decent place to stay, and I knew I'd be away and unable to keep an eye on the place. Seemed the thing to do, Joseph's cabin sittin' empty and all."

"If he'd been another sort of man, he might have harmed

Charlotte." Ma turned in her direction and shuddered, convincing Charlotte it was best not to share the full events of yesterday.

Pa raised a finger, a lilt in his voice. "Ah, but he didn't."

Charlotte suppressed a grin at her mother's audible sigh. She had to admit, other than the aches and bruises he'd given her, Mr. Avery appeared to be the trustworthy sort. He'd given her no qualms about leaving when asked and even had the courtesy to stop by to check on her. Perhaps, outside of his air of secrecy, Pa had him pegged right.

She braced her hands on her father's shoulders, coming to his defense. "No harm done. He's gone now. I told him Uncle Joseph is returning, and he packed up and left."

Pa patted her hand. "There, you see? All's taken care of."

Ma's lips worked back and forth as though she were going to speak, then a slight grin edged across them. She reached to tousle Pa's wavy, red hair. "You've more nerve than you're deserving of, the both of you."

Lifting his head, Pa winked at Charlotte. She leaned to kiss his cheek, her angst forgotten. There was something about her father that wouldn't let her stay upset.

She glanced through the window at the tiny figure on the horizon. Given time, perhaps the same could prove true of Mr. Avery.

Chapter Three

"HELLO IN THE HOUSE!" Pastor Brody's familiar deep voice called from outside the cabin.

With a glance out the window, Ma unfastened her apron. "They're here."

An uncomfortable tingle trickled through Charlotte at the sound of the wagon coming to a stop in front of the cabin. The terrible way she and Becky had parted bludgeoned her thoughts. They'd barely spoken for weeks before Becky left, then she was gone, without a chance for Charlotte to voice her regrets.

Tempering her uncertainty, she followed the rest of the family out to greet the travelers. She stood at a distance as Pastor Brody helped Becky from the wagon. In her fine dress and with her hair swirled beneath her bonnet, her cousin looked far different from the sorrowful country girl of a year ago. Instead, she looked vibrant and alive, almost glowing. Even Uncle Joseph seemed the picture of health, though his eyes remained downcast and his hair a shade grayer.

Quick strides landed Pa beside Becky. His jade-green eyes widened as he took her in head to toe. "Well now, ain't you a sight for sore eyes, all growed up and purtier than moon glow?"

He lifted her in a spin, and a soft giggle spilled from Becky. She tugged her bonnet into place as her feet landed on the ground. "It's great to be home."

Ma reached to hug her, followed by Esther, both bearing huge smiles. Something within Charlotte balked. Try as she may, she couldn't get past the awkwardness her cousin's presence emanated. Hopefully, in time, things would get easier.

As the others moved to greet her uncle, Charlotte forced a grin and edged toward Becky. "Welcome back."

"Thank you, Charlotte." Becky leaned forward, arms extended. Charlotte met her cousin with a stiff embrace. Why could she not shake this stilted feeling? Would she never get past it?

They parted just as Pa gave Uncle Joseph a hearty slap on the back. His gaze shifted to Becky. "Sure am glad to have you folks back. Just wasn't the same around here without you."

Uncle Joseph grinned and leaned against the wagon wheel. "Not half so glad as we are to be here."

Ma tugged on his arm. "Come in and sit a spell. We've a lot of catching up to do."

"If you don't mind, we'd like to head on home and rest up. Just wanted you to know we made it back. We'll visit another time."

"We'll count on it. In fact, we'll have us a coming home shindig you'll not soon forget."

Uncle Joseph scratched at his chin. "No need for a lot of fuss."

Pa's light-hearted chuckle split the air. "Now you know Clara ain't gonna let a chance to celebrate slip by. She and the girls have had their hearts set on it ever since you sent word you were comin'."

Uncle Joseph pursed his lips and gave an affirming nod. "Reckon it would be nice to catch up with folks. Just give us a few days to get settled."

"Will do. That'll give us time to spread the word."

Pastor Brody pushed back his broad-brimmed hat. "While you're at it, let it be known we'll have services this Sunday. I guarantee it'll be worth everyone's while to be there."

"What is it? What's the news?" Ma never could let a good secret go unrevealed.

He held up a hand. "Sunday."

Pink rose in Becky's cheeks as she shared a playful grin with the pastor. Charlotte gnawed at her lip. What hidden secret did they share? Judging by Uncle Joseph's wide smile, he seemed in on the little ruse. Yet it was clear the rest of them would have to wait.

CHAD PULLED BACK on the drawknife, sending another shaving of bark to the ground. The shaft of white oak was among the straightest and finest he'd cut yet. He wiped his sweaty brow with his sleeve and stared down the lengthening row of split-rail fence. If all went well, in a few weeks he'd be ready for his herd. Thirty head would be a good start for his eighty-acre plot. It would take nearly all he and Lauren had scraped together, along with what little he had left from the sale of their property in Tennessee.

He blew out a long breath and returned to work. The dream of a cattle ranch seemed hollow without Lauren. He'd been missing her more of late. Their young son too. Charlotte Stanton reminded him so much of Lauren. Not in appearance as much as in her zest for life and her fiery nature. A woman needed a lot of grit out here on the prairie. Anything less wouldn't hold up.

He tossed the bare log aside and reached for another. A cantering horse sounded in the distance, and Chad stood upright, rifle at the ready. His tense muscles relaxed as the rider raised a hand in greeting. The red beard could belong to none other than Jed Stanton.

Laying his tool aside, Chad strode to meet him, the unexpected visit a welcome interruption to his day. "Didn't expect to see you quite so soon."

Jed brought his horse to a stop and leaned forward in his saddle. "I'm afraid I can't stay. Just wanted to let you know Pastor Brody made it back with the Hollisters. We're planning a homecoming shindig for them next Saturday evening. You're more than welcome to join us."

"Much obliged." The invitation couldn't be more than a polite gesture on Jed's part. Chad hadn't even met the Hollisters. Though, having stayed out on their place a number of weeks, he almost felt as though he knew them.

"The preacher says there's to be church services in the morning and that whoever comes won't be disappointed."

"Is that so?" Truth was, any more, being around people didn't set right with Chad. They asked too many questions. Communing with God alone in nature suited him much better. Yet, totally isolating himself wasn't right either.

Jed glanced over the property. "Looks like you've got your work cut out for you."

"That I do." He'd been torn knowing where to start first. Fencing in the yard and repairing the barn had won out over fixing up the rundown cabin. Any roof over his head would do for the time being, at least till cold weather hit. His first priority was getting the barn and pasture ready for his cattle.

Jed sat taller in the saddle, tightening his hold on the reins. "Wish I could stay and help, but Clara wants me to spread the word. I'll do my best to lend a hand early next week." He chuckled. "That is if Clara doesn't claim me first."

With a grin, Chad took up his drawknife.

Jed clicked his tongue and wheeled his horse eastward. "Gotta keep the womenfolk happy." He let out a laugh, calling over his shoulder as he trotted away. "But then, I don't guess you've had to worry about a wife to please."

Chad nodded, his smile dying away. A vision of Lauren dressed in her wedding gown flashed across his mind, her wide smile and blue eyes slicing through him even now. No bride ever looked lovelier.

He scuffed the toe of his boot against the ground. Being alone hadn't been his choice. Scripture said it wasn't good for man to be alone. If that were true, why had the Lord allowed Lauren to be taken?

Engaged?

Had Charlotte heard right? Pastor Brody and Becky were to be married?

Whispered silence swept through the congregation, hinting others too were dumbfounded by the unexpected announcement. No wonder Miss Prescott had left town in a hurry, leaving students without a teacher. Everyone had anticipated she and Pastor Brody were headed for matrimony. How could they have been so wrong?

Pastor Brody held his hand out to Becky on the front row, and she rose to stand beside him. He slid an arm around her waist, a brilliant smile lining his lips. Charlotte gave a half-hearted clap as the congregation broke into thunderous applause. Her father put his fingers to his mouth, producing a shrill whistle. With a chuckle, he nudged her arm. "If that don't beat all."

Charlotte pasted on a smile, inwardly chiding herself for not being happy for her cousin. After all the hardship Becky had suffered, the Lord seemed to be blessing her beyond measure. Charlotte felt a bit like one of Job's disgruntled friends, casting blame onto Becky when the Lord seemed pleased with her.

"When's the wedding, preacher?" someone shouted, pulling Charlotte from her thoughts.

Pastor Brody shared a tender look with Becky, then glanced over the congregation. "We'll let you know."

Charlotte peered over the shoulders of those seated in front of her, drawn by the sparkle on Becky's collar. Though she couldn't quite make out the shiny object, it appeared to be some sort of brooch or pendent. Its shape resembled the jeweled cross Pastor Brody had given Miss Prescott.

Charlotte laced her fingers together in her lap. Surely he hadn't given the same brooch to two women. There was something odd about the whole situation. Away for nearly a year, how could Becky have possibly won the pastor's heart?

The congregation began to filter out into the aisles, forming a line to congratulate the couple. Esther pulled at Charlotte's arm. "Isn't it wonderful? Let's go greet them."

With bated steps, Charlotte followed Esther to the end of the line. Her sister's charitable spirit never ceased to amaze her. Perhaps that was some of the reason Esther's company was so sought after. In her soft, gentle way, she continually put others ahead of herself.

Several of Esther's school friends waved to her or stopped to chat. Charlotte had nothing else to do but edge forward in line and glance around the crowded room. She craned her neck toward the back of the church, catching a glimpse of Mr. Avery's back as he slipped out the door. There was no mistaking his smooth, sandy hair and muscular frame.

She stared after him, wondering what incited him to go against the flow of people to rush away. Was he in such a hurry to return home, or did he have plans to meet someone? Mystery seemed to shroud their new neighbor.

"If I may have everyone's attention a moment." Her father stepped to the front. "For those of you who haven't heard, Clara asked me to invite you all to our place this Saturday to celebrate

Joseph and Becky's return." He pointed toward Pastor Brody and Becky. "Now the preacher's given us one more reason to kick up our heels."

Laughter rippled through the congregation. Charlotte glanced out the window in time to see Mr. Avery mount and ride away. Part of her couldn't help but wish he'd heard the announcement. But, with the awkward way she felt around him, perhaps it was just as well he wouldn't be there.

A flash of orange to her left caught Charlotte's eye. Trapped in a web of well-wishers, Norris Pickford simply smiled at her and waved. Charlotte lifted her hand in a half-hearted gesture.

Then again, the newcomer's presence might have proven interesting.

Chapter Four

CHAD TIGHTENED the cinch on Buck's saddle, then slid the stirrup into place. No doubt he'd be a bit late for the Hollister coming home party. Why Jed had gone out of his way to invite him Chad couldn't say. He had no business going. After all, he didn't even know the Hollisters. But to decline wouldn't seem neighborly. Jed had been good to him.

Still, the last thing he wanted was to tangle with Miss Stanton again. Attractive as Charlotte was, she seemed spoiled and petty, not the type he'd pursue, even if he was in the market for a wife.

Which he wasn't.

The best he could do was to make himself scarce when she was around.

He mounted and glanced over the section of fence he'd been working on. Even with Jed's help earlier in the week, it had taken longer than expected to finish. Clara Stanton was right. The place wasn't fit for coons. The entire homestead was badly in need of repair. Once he'd built the yard fence, fixed up the barn, and purchased supplies, he'd worry about the cabin. There was nothing much of value in it anyway. Other than the picture of Lauren and their son and the few items they'd shared. Nothing else mattered. It could be carried off, and he'd hardly miss it.

With a sigh, he tapped his heels in Buck's flanks. Best to get this over with. He'd arrive late and leave early, same as church service. The less opportunity people had to probe into his past, the better.

CHARLOTTE STEPPED OUTSIDE THE CABIN, a bowl of cider clasped in her hands. The air was thick with the spicy scent of pork from the hog roasting on a spit at the front of the cabin. Several neighbors had already gathered, awaiting Uncle Joseph and Becky's arrival. Esther flitted around like a butterfly decorating the row of tables with jars of blue phlox laced with spring beauties. Charlotte shook her head. Must her younger sister be in such high spirits?

She set the bowl of cider at the center of the far table and scooped some of the liquid refreshment into tin cups. A soft breeze heralded the array of instruments being strummed and tuned for the outdoor festivities. Spurts of laughter and spry conversation drifted from various corners of the yard. Charlotte swiped at a spilled drop of cider on the table. Everyone seemed enamored by the reason for the gathering.

Not her. She would just as soon be somewhere else.

The sound of a wagon, followed by excited voices, alerted her that the guests of honor had arrived. Pa gave the hog spit a turn, then bounded over to greet them along with the rest. Charlotte lingered behind, straightening the cups of cider. Her cousin's return drudged up unwanted memories that left her stomach in knots. Her shoulders sagged. Was she so wrought with jealousy that she couldn't forget past grievances and be happy for Becky?

Pastor Brody slowed the rig to a stop at the edge of the cabin, a huge grin lining his lips. Like the soon-to-be groom he was, he sat tall on the wagon seat, Becky and Joseph wedged in beside him. It was all too incredible. Soon Becky would be a pastor's wife, holding a position of respect and high-esteem within the community. Already Charlotte sensed the excitement in the air. Could she stomach all the attention her cousin was certain to garner?

All smiles, Becky lifted her hand in greeting. Pastor Brody hopped from the wagon, then turned to help her down. The tender look they shared left no doubt to their affection for each other. How it had all come about was a mystery Charlotte had yet to unravel. She lifted a brow, her gaze again darting to the brooch on Becky's collar. Had Miss Prescott chosen to give it back, making Becky the pastor's second choice?

Pastor Brody helped Charlotte's uncle find his footing, but allowed him to climb from the wagon on his own. His hair had grown back, making it difficult to distinguish a scar left by his head wound. Though his blinded eyes tipped downward, he bore a confidence he'd lacked when he'd left a year ago for the school for the blind.

Becky moved to her father's side, looping her arm through his while Pastor Brody drove the wagon out back of the cabin.

Esther gave their cousin a heartwarming hug. "It's so good to have you back. I can't wait to hear more about your trip."

"I look forward to it." Becky released her hold and stood at arm's length, gingerly clasping Esther's fingertips. "My, but you've changed."

A wide smile played on her lips. "What about you? You're so lady-like."

Becky tugged at her dress sleeve. "A bit of my Aunt Ellen's talented handiwork."

Charlotte dropped her gaze, aching to feel a part of their closeness. But how could she? She'd done nothing to warrant such a bond. Nor had she any wish to.

Until now.

As others swarmed to welcome them, Charlotte stood back, suppressing the urge to hideaway inside the cabin until the guests had left. Ma strolled up beside her and held out a pot of boiled potatoes. "Set this on the table over there, will you? I want to go say hello to Joseph and Becky."

Taking the warm crock, Charlotte stared after her. Cheerful shouts rang out as her mother pushed her way through to the newcomers. A pang of envy trickled through Charlotte. Here she was a mere servant in her own home, while Becky was being treated like a queen. She turned away and trudged to the tables with the crock of potatoes.

Others arrived, toting savory dishes, until the tables teemed with fried chicken, sweet potatoes, corn fritters, homemade bread, and every sort of pie imaginable. One by one, neighbors filed by to pay their respects to the travelers. Not yet ready to face her cousin, Charlotte busied herself arranging the food and visiting with those she hadn't seen in some time.

At last, Pa strode to the forefront, his shrill whistle cutting through the chatter. "Well now that everyone's here, we'll have the blessing and dig in. Pastor Brody, will you do the honors?"

"Gladly," the preacher's familiar baritone voice hailed from across the yard.

Pink spilled into Becky's cheeks as he clasped her hand. Charlotte bowed her head. What would it be like to truly hold someone's heart? Would she ever know true love?

The blessing said, Charlotte opened her eyes and edged back, allowing the guests to file in first. As she surveyed the crowd, she found herself inadvertently seeking out a certain sandy-headed stranger. Instead, Norris Pickford's orange hair flashed at her from across the yard. Though steeped in conversation with Lola Brimmer, he motioned as though trying to catch Charlotte's eye. She pretended not to notice, allowing her gaze to drift past him. Though a bit rotund, Miss Brimmer had a pleasant personality and, as far as Charlotte knew, was unattached. Perhaps if left to themselves, the young lady might eventually win him over and throw him off Charlotte's trail.

One could only hope.

Charlotte spied Becky mingling about, her wheat-blond hair tied in a loose bun beneath her bonnet and her well-fitted dress accenting her slender frame. She had to admit, her cousin looked the part of a pastor's wife, flitting from one person to the next.

Becky's eyes locked on hers, and a lump rose in Charlotte's throat. She averted her gaze, hoping the strain between them wasn't evident to anyone who might be looking on.

By now, the line had depleted enough that she was able to move through to fill her plate. Peals of laughter filled the night air as the band instigated a lively tune. The tables full, Charlotte found a spot at the corner of the cabin to stand and eat. She tapped her foot, smiling as old Doc Pruitt tugged silvery-haired Annabelle to her feet for a dance. Other couples soon followed suit. Charlotte swayed to the music as she nibbled her chicken leg, savoring the first moment of true enjoyment she'd had.

"Hey, Charlotte," a man's nasal voice rang out above the music.

She tensed at sight of Norris strolling toward her. Perhaps she could slip around the corner of the cabin and lose herself among the horses and wagons. But, Norris already had her in his sights. Unless she intended on being completely rude, there was no getting around him. Pasting on a smile, she squared her shoulders and turned to greet him.

"How about a dance, Charlotte?"

She motioned to her plate. "I'm afraid I'm not finished eating."

Norris' smile deepened. "Oh, I can wait."

Charlotte grinned and stifled a chuckle as she focused on what looked to be either dandelion greens or spinach wedged in his teeth. Glancing at her plate, she pinched off a bite of chicken.

Perhaps if she stalled, Norris would lose interest and find another dance partner.

"Mighty fine night for a hog roast." He leaned in closer, gripping his suspenders.

"Yes it is." Charlotte veered back, still toying with the sliver of meat between her fingertips. She had a feeling her companion wasn't going anywhere without a little prompting. She ventured a glance in his direction, then immediately looked away. "I noticed you and Lola Brimmer were enjoying nice conversation. Perhaps she's finished eating and would like to share a dance."

"Mmm, after a while, maybe. I'm saving my first dance for you."

Heat rose in Charlotte's cheeks as he edged still closer. Popping the chicken in her mouth, she chewed much faster than necessary. She shifted her weight to the side, and her shoulder knocked against a passerby, throwing her off balance.

A strong hand gripped her forearm, steadying her. "Pardon me."

Turning, she gave a soft gasp at sight of Mr. Avery standing beside her. No longer clad in buckskin, he wore a loose-fitting white shirt and necktie. He stood a full head taller than she, with firm, broad shoulders. Even in the dim light of evening, his silvery eyes seemed to bore into her.

Releasing his hold, he tipped the brim of his hat, his expression somber. "Miss Stanton."

Charlotte gave a slow nod. In the flurry of activity, somehow she'd missed his arrival. Had he just now come?

Without another word, he turned and sauntered in her father's direction. Charlotte stared after him, a bit breathless and unable to determine if she were happy to see him or if the pitch in her middle had more to do with her waning appetite. Mr. Avery looked about as enthused to be here as she was. At sight of him, a smile lit her father's face, and he strolled to meet the newcomer. Mr. Avery's expression eased slightly as her father directed him to the tables of food.

"Who's that feller?"

Charlotte broke off her stare and returned her attention to Norris. "What? Oh. Mr. Chad Avery. A new neighbor of ours. Just recently moved here from Tennessee."

Norris watched the newcomer with guarded interest. "Seems awful friendly with your pa." There was an edge in his voice that hadn't been there before.

Charlotte took a sip of cider and followed his gaze. "They seem to have hit it off."

Turning to face her, Norris let out a sigh. "If you ain't gonna eat, we may as well dance."

Charlotte glanced at her half-full plate. He was right. She had no appetite. And obviously he wasn't going to leave without a dance. May as well get it over with. She set her cup and plate on the edge of a table and allowed him to take her hand. As his clammy fingers fastened around hers, she wished more than ever she could persuade him to take up with Lola Brimmer.

The setting sun cast a shadow over the prairie as she and Norris moved to the lively beat. His smile returned, along with the smidgen of green wedged in his teeth. Stifling a grin, Charlotte fixed her gaze over his shoulder. She ran her tongue over her own teeth to ensure she wasn't displaying a similar distraction.

At the corner of the yard, Pastor Brody, Becky, and Charlotte's uncle had joined her father and Mr. Avery in conversation. He paused from eating long enough to shake the pastor's hand. As other prominent members of the community joined the gathering, Charlotte itched to be included. Could she somehow shorten the dance or persuade Norris to abandon her for someone else?

A sudden scuff of her partner's shoe against the toe of her

boot gave birth to inspiration. Perhaps she could carelessly allow him to step on her.

No. He would never leave her side if he thought he'd injured her. It would be more profitable to convince him she'd done something foolish to injure herself.

That was it. The perfect solution. Another twirl about, and she'd have her out.

Following Norris's lead, she widened her smile and swayed to the music. Then, with a quiet gasp, she stumbled forward.

He clutched her arm, his brow creased. "You all right?"

Cringing, Charlotte leaned to one side and held her foot at an angle. "I'm afraid I've twisted my ankle."

His worried gaze shifted from her to the line of tables. "Can you walk?"

"I think so." With his assistance, she hobbled to an empty seat. It was easy to feign injury, for in her attempt to fool Norris, she'd put enough strain on her ankle to feel the pull. She plopped down on the wooden bench with a sigh and scanned the crowd for the one person she hoped would prove a worthy diversion.

Warm relief flowed through Charlotte as she spied Lola standing along the sidelines, looking a bit forlorn. She glanced their way, and her mouth grew taut, almost pouty. She seemed to watch them with interest.

Charlotte arched a brow. This looked promising. Was Lola envious of the attention Norris was giving her?

Norris bent to take a seat beside her, and Charlotte gave him a gentle upward nudge, pointing in Lola's direction. "N-no need for you to miss out on account of me. I'm sure Miss Brimmer would be most willing to dance in my stead."

His gaze flicked from Charlotte to Lola, then back again. "Oh, but I couldn't just leave you here."

Charlotte stopped rubbing her ankle and straightened. "Nonsense. I'll be fine."

He took a step forward, then hesitated.

Charlotte flashed a smile and waved him on like a mother prompting a young child. She liked to think she wasn't manipulating him, simply spurring him toward a better option.

He made a slow turn, then sauntered away. Charlotte breathed a relieved sigh, watching Lola's face blossom at his approach. As they took to dancing, Norris cast an occasional glance in Charlotte's direction. Halfway through the song, he seemed less preoccupied with her and more engrossed in his partner. Charlotte waited until the song ended and another began before slowly sliding from her place on the bench and making her way to the group of well-wishers surrounding the betrothed couple.

She slipped to her father's side seemingly unnoticed — but for Mr. Avery. His silvery eyes found hers for a brief instant, then darted away. Did he find her presence intrusive, bothersome? His stony expression made it difficult to deduce.

"It would only be a short while, just until it lets out for the summer." Charlotte's father directed the statement at Becky.

She cast a glance at Pastor Brody before answering. "I-I don't know, we've only just returned, and we've the wedding to plan. Besides, who would stay with Pa?"

"I'm sure something could be worked out. At least give it some thought."

At her father's words, Charlotte edged forward. What had she missed? Was he suggesting Becky take over the teaching position for the remainder of the school year? The thought was almost humorous, seeing as she was most likely the reason Miss Prescott hadn't finished her term.

Uncle Joseph crossed his arms in front of him. "Don't let me stop you. If you wanna teach, I'll find some way to bide my time."

Charlotte couldn't resist chiding in. "Becky a teacher? Why, she never even attended school." She sensed Mr. Avery's eyes upon her and could almost feel his displeasure. She dropped her gaze, wondering why it mattered to her.

Her uncle cleared his throat. "Well, she did her fair share of it in St. Louis. Was even asked to stay on to help instruct the blind students. But I reckon Matthew and the Lord had other plans."

Quiet laughter rippled through the group as Becky and Pastor Brody shared a tender smile. Charlotte's cheeks warmed. It seemed, regardless of her ribbing, her cousin wouldn't be discredited in the eyes of the community.

Charlotte's father turned to her as if noticing her for the first time. "What about Charlotte here? She'd make Joseph a right nice companion while you're away."

Charlotte stiffened, meeting her cousin's startled gaze. It was difficult to say whose eyes grew wider, Becky's or her own. Both knew such an arrangement was less than ideal, given their strained relationship.

Charlotte bit at her cheek. Perhaps she'd agree to the idea just to nettle her cousin. She clasped her hands behind her back. "Why, I'd be pleased to spend my days with Uncle Joseph."

Her father grinned, hooking his thumbs in his suspenders. "There now, you see? Problem solved."

Most of the onlookers smiled, apparently thinking Charlotte heroic in her offer. Becky winced, however, and stared at the hem of her dress as though warring within.

Pastor Brody stepped forward, his gaze fixed upon his future bride. Just how familiar he was with her and Becky's past grievances Charlotte couldn't guess. His puzzled expression hinted he knew little.

At last, Becky's eyes lifted. "Can I think about it and let you know?"

"Sure. You just give the word when you're ready." The wide grin on Pa's face sliced through Charlotte like a sharpened blade. Any thoughts she'd had of mending the rift with her cousin fell away.

She cleared her throat. "It's a shame you and our previous teacher, Miss Prescott, didn't have the chance to meet. Not only did you have teaching in common, but an uncanny similar taste in jewelry." She pointed to the brooch on Becky's collar. "I seem to recall Miss Prescott having a jeweled cross just like that one."

All eyes shifted to Becky. They were all witnesses to the fact Charlotte spoke the truth. Becky drew a hand to her brooch, her face paling as she turned a wide-eyed gaze on her fiancé.

Now it was Pastor Brody's turn to redden, but the set of his jaw bordered on irritation rather than embarrassment. He shared a long and loving look with Becky, then slipped an arm around her shoulders. "The brooch was my birthday gift to Becky."

Straightening, Becky drew in a decided breath. "Miss Prescott mistakenly thought it belonged to her."

Charlotte gave a slow nod. "Then it seems only fitting you take her place, since it's more than likely on your account she left."

Becky's eyes flashed, turning fawn-like as she lowered her gaze.

A nervous twinge pricked Charlotte's middle. Even as she spoke the words, she knew she shouldn't have said them. She was making matters worse not better.

"Enough, Charlotte." Her father's reprimand did less to silence her than the unexpected grip on her arm. She teetered sideways, her smile fading at the stern expression lining Mr. Avery's brow. Without a word, he pulled her toward the dancers and drew her into his embrace.

But something told Charlotte he had anything but socializing on his mind.

Chapter Five

CHAD TIGHTENED his hold on Charlotte. This was the second time she'd fought to free herself from his grasp in little more than a week. The first time he'd been more than willing to accommodate. But not this time. Not the way she was treating Miss Hollister.

Someone had to put a stop to her shenanigans. Neither her father nor the pastor seemed to have the heart to. Chad, himself, had nothing to lose. Let Charlotte think of him what she wished.

The least he could do was keep her where she could do no further harm.

Her eyes shot daggers at him as they swayed to the music. At last, her chin lifted. "I had no wish to dance with you, Mr. Avery."

He met her gaze, jaw clenched. "That's not important. What matters is you'll no longer be troubling Miss Hollister."

Her lips parted, and her angry glare softened a bit, taking on a more defensive air. "What do you mean troubling her?"

"I don't know what you were referring to back there, but it's plain you meant to embarrass her."

The truth of his words must have swept through his dance

partner for the fire in her eyes extinguished, and her gaze drifted to his shirt. Had she seen the error of her ways?

Heat singed his own cheeks when he realized how close he was holding her. He pulled back, keeping her at arm's length. He'd not danced with anyone but Lauren, before or since.

Until now.

What had possessed him to react so? Was it out of concern for Miss Hollister or a desire to instill a sense of fairness in this spirited young woman who seemed concerned only for herself?

Her head lifted. "You had no right to interfere. You know nothing about me or my cousin."

"I know you well enough to realize you resort to trickery when it serves your purpose."

Her eyes narrowed. "Don't be ridiculous."

Cocking his head to the side, he glanced at her feet. "How's your ankle?"

Her cheeks pinked. "Must you watch my every move, Mr. Avery?"

With a shrug, he nodded to his right. "It appears I'm not the only one curious as to your progress. There's a fella over there who seems a bit intrigued that you've recovered so soon from your injury."

Charlotte followed his gaze, her grip on his shoulder tightening at sight of the orange-headed young man watching them.

The music faded, and Chad loosened his hold on her waist. "If you no longer wish to dance with me, Miss Stanton, I'd be happy to escort you over to your friend."

Chin quivering, Charlotte took a step back. "Excuse me." Her eyes remained downcast as she skirted away from the festivities and rounded the corner of the wood shed.

As the musicians struck up another tune, Chad ambled his way to the sidelines. Perhaps he'd been a bit hard on Charlotte. But then, she seemed the sort who knew how to give a rebuke but was unwilling to take one in return. He'd most likely done her a favor, allowing her the opportunity to see herself through the eyes of a stranger. Beautiful as she was on the outside, it meant nothing if her heart was mean-spirited and self-seeking.

Still, he had to wonder if there was a caring person locked deep inside Charlotte just itching to get out. He just wasn't sure he was the one who needed to find her.

THE NERVE OF THAT MAN.

Charlotte sagged against the buckboard with a frustrated groan. What right did Mr. Avery have to scold her for things he had no part in? He was a mere stranger, a newcomer to these parts. What did he know of the goings on around here?

She dabbed her eyes with her handkerchief and hung her head. Yet, his insight into her was alarming. Had others seen through her insecurities so easily?

Alone, but for the spattering of horses and wagons, she leaned her head against the buckboard and closed her eyes. The faint sound of music and laughter from the front of the cabin ate at her like soured milk. Truth be known, she was as aggravated with herself as she was Mr. Avery. Here she'd vowed to try harder to mend her differences with Becky. And what had she done but fall right back into her old ways.

Forgive me, Lord.

She opened her eyes and stared into the starry sky. Only a faint glimmer of light remained on the western horizon. Before long, she'd be engulfed in darkness, and grateful for it. She didn't deserve to celebrate. Instead, she longed to fade into the vastness of the prairie.

Crossing her arms, she breathed a deep sigh. She didn't need some stranger pointing out her faults. She knew well enough she had flaws. If she had any gumption, she'd offer Becky an apology.

"Charlotte?"

Esther's gentle voice startled Charlotte from her reverie. She swiped a tear from her cheek and stepped from the shadows.

Her sister edged closer. "What are you doing back here?"

"I-I got winded dancing. I needed some air."

A smile lit Esther's face. "He's handsome, isn't he?"

"Who?"

"Mr. Avery. I saw you dancing with him."

Charlotte's face flamed hot. It seemed nothing she did went unnoticed. With a shrug, she set her jaw. "I truly hadn't noticed."

It was a lie. She knew better than Esther how handsome he was. She'd been close enough to see the specks of black in his silvery eyes and feel the warmth of his arm wrapped around her waist. Given other circumstances, she might have melted into his strong embrace.

But as things were, good looking or not, she wanted nothing more to do with him.

CHAD TAPPED his gelding's flanks, prodding him to a trot toward home unable to get the encounter with Charlotte Stanton out of his head. The hurt in her eyes when he'd chided her had settled like bad meat in his stomach. Had he been too hard on her?

She was like a raw piece of wood in need of finishing. Why he'd taken it upon himself to attempt to shave off her rough edges he couldn't say. It seemed the right thing to do at the time. Maybe something he'd said would sink in.

Lauren would have taken to her like an older sister. He leaned back in his saddle, letting his free hand drop to his thigh. Why was it he still filtered everything through his wife's eyes? When you'd pledged your heart to someone for a lifetime, it was hard to let go.

Shifting in his saddle, he peered into the night sky. He'd

stayed longer at the party than planned. Maybe too long where Charlotte was concerned. He'd watched for her to reemerge after disappearing around the corner of the cabin, but to his knowledge, she'd never shown herself. If he'd spoiled her evening, he was sorry. Yet, there were worse things. Like living your life to please yourself at others' expense.

Iron sharpeneth iron, so a man sharpeneth the countenance of his friend. All he'd wanted was for Charlotte to take a look inside herself. He had an inkling if she did, she'd not like what she saw. Despite her angry glares and biting words, for a brief moment, he'd caught a glimpse of shame and remorse in her eyes as though he'd tapped into her hidden spirit.

Only time would tell if he'd ever glimpse it again. Or even if he should.

Chapter Six

CHARLOTTE'S STOMACH lurched as she eyed her cousin standing alongside Pastor Brody at the back of the church building. The service over, Becky greeted the congregation with a warm smile and a handshake as they exited. Her sparkling blue eyes fostered friendliness worthy of a pastor's wife. Pastor Brody gazed down at her in seeming admiration. It was plain the two were deeply in love.

Charlotte held back, letting her parents and sister file out ahead. She knew what she needed to do. Her sleepless night and restless spirit demanded it. Yet the shame of it gnawed at her. Last night, she'd failed miserably. Would she fare any better today?

In attempt to stay preoccupied, she exchanged pleasantries with Mr. and Mrs. Brimmer in line behind her. As she edged closer to the open doorway, she wiped damp palms on her skirt. She didn't quite catch what her father said to cause Pastor Brody and Becky to share a soft chuckle, but their smiles faded as they turned in her direction. Charlotte gave a slight cough, choking down the lump in her throat.

Before Charlotte could find her voice, Becky reached out a

hand. "Good to see you, Charlotte. Would you mind waiting until the others have gone? There's a matter I wish to discuss with you."

Charlotte met her cousin's gaze, caught off guard by the unexpected request. Did Becky plan to put her in her place? She hesitated, then gave a brief nod. The plea seemed innocent enough. It was the unknown reason behind it that bothered her. With a quick shake of Pastor Brody's hand, she pressed forward, abandoning her hopes of trying to make amends.

Finding a quiet spot outside to wait, Charlotte waved her family on to their wagon. The mile and a half walk home would likely be just what she needed after what could prove a heated exchange. She leaned against the sideboards of the church build-ing, sifting through her thoughts. Her planned words having escaped her, she tried to determine why Becky wished to speak with her. To scold her? To implore her to get along?

Chad Avery's chiding words forced their way into her thoughts. She burned inwardly at memory of his candidness. Much as she hated to admit it, he'd been right, not only about the way she'd treated Becky, but Norris as well. Thankfully, Char-lotte hadn't had to face him or Mr. Avery this morning. Norris was either ignoring her out of spite or her hopes of boosting his interest in Lola Brimmer had paid off for they'd sat together in the pew and left in each other's company without so much as a word to Charlotte.

She'd caught a glimpse of Chad after the service, but he'd soon slipped out the door. What a strange sort he was, sneaking off without a word to anyone. Still, she couldn't consider him unsociable or else he wouldn't have come to last night's party or stayed for breakfast at her father's request. He seemed a man of few words, but when he did speak, he had a tendency to cut to the heart of a matter. Those silvery eyes of his possessed a depth that reached inside of her to expose her very soul.

"Thanks for waiting." The gentle voice pulled Charlotte from her thoughts.

She turned, trying not to perceive the worst of her estranged cousin's reasons for wanting to speak with her. Charlotte threw back her shoulders. She had no intention of going through with an apology without knowing why Becky had called her aside. "What is it you wish to speak to me about?"

Becky drew in a breath and wet her lips. Whatever she had to say wasn't proving easy. She squinted against the mid-day sun as she tied on her bonnet. "Were you sincere in saying you'd stay with Pa if I were to finish out the school term?"

Charlotte's eyes widened. Of all the things she'd imagined Becky saying, this wasn't one of them. After all their feuding, would she really entrust her father to Charlotte's care? "I suppose so. Are you considering taking the position?"

"It seems the only way for students to finish their schooling. It's less than a month until classes let out for summer. I'll still have a couple of weeks to plan for our wedding."

"When is it?"

Becky's eyes sparkled, and her face parted in a smile. "The fifteenth of June."

With a slight nod, Charlotte's stomach gripped. Why was it she couldn't rid herself of jealousies where Becky was concerned? She willed herself to shake them off, but couldn't quite bring herself to voice regrets for last night's disgraceful behavior.

"I told Uncle Jed that if you'd be willing to stay with Pa, I'd take the position. Matthew would be happy to escort you to and from my place."

"That won't be necessary. I can ride there just as quick."

"Then you're willing?" Becky's fluctuating tone made it difficult to distinguish if she were happy about the arrangement or amazed.

Charlotte rolled her shoulders. "I reckon, so long as Uncle Joseph doesn't mind."

"He's agreeable. It may take him a bit to readjust to the smallness of the cabin, but he'll do fine, even if you're not yet there when I leave." Becky glanced across the church yard to where Pastor Brody waited with her father. Taking a step back, she gave a slight smile. "I'd best be going. Could you let Uncle Jed know I'll be set to start tomorrow morning?"

Charlotte bobbed her head, unsure how this had all come about. When she mentioned staying with her uncle, she'd merely been jesting in attempt to gall Becky. She never imagined her cousin would consider it. Now Charlotte found herself in the midst of a situation she hadn't planned on. Somehow she'd managed to sidestep her apology. But then, Becky couldn't be too upset with her or she wouldn't have asked her to tend her father.

Perhaps it was best to leave it at that.

CHAD SAT BACK in his chair on the porch cleaning his rifle barrel. Thanks to last night's shindig, he'd neglected to hunt down his Sunday dinner. So he'd made do on day-old pan bread and a couple strips of venison jerky. Tomorrow morning he'd rise early and head for the timber. Anyway, he'd eaten enough last night to ensure he wouldn't go hungry.

The churning sound of wagon wheels pulled his attention. It wasn't often he had visitors. In fact, outside of Jed Stanton, he couldn't recall a soul. Who'd be out his way on a warm Sunday afternoon?

As the wagon neared, he recognized Joseph and Becky Hollister atop the seat still dressed in their Sunday best. Hours had passed since the service ended. They must have stayed in town a while and taken lunch with the preacher. What could have spurred them to make the detour past his place? He could think of no reason other than pure neighborliness. Standing, he set his rifle aside, then stepped from the porch to meet them.

Miss Hollister pulled the team to a stop before his cabin, a pleasant smile lining her lips. "Good afternoon, Mr. Avery."

He tipped the brim of his hat. "Miss Hollister."

At his voice, Joseph Hollister's head lifted. "Sorry to barge in on your Sunday, but we have a matter to run by you that couldn't be put off."

"How can I help you?"

Mr. Hollister cleared his throat. "We've a crop that needs put in, Mr. Avery, and as you know, I'm limited in what I can do. Jed tells us you're a hard worker and might consider lending us a hand."

A smidgen of sadness washed through Chad as his gaze flicked to the man's unseeing eyes. It wasn't easy for a man to admit he needed help. Joseph had made his request with both dignity and humility.

His mind filled with dozens of reasons he should decline the request. His fence and cabin were in sad need of repair. His smokehouse was empty. He had his own crops to tend. And there were plans to finalize before his cattle came. Yet, how could he refuse a neighbor in need? "I'd be willing to work mornings, so long as I could have the afternoons to tend to my own duties."

"Fair enough. Would you be willin' to start tomorrow morning?" There was a noticeable upswing in the man's tone.

"That'll work."

Joseph sat taller on the wagon seat. "Now, we'll make it worth your time. We've not a lot of cash, but I've some skill with a lathe. If there's something you're in need of you just say and maybe we can make a trade."

Chad crossed his arms, envisioning his empty cabin filled with furnishings. He'd grown accustomed to perching on the hearth for his meals. Alone, he had no need for a sit-down table, but then he couldn't deny it might help ease the void of the empty cabin.

Too bad it couldn't fill the void in his heart.

He drew in a breath. "If you could manage a table and chairs, that would suit me fine as payment."

With a satisfied nod, Joseph stuck out his palm. "Much obliged."

Chad strode forward and clasped his hand. "I'll be over first thing in the morning."

"Good. You'll find the plow and harrow beneath the barn lean-to."

Miss Hollister's smile widened. "Thank you, Mr. Avery. I can't tell you what a help you'll be."

Chad tipped his hat. "My pleasure."

She took up the reins. "I'll be gone to teach at school while you're there, but my cousin, Charlotte, has agreed to stay with Pa in my absence."

Chad gave a slight nod, suppressing his surprise. So, Charlotte had a heart after all. He hadn't supposed she'd meant last night's offer. It appeared he'd either misjudged her or, more likely, Miss Hollister had been shrewd enough to beat her at her own game.

He watched them leave, then returned to his seat on the porch and took up his rifle. So much for his plans to restock his food supply. He'd have to start plowing early in the morning to get much accomplished before the sun peaked. Depending on how many acres the Hollisters had, if he worked half days, it would likely take a couple of weeks or more to plow and plant their fields. He could spare that much time.

But something told him Charlotte might not be so thrilled with the arrangement.

Chapter Seven

CHARLOTTE DREW a calming breath and reined Willow closer to her uncle's cabin. A thin plume of smoke from its stone chimney swirled in the distance. She shivered in the cool air. Or was it the thought of putting herself in a situation she knew nothing about?

The early morning ride had given her time to consider her rash agreement to look after her uncle. The arrangement made sense, yet she couldn't quite fathom why Becky had been so willing to allow it. Either her desire to teach was stronger than any grievances she had toward Charlotte or she'd chosen to let bygones be bygones. Regardless, time spent at her uncle's would prove a welcome change from her usual routine.

She pressed her heels into Willow's flanks, certain by now Becky and Pastor Brody would have left for town. Assured her uncle could manage on his own a short time, Charlotte hadn't rushed to arrive. No sense enduring the strain with her cousin if she didn't have to.

The sound of clanking metal pulled her attention to the field up ahead. She caught a glimpse of a man behind a plow just as he disappeared behind the back side of the barn. She brushed a strand of hair from her cheek. Surely Uncle Joseph wasn't working the field.

He couldn't.

Reining Willow closer, Charlotte waited for the team to reappear on the opposite end of the barn. Heads bowed, the horses lumbered into view, then the moldboard plow. She shielded her eyes from the morning sun, her gaze intent on the corner of the barn.

Buckskin clad arms came into view, followed by Chad Avery's muscular frame. Charlotte tugged Willow to a stop. What was he doing working her uncle's field? Not that she'd expected Uncle Joseph to be at the reins, but Mr. Avery's presence proved almost as unsettling.

She pressed her heels in the mare's sides, curiosity spurring her forward. Mr. Avery's back was to her now, and he'd given no indication that he'd seen her approaching. Would he be as astonished to see her as she was him? After all, it was obvious he considered her selfish and petty. Perhaps his opinion of her would shift if he saw her helping her uncle.

Not that she cared.

His buckskin gelding stood grazing outside the barn. As Charlotte edged Willow up beside him, he raised his head and nickered. He was truly a magnificent animal, sleek and spirited. No doubt about it, Mr. Avery had an eye for quality, an attribute which would serve him well in choosing his cattle stock.

Charlotte dismounted and loosened her saddle. Sliding it from Willow's back, she did her best to keep hidden from Chad's view. Something within her relished the thought of shocking him. Abreast to the troubles between her and Becky, most likely Charlotte was the last person he expected to see here.

She set the saddle over the side of the stall next to Chad's black and silver one and stood at the corner of the barn. The sound of the plow slicing through the crusted earth indicated Chad had turned and started back in her direction. She stifled a grin. This would be the second time in their short acquaintance she'd caught him off guard.

She waited until the team neared before stepping into the open, a touch of a grin lining her lips. Instead of a wide-eyed stare, Chad barely glanced her way. The team of horses seemed more startled than he. With a slight nod of his head, he offered a mere, "Miss Stanton," like she was a permanent fixture on the place. Without the slightest pause, he turned the team around and kept going, the long harness reins stretched over his broad shoulders.

Charlotte swiveled toward the cabin with a disgruntled "humph", miffed, not only that he'd shown no surprise, but also that he displayed no reaction at all. Hopefully she'd receive a more enthusiastic reception from her uncle.

THE MID-DAY SUN, along with Chad's growling belly hinted it was quitting time. He wiped his sweaty brow with his sleeve and glanced over the partially-worked field. Nearly a quarter of the way finished plowing. Not a bad morning's work. By the week's end, he'd be set to harrow.

He unhitched the horses, giving them each a pat on the neck. They were a strong, able team. It was tempting to take a short break and continue working, but his duties at home called to him. He stripped the horses of their harnesses and set them free to roam the pasture. They rolled on the ground, bits of prairie grass and dirt clinging to their sweaty coats, then trotted to the creek for a well-deserved drink. Chad looped the harnesses over his shoulders and started for the barn, a bit amused by his brief encounter with Charlotte. She'd seemed miffed he hadn't paused to chat. After his rebuff, it amazed him she'd even made an effort to acknowledge him.

It was just as well. He'd said all he had to say to her at the party. Though he had to admit he was pleased, and a mite surprised, at her willingness to help the Hollisters. It was a step in the right direction anyway. Perhaps, Lord willing, his words had found their mark.

He left the harnesses on the pegs where he'd found them and slid his saddle from the stall. As he carried it outside to Buck, the door to the cabin eased open, and Joseph stepped onto the porch. "Will you join us for lunch, Mr. Avery? We've nothing fancy to offer, but Charlotte's making do with what we have."

Chad paused from fastening the saddle cinch. "Much obliged, but I'd best be going. Another time perhaps."

Joseph's slow nod hinted of regret. "How'd you get along?"

He mounted and rode over. "If all goes well, I should be done plowing by the week's end. That's a fine team you've got there."

Joseph stood taller, a hint of a smile crossing his lips. "They've pulled together a number of years now."

"It shows."

Joseph stepped from the doorway, allowing Chad a glimpse of Charlotte bent over the fire, stirring something in a kettle. She glanced his way and then stood and moved out of sight. If she was that out of sorts, he'd done right in declining to stay.

Though the savory scent wafting out at him begged his deprived stomach to reconsider.

Widening his stance, Joseph leaned on his cane. "You'll be back tomorrow then?"

"At first light." Chad reined Buck to the left. Out of the corner of his eye, he glimpsed Charlotte peering from behind the curtained windowpane. He had half a mind to tip his hat and toss her a wink. But then what would it accomplish? She was frustrated enough at him already. Best thing to do was forget they'd ever crossed paths.

UNCLE JOSEPH'S grip on Charlotte's arm wasn't as firm as the day before. He seemed to be gaining confidence in her ability to guide him. The stroll to the barn had fast become a morning routine for them. A couple of hours working the lathe, a skill he'd achieved in St. Louis, not only gave her uncle something to do while she prepared the noon meal, but also seemed to curb his angst at not being able to help Mr. Avery with the fieldwork.

Charlotte's eyes pulled in Chad's direction. Even from a distance, she sensed his strength and vitality. He'd made great strides in the three mornings he'd been here, working as though his very life depended on it and then leaving with nary a word. Was he merely a hard worker or, like her uncle, driven by some unspoken void?

He'd shared little about himself, other than where he'd come from and that he intended to own a cattle farm. Despite her intention to have nothing to do with him, an insatiable curiosity nipped at her, begging her to delve deeper into this handsome stranger. Why did he keep to himself so much? How could he say so little and yet pierce her soul with his words?

Shaking off her inquisitiveness, she widened the barn door and helped her uncle find his spot at the lathe. As he fastened a block of wood in the clamp, Charlotte picked up one of the table legs he'd completed and ran her fingertips over the smooth design. "My, but you do fine work, Uncle Joseph."

He shrugged, a slight grin seeping onto his lips. "Don't know as any leg matches another, but I try."

"No, truly. It's amazing how well you do without your sight."

"Well, I reckon it's something anyway." His jaw tensed ever so slightly as he put his foot to the treadle, sending the block of wood into a spin.

Charlotte set the table leg back in its place, fearing her compliment had inadvertently caused him grief. "Well, it's something I'm sure I could never do."

"Learned a lot at that there school for the blind." He paused, a hint of sentiment in his voice. "Truth be told, I'm sort of home-sick for the folks we left behind."

Plucking a piece of straw from the pile in the corner, Charlotte leaned against the stall. "You liked St. Louis then?"

"Oh, not the city so much. I've hankered for the freedom and openness of the prairie for a good long while. But the Lord took care of us there. Met some mighty fine people. 'Course they don't have anything on the folks around here."

"Well, we're glad you're back."

He gave a decided nod and returned to his work, the smidgen of sadness Charlotte had detected earlier all but gone. She studied his face, not recalling ever once having the opportunity to visit with him alone. Before his blindness, he'd always been busy working with little time for idle chitchat. Truth was, until now, she'd taken little opportunity to get to know him — or Becky. She and her cousin had shared a politeness, but not friendship.

A stab of anger burned in Charlotte's chest. Until Becky had moved in after the storm and stolen her family away. Then all they'd shared was animosity.

Her mouth twisted. How jealous she'd been on her father's account. She'd tried every which way to make Becky's life miserable. How ironic she now sat visiting with Becky's father, at her cousin's consent. Had she misjudged Becky? It pained Charlotte to think how spiteful she'd been. Had jealousy been to blame for their troubles all along? Regardless, it was high time she put such foolishness aside.

And perhaps treat Mr. Avery a bit kinder as well.

She brushed bits of straw from her hands and edged toward the door. "Well, I'd best get to dinner. If you need anything holler."

The lathe fell silent and her uncle cocked his head to the side. "You know, I was of a notion that you and Becky didn't get on so well. I feared this arrangement wouldn't work. But I think we'll make out just fine."

Charlotte's lips tipped upward. "I believe we will."

CHAD DID his best to ignore the slender red-headed woman tramping toward him through the tall grass. It seemed Miss Stanton had finally emerged from her hiding place. Each morning he'd seen her help Joseph to and from the barn or fetching water from the creek, but other than that she'd remained in the cabin. Why was she so bold as to approach him now?

If he paid her no mind, maybe she'd trek past or disappear altogether. But the figure walking toward him was no mirage and seemed to be headed straight for him. She hiked her skirt as she crossed the field, toting a small drinking vessel.

Chad halted the team at her approach. He straightened, squinting against the late-morning sun. Charlotte held out the jar of water, eyes sparkling in the glow of the sun. "I thought you might be thirsty."

She nodded toward the empty canteen at the edge of the field. She was right. He was bone dry.

"Much obliged." Meeting her gaze, he removed his glove and took the jar of water. The last time he'd stared into those emerald eyes, they'd been tainted by a fiery glare. Today, they seemed much tamer.

She planted her hands on her hips, shifting her eyes to the field beyond. "Uncle Joseph will be pleased with your progress."

Chad chugged some of the cool water, then dried his mouth with his sleeve, curious as to Charlotte's sudden amiable nature. Had she forgiven him for the irritation he'd caused her or was she softening him for a blow? "It's been my pleasure to help. Your uncle seems a right fine man."

"I'm finding that out."

Chad leaned on the plow handle. "Haven't you known him all your life?"

"Until now I guess I haven't taken time to really know him at all."

The genuineness in her voice surprised him. Was he getting another glimpse of the deeper Charlotte? The one he'd sensed for a brief instant at the homecoming?

He took another swig, his thoughts turning to Lauren. They'd had so little time together, yet he'd known her every thought, sensed her every mood. His vision clouded, his words spilling out in a whisper. "Sometimes it pays to make the effort."

Quietness settled over them and Charlotte crossed her arms over her middle. A gentle breeze tossed a wavy strand of hair that had fallen free from her bonnet. She cleared her throat, her eyelids flicking to the newly plowed earth beneath her. "Will you stay for lunch today?"

He tensed at the unexpected request. For three days now he'd declined her uncle's offer, thinking she'd not wished him there. But, how could he refuse when she'd made the offer first hand? He clenched his jaw and held out the empty jar. "Reckon I could."

A faint blush touched her cheeks as her face lifted. She clasped the jar and took a step back, a slight grin playing on her lips. "I'd best go finish readying it then." With that, she turned and started toward the cabin.

Taking up the reins, Chad stared after her. Had he done the right thing?

Or would he live to regret it?

CHARLOTTE'S STOMACH CHURNED. What had gotten into her?

She hadn't given a thought to asking Mr. Avery to join them for a meal until the words rolled off her tongue. Nor had she expected him to accept. Now, here they sat, spoons scraping bowls in uncomfortable silence. Days earlier she'd vowed to have nothing more to do with him. What had changed?

She stole a glance in his direction across from her, noting his chiseled jaw and tanned complexion. Perhaps she'd decided he meant no harm in reprimanding her. It was the commanding way he'd handled the situation that baffled her. After all, it wasn't just anyone she'd allow to openly point out her faults.

Least of all a stranger.

But something within had nudged her to give him another chance. To give herself another chance.

"Soup's good, Charlotte. Just wish we'd had a ham hock to add." It was her uncle's voice which finally broke the quiet.

"Thank you." For lack of meat in the smokehouse, she'd had to season the potato soup with cream, a few sprigs of parsley, and some garlic mustard leaves. She only hoped it would be filling enough for their guest.

Swiping a chunk of cornbread through the remnants in his bowl, Uncle Joseph turned toward Chad. "How soon will you get your cattle?"

Eager for his answer, Charlotte laid down her spoon and listened in quiet expectation. The prospect of cattle ranching had interested her from the start.

With a final swallow, Chad pushed back from the table and crossed his legs at the ankles. "I'll be traveling up north in a few weeks to meet up with the cattle drive. I've still a lot to do to ready the place before then."

"I hope we've not put you behind askin' you to help out here."

"Not really."

By the flinch of Chad's cheek, Charlotte suspected he was being more polite than truthful. She laced her fingers together in her lap. "If you're pressed for time, maybe I could help with the planting."

Chad shot her a surprised look, but said nothing. Did he think her incapable of such work or was the thought of her company so unpleasant to him? Ignoring his stunned reaction, she turned to her uncle. "After all, I've only the noon meal to tend to while you're working at your lathe. Surely I could help part of the morning."

Uncle Joseph crossed his arms over his chest, lips pursed. "Well now, I reckon that's a thought, if Chad's not opposed to the idea."

Charlotte shifted her eyes in his direction, daring him to refuse. For every reason he could come up with not to let her help, she'd think of a better one why she should.

Straightening, he cleared his throat. "I reckon that would be all right. But I won't be ready for planting till sometime next week."

Charlotte tipped her chin upward, a slight smile spilling onto her lips. One way or another, she'd learn who this man was.

Chapter Eight

PART TWO · AWAKENINGS

May, 1855

THE STEADY SCRAPE of the harrow's iron teeth pulling over the field played like sweet music in Charlotte's ears. After being cooped up in the cabin, it was grand just to breathe in the earthy smell of fresh-turned soil and feel the soft breeze against her skin. Reaching in her shoulder pouch, she clasped another handful of wheat. With a swing of her arm, she scattered the tiny seeds in all directions. There it would sit, until the harrow worked it into the fertile ground.

Across the field, the harnesses clanked as Chad's masculine voice spurred the team on. Charlotte stole a glance in his direction, a wave of uncertainty washing over her. Is this what it would be like to work alongside a husband? Would even mundane tasks such as cooking and mending hold new appeal when spawned by love for a man?

She sighed as a drove of blackbirds landed at the center of the field, heads bobbing as they scavenged what they could of the exposed seeds. With another pass of the harrow, the brood flew up only to land again as Chad and the horses trudged to the opposite end of the field. It was a good thing he followed her so soon after sowing, else the harvest would be thinned considerably by the persistent flock of birds.

Wiping sweat from her brow, Charlotte emptied the remnants of her seed pouch at the edge of the field. She brushed chaff from her hands, squinting against the cresting sun. Chad had supplied them with a bundle of good-sized bass, cleaned and ready for frying. The least she could do was have them ready when he finished.

His halting command on the horses caused her to pivot in his direction. The team lurched to a stop, nickering and wagging their heads. A meadowlark's sweet song pealed overhead as the harrow stilled. Was something wrong?

Chad loosened the lid of his canteen and raised it high as though draining its final drop.

Charlotte strode toward him, noting his parched lips and sweat-drenched shirt. May had brought unwelcome heat, each day more blistering than the last. "Can I get you more water?"

He swallowed and nodded toward the horses. "The team could use a drink as well."

She patted their damp withers, heat rising from their chestnut coats. "Then we'll walk them to the creek, and you can fill your canteen."

He gave a quick nod and, with gloved hands, loosened the leather straps that bound the team to the harrow.

Charlotte stood at the horses' heads, gripping their harnesses, her eyes fixed on the handsome newcomer. Try as she may, she couldn't get him to meet her gaze. Why was it he seemed to distance himself from her just when she was beginning to warm to him?

She strolled alongside as Chad led the horses to the creek. The chatter of birds and the sound of hooves dragging through the thick prairie grass helped ease the silence. They worked their way along the shady path that led to the creek. Charlotte hiked her skirt and waded in, cool relief sweeping over her. The horses pawed at the stream, sending a spray of water onto her, stealing her breath away. With a gasp, she retreated onto the bank and tugged at her damp frock. She sensed Chad's eyes upon her and turned in time to see a rare grin line his lips. He *would* find it funny.

But then, his smile was worth it.

Bits of sunlight shone through the jumble of leaves above, creating a lacy pattern across the rippled stream. Charlotte lifted her gaze to the grass-covered plains beyond.

Chad's land.

What would it be like to see cattle roaming the countryside? She turned to him, the gentle breeze cool against her dampened skin. "Did you raise cattle in Tennessee?"

"Nope." Stepping a couple paces upstream, he dipped his canteen into the flowing brook.

Charlotte slumped against a hickory tree, its rough bark digging into her shoulder blades. Was there no way to entice this man into conversation? She'd try another approach. "Have you any family?"

A shadow fell across his face. "None to speak of."

Charlotte knit her brow. Did he or didn't he? Or was he just unwilling to say?

Straightening, he took a long swig from his canteen before popping on the lid. He trudged back to the horses and gave them each a firm pat on the neck. "They're a good team."

"So, you not only have an eye for cattle but horses as well." Charlotte stepped up beside him, surprised at the drumming of her heart as she took in his handsome profile. "What else do you know about besides horses and cattle?"

His eyes found hers. "Nothin' much."

Charlotte gave a soft chuckle. "Oh, I have a feeling there's a lot more to you than you're saying."

His cheek flinched as his gray eyes pried from hers. "Best get back to work." With that, he gathered up the reins and led the horses out of the undergrowth and up the rise.

Charlotte stared after him, brushing a strand of hair from her cheek. The man was holding back, as though a shadow cloaked his heart keeping his true self captive. What secrets did he keep pent inside? And was there a way to draw them out?

If so, she intended to find it.

A RAW ACHE nipped at Chad's insides as he neared the Hollister farm once again. Charlotte asked far too many questions, drudging up memories he'd just as soon stay hidden. For two days he'd avoided her, unwilling to remain any longer than he had to. Twice now he'd declined her offers to stay for lunch. Both times hurt shone in her emerald eyes.

He slumped forward in his saddle, shifting with the rhythm of his horse. If he were honest, he'd admit there was more to his dodging her than the thought of painful memories. He'd begun to enjoy Charlotte's company a bit too much. He couldn't afford to let her get too close and risk hurting her.

Risk hurting himself.

Shaking off his sullen mood, he glanced down at the rabbit tied to his saddle horn. If she offered again would he stay? Probably. After all, all he had to return home to was an empty, broken-down shack and shattered dreams. The Lord's presence was a comfort of sorts. Nothing calmed his bruised spirit like the Word of God. But now and then, he yearned for the company of voices and the stir of people.

He reined Buck to a stop outside the barn and dismounted. The buckskin gelding set to grazing as Chad removed his saddle and carried it into the barn. Coming here had become routine. Joseph's dog, Nugget, now greeted him like a trusted friend, with a wag of his tail and a welcoming bark. Soon the planting would be finished. Would he miss it?

Would he miss Charlotte?

Soft, hurried footsteps sounded behind him. Turning, he took in Charlotte's fiery hair draped about her shoulders, her rounded face and full lips. She'd not arrived ahead of him before. Had she come early on his account? Morning sunlight filtered through the open doorway, accentuating her trim silhouette. Moisture coated his palms as he tried unsuccessfully to pry his eyes away.

She took a step toward him, her fawn-like eyes fixed on his. "I . . . I fear I must have offended you. You've not said a half-dozen words to me these past couple days, nor have you stayed to lunch. Or is it my cooking that's kept you away?"

One corner of his mouth flinched. "Had a lot on my mind's all." He set Buck's saddle on the stall and reached for a harness.

"Then I've come . . . that is Uncle Joseph wanted me to tell you he insists you join us today."

Pausing, Chad tilted his head toward her, then nodded toward the saddle. "Can you stew rabbit?"

Charlotte followed his gaze, a hint of a smile playing on her lips as she spied the skinned rabbit dangling from the saddle horn. "I can try."

Her earnest expression melted his resolve. He hadn't the heart to disappoint her again. Right or wrong, something inside him reveled in the thought she wanted him to stay.

CHAD'S teeth bit into something hard, and he cringed. His gaze met Charlotte's, her green eyes full of question. He forced a grin, waiting until she turned away to remove the tiny bone from his mouth. Rabbits were known for their many small bones. At least one had made it into his stew.

"How's the fieldwork coming?" Joseph pushed his empty

plate away and rested his elbows on the table, his deep voice cutting through the quiet.

Chad straightened and cleared his throat. "Should finish up sometime tomorrow."

The clank of metal pulled his attention to Charlotte. She scrambled to retrieve the fork she'd dropped, a hint of red staining her cheeks. Not quite meeting his gaze, she traced her fingertips along the edge of the table. "So soon?"

The disappointment in her voice confused him. Having helped with much of the planting, she should know his time here was short-lived. Would she be sorry to see him go? "A few more passes along the east side with the harrow should do it."

Joseph leaned back in his chair. "Good. Much obliged for all your help. All we need now is for the good Lord to send a rain to set the seed to growing."

"My pleasure." It truly had been. Despite it throwing him behind schedule, he'd enjoyed the break from solitude, not to mention the chance to help a neighbor. Though he'd plenty to keep him occupied at home, the thought of long days in isolation didn't seem as appealing as it once had.

"I'm afraid I'm not quite finished with your table and chairs."

A weak grin pulled at Chad's lips. "Done without 'em this long. A while longer won't matter."

Charlotte stood and gathered their empty dishes. "Perhaps there are some other chores around here Mr. Avery could do until you finish. Chopping wood for instance."

Chad stared up at her, thankful her attention was stayed on the plates in her hands. That Charlotte would initiate such a suggestion both intrigued and baffled him. If he didn't know better, he'd swear she was trying to conjure up a way to keep him around. Was this the same young lady who days earlier had treated him with such disdain?

Thankfully, Joseph put a quick end to the notion. With a

shake of his head, he leaned back in his chair. "We've taken enough of the young man's time. Besides, once Becky marries, she and I will move to Matthew's place on the outskirts of town."

Charlotte retraced her steps. "What will you do with this place?"

"Haven't quite figured that out yet." Her uncle gave a soft chuckle. "If-en your pa's not interested, we may just wind up selling it to Chad here."

The unexpected notion rumbled through Chad like a crack of thunder. What a spread the jointed lands would make for his herd. He glanced around the sturdy cabin. This place certainly had his old broken-down shack beat. But he barely had enough saved to buy his cattle. And anyway, what would a man alone need with such a fine arrangement?

Best he squelch this dream before it took root.

CONCEALED BEHIND THE LINEN CURTAIN, Charlotte watched Chad clasp hands with her uncle and turn to leave, the young man's winsome smile spilling over her like summer rain. He had such an alluring quality about him, with his piercing gray eyes and good-natured ways. Over the past couple of weeks, she'd come to like him a bit too much, she feared. Now that his duties here had ended, would she see him other than a brief moment on Sundays as he exited the church building?

Soon he'd be off on his cattle venture, and she'd not see him at all. The thought initiated an unwelcome hollowness in her chest. She'd grown accustomed to his presence, looked forward to it even. Without him around, would her time here prove less appealing? Up until now, she hadn't minded her commitment to watch after her uncle. To be truthful, she'd been stunned at how amiably they'd gotten along. Even she and Becky had fallen into a cordial pattern of greeting, though Charlotte made a point not to linger once Becky arrived. It just seemed easier that way.

Without Chad, things would be different. Less eventful for certain.

Dull even.

Now that the crops were in, how would she bide her time while Uncle Joseph was at the lathe? Outdoor work, or work in general, had never been her strong-suit, yet somehow helping in the field hadn't seemed so much like work alongside Chad. She'd been utterly exhausted when she'd returned home. But it had been a good tired.

Come to think of it, Norris had only called on her once in the past two weeks and had left early when she yawned and made mention of how tired she was. He hadn't put up much of a fuss at leaving. Neither had he returned.

As Chad slipped from view, Charlotte eased back from the window, a fragile smile touching her lips. How different he was from Norris. Comparing the two was similar to likening a spirited stallion to a foundered pony, one safe and docile, the other challenging and elusive.

The trouble was, like that wild stallion, Chad skittered away every time Charlotte tried to get close.

Chapter Nine

CHAD TAPPED THE WOODEN NAIL, securing the final clapboard shingle in place. He wiped his brow and eased back on his haunches as he surveyed his handiwork. Repairing the ramshackle old cabin was proving almost as much work as constructing a new one. He'd hoped to put it off, but what else could he do? He'd have more time to work at it now than after the cattle came. There were still several logs to repair and chinking to be done, but at least he'd have a dry roof over his head.

He tossed his mallet to the ground and stuffed the leftover wooden nails in his leather pouch. The sun had lost its harshness as it sank lower in the western sky. Chad's stomach rumbled, reminding him he'd had nothing to eat since breakfast. With this morning's traps empty and no time to hunt or cook a meal, it would be venison jerky for supper again. A sigh escaped him as he made his way down the ladder. He could almost taste the venison stew Lauren would have readied for him . . . if only she'd been there.

He gathered his supplies and trekked to the barn, hounded by the stillness surrounding him. It'd been nearly a week since he'd set eyes on anyone . . . save his horse. For a time, being alone had suited him. Now, the quiet brought an emptiness he couldn't comprehend. Having grown accustomed to Charlotte and Joseph's company, it didn't seem right not to join them each morning. Going there had given him reason to rise and start his day. Now, getting up seemed more a chore. He shook his head, pushing his hat back with his forefinger. Maybe he just needed a dog, someone to jaw at.

A cool breeze swept over his face as he made his way inside the cabin. Rain clouds loomed on the horizon. It seemed he'd repaired his roof just in time. He scanned the solid ceiling, then let his gaze drift to the holes in the log walls. With any sort of wind, rain would seep in. No matter. Until his new table and chairs arrived, he had little of value.

His gaze flicked to the photo atop the mantel. The only things truly precious to him he'd lost.

THE AFTERNOON SUN hid behind a passing cloud. Charlotte tossed the dish water over the porch rail and squinted at the thickening sky. If a storm blew in, the three-mile ride home would be grueling. In an hour or so, Becky would return. Perhaps having Willow saddled and ready couldn't hurt.

Charlotte set the dish pan on the porch rocker and hollered in at her uncle. "It looks like rain. I think I'll saddle my horse."

"Go on home. I'll be all right."

Uncle Joseph's words were like a soothing melody. Still, she didn't feel right leaving him alone so long. "You sure?"

"I'll be fine. Now get goin'. Don't want you gettin' caught in a storm." The tension in her uncle's tone was out of concern, not irritation. Having lost a wife and daughter to the clutches of nature, her uncle had good reason to be on edge where storms were concerned.

A bit hesitant, she strolled to the barn and placed a hand on the wooden door. It hung open slightly. Odd. Hadn't she bolted it earlier?

Turning, she stepped inside and took a tentative glance around. Willow gave a soft whinny at her approach. Dismissing her qualms, she smoothed a hand over the horse's muzzle. The ten-year-old roan still had plenty of spunk. Raised from a foal, she'd been an added blessing when Charlotte's father had purchased his team of horses. Willow had the distinction of being utilized as more of a riding horse than a work horse.

A slight noise drew Charlotte's attention to the loft above. She paused to listen, finally dismissing the sound as some small varmint. With a shrug, she lifted the saddle from its place on the stall and set it atop Willow. A second thump, louder than the first, sent Charlotte's fingers digging into the leather saddle.

No critter was that careless—lest it be human.

"Who's up there?"

Silence.

She gnawed at her lip, her heart drumming in her ears. She couldn't leave now, knowing the intruder might pose a threat to her blind uncle. She scanned the barn for some sort of defense and spied the wooden table legs her uncle had made for Chad propped against the wall. For lack of anything better, she reached for one. Hopefully they'd forgive her if she splintered it over the intruder's head. Clutching it in her hand like a club, she started up the loft ladder.

Stifling heat smacked her in the face as she peered over the top rung. She held the table leg out in front of her and glanced over the piles of straw and hay. Movement to her right set her heart beating faster. A youthful face peeked from behind the heap of straw. A boy?

Charlotte lowered her weapon and expelled the breath she'd held. "Come out of there."

In response, the boy burrowed deeper into the pile. With a

sigh, Charlotte climbed into the loft, the air thick with the scent of hay. Taking hold of the child's foot, she pulled him from the straw pile only to have him twist and squirm until she lost her grip. He skittered out of reach, his scraggly blond hair nearly obscuring his widened eyes. Yet, in the brief moment their blueness locked onto hers, Charlotte sensed not only fear but desperation.

"It's all right. I mean you no harm." She reached for him, her voice gentle.

Ignoring her plea, he groped his way to the ladder and started down it, taking a frantic leap to the barn floor half-way down.

Charlotte peered over the edge of the loft just as he scrambled to his feet and fled toward the door. "Wait!" Hiking her skirt, she climbed down the ladder. With hurried breaths, she rushed after him. Pushing through the door, she stepped outside and scanned the yard to no avail.

He was gone.

The youngster's ruddy face churned in her mind. Who was he, and what had he been doing here miles from nowhere? Why wasn't he in school? If she described him, maybe Becky would know who he was and what had brought him here.

Charlotte glanced at the darkened clouds, torn between staying and going. Willow's soft nicker pulled her back inside the barn. She finished tightening the saddle cinch, weighing her options. If she stayed, more than likely she'd get drenched. But if she didn't, curiosity would plague her.

She breathed a soft sigh, her mouth twisting. Perhaps it would be best to wait after all.

"HE WAS IN OUR LOFT?" Becky seemed as surprised as Charlotte the youngster had strayed so far from home.

"Yes. I'd guess him to be six or seven with scraggly blond

hair, blue eyes, and of slight build for his age. Does he sound like one of your students?"

Becky slid her bonnet off and eased into a chair. "Young Johnny Langston missed school today. I suppose it could be him. He fits your description."

Charlotte joined her at the table, reveling in the fact that for once she and Becky were on the same side. "What would he be doing out this way alone? Do you know where he lives?"

"He and his father live a couple miles east of here. I don't know much else other than they moved here after his mother died some months ago."

His mother being gone would explain his unkempt appearance but not why he was running around unattended. Something in Becky's demeanor begged Charlotte to pry for more. "But why would he be hiding out here instead of attending school?"

A shadow fell over her cousin's face. "I'm afraid Johnny misses school quite often. From what I hear, his father is given to drinking."

Charlotte burned inwardly. Had the boy's father mistreated him? At the very least he'd neglected him. "What sort of father allows his young son to roam the countryside?"

Becky hung her head. "His father isn't well, whether from the effects of drinking or illness, Doc Pruitt says the man hasn't long to live."

The desperation in young Johnny's blue eyes resurrected in Charlotte's mind. How her heart ached for the boy "The poor child. Has he any other family?"

"None that we know of. Matthew and I have spoken with Johnny's father, but he's not the easiest person to talk to. He keeps to himself and refuses help of any sort."

"But why would the boy run off? He must have been frightened of something."

Becky rolled her shoulders. "I'm not sure what causes him to miss so much school either, but Mr. Langston insists he and Johnny are fine."

A faint rumble of thunder pulled Charlotte's attention to the window where gray clouds blanketed the sky. "I'd best be going."

"Maybe you should stay and wait out the storm." Her uncle's protective tone flared in his voice.

She stood and smoothed the creases from her dress. It didn't take much for the uncomfortable feeling between her and Becky to seep back into the room. "Thank you, but Ma will fret if I don't come home."

Becky rose from her chair. "Thanks for telling us about Johnny. I'll let you know if I hear anything."

With a nod, Charlotte opened the door. A swelling breeze wafted through, the air a bit cooler than when she'd entered. As she started for the barn, a sprinkle dampened her cheek. Chances were slim she'd make it home without getting soaked. The only shelter along the way, outside of a grove of trees, would be Chad's place to the west. Even it was a mite out of the way. Still, his place would be closest if she needed protection from the storm.

A smile touched her lips. Wouldn't that be a shame?

HEAVY RAIN PELTED Chad's cabin, drowning out the quiet. He kept a watchful eye on his roof for leaks, but the new clapboard shingles appeared to be holding. Unlike the sidewalls where rain had seeped in to form puddles along the edges. Dropping to his knees, he sopped up the rain-water with a rag and squeezed it into a bucket. Debris from the damp logs sprayed in at him along with the rain, littering the floorboards. The thought of chinking and daubing all these crevices was about as inviting as plowing a field with a spoon. There'd be no end to it.

A sigh escaped him. If Lauren and their son were here, it wouldn't seem such a chore. A family to protect and provide for made all the difference. Now, even jobs he used to enjoy seemed burdensome.

His bucket full, he stood and glanced out the rain splattered window. A dark object outside the barn drew his attention. He squinted, trying to determine between splashes of raindrops what it could be. The rain slowed momentarily, just long enough for him to recognize a horse.

Not just any horse. Charlotte's roan.

Another spray of rain hit the windowpane as the horse slipped from view, either into the barn or under the lean-to. Chad ran a hand over his jaw. What would Charlotte's horse be doing here? Worse yet, where was Charlotte?

Hair rose on the back of his neck. Had her horse gotten spooked by the storm and thrown her?

He dropped his bucket and rushed outside. Sheets of rain soaked through his clothing, cold against his skin, as he splashed his way through the muddy yard. Stranded beneath the lean-to, Charlotte's horse looked a sight, drenched from mane to hoof. As Chad neared the barn, he slowed his pace, so as not to frighten her. The roan nickered and raised her head at Chad's approach. Slowly, he reached for the reins. There was no way he'd find Charlotte in this storm. Once it let up, he'd search.

All night if he had to.

He eased open the barn door and urged the mare inside. The horse whinnied and pulled back, snapping the damp reins out of Chad's slippery hands before retreating back to the lean-to. With a groan, he started after her.

"It's no use. The fool horse would rather get drenched than set foot in a strange barn. She's funny that way."

Chad stopped in mid stride. He pivoted, stunned to see Charlotte perched atop a pile of straw, soaked from head to toe. "I thought you'd . . . How'd you wind up here?"

Charlotte stood, brushing straw from her damp dress. "I thought I could make it home. I was wrong."

She stepped toward him, her long, crimson hair cascading over her shoulders. Its wetness somehow only accentuated her natural beauty. How he'd missed the softness of a woman. Charlotte's presence here confused him.

He cleared his throat and turned to peek out at the rain-whitened sky. "Hopefully this storm will let up soon so you can be on your way."

Her frustrated "humph" told him he'd said something he shouldn't have. "Since you're so eager for me to leave and my horse and I are soaked anyway, perhaps I'd just as well go."

Chad turned, startled to have her standing beside him, the fire in her green eyes lit once again. He had to admit he'd missed her feistiness. The Lord had sure given her flaming hair to match her spirit. As she moved toward the door, he caught her by the arm. "You're welcome to stay as long as you need. I was merely thinking of the worry you'll be causing your folks."

Like a squall running out of strength, the comment seemed to settle her. She eased back as he loosened his hold on her arm. "Oh. Then, I thank you for your concern, Mr. Avery."

"I'd rather you called me Chad."

Her lips curved into an attractive smile. "All right. Chad."

He swallowed. His name sounded different when Charlotte spoke it. He took a step back, almost wishing he hadn't made the suggestion. Somehow he felt safer when she was angry with him.

Chapter Ten

"Aa-choo!" Charlotte covered her mouth as she sneezed. Yesterday's wet ride had left her chilled to the bone. Yet it had been worth it to spend a few quiet moments alone with Chad.

Ma shook her head and handed Charlotte a pot of chicken and noodles to set on the table. "It's a wonder you didn't catch pneumonia. Whatever possessed you to ride home ahead of a rainstorm?"

"I figured you'd fret if I didn't come."

Ma stood and wiped her brow with her apron. "Well, you were late enough as it was. You must've held up somewhere along the way."

Chad's handsome face rose to the forefront of Charlotte's mind, and she couldn't hold back a grin. "Just for a bit."

"Where was that? There ain't much but prairie between here and Joseph's."

She hesitated. Innocent as it was, Ma wouldn't take kindly to knowing Charlotte had been alone with a fellow they knew so little about. She could sense Esther's eyes upon her, and her face warmed. Esther knew Chad had taken up residence in the old

Randall place and had mentioned herself how handsome he was. Had she guessed Charlotte's secret?

The door creaked open and spared Charlotte from answering. Her father entered, stealing Ma's attention. "Bout time you're home from town. What kept you?"

He took a seat at the table and held out a slip of paper, his usual cheery disposition tainted by a frown. "This telegram came, so I stopped back by the mercantile to get a few more things."

Questions formed in Ma's blue eyes. She took the note from him, her complexion paling as she read it.

"What is it, Pa?" Esther's tender voice sliced through the stillness.

He shifted in his chair, his attempt at a smile failing. "Seems I'm needed up north again."

The pleasant thoughts Charlotte had entertained moments earlier vanished like summer dew. "So soon? But you've hardly been home a month."

"It's not my wish to leave. I'm needed." His gentle eyes pierced her heart as he cupped his hand under her chin. No matter how old she got, she'd always be his little girl.

Moisture brimmed in her younger sister's eyes. "When do you have to leave?"

Pa sat back, releasing a long breath. "First thing Monday morning."

"But you'll miss Becky's wedding."

He raked a hand through his hair. "I know, but it can't be helped."

Ma tossed the telegram on the table, her expression hardening. "They call and you come a runnin'."

"Now, Clara, you know I don't relish leavin' you. Can I help it they're short a man?" Pa stood, strain telling in his voice.

"Next time it could be you." Ma turned her back to him, a quiver in her voice.

Curious what had her mother so distraught, Charlotte swiveled the telegram around where she could read it. A chill, much worse than yesterday's rain, ran through her as she soaked in the words.

SHORT-HANDED DUE TO LOGGING ACCIDENT

INJURED WORKER UNABLE TO RETURN DUE TO SEVERITY OF INJURIES

REQUEST YOU COME AT ONCE

BENJAMIN S. CRAIG

Charlotte's eyes met her father's, and he managed a slight grin. "Don't look so worried. I'll be back before you can miss me."

It wasn't so. She missed the very thought of him leaving. They all knew the dangers loggers faced. Her father making light of the situation didn't lessen them.

Ma sniffled as she stooped to remove biscuits from the Dutch oven. "Why does it have to be you? Why can't someone else go?"

He placed his hands on her shoulders. "Skilled loggers are hard to come by, Clara."

She stood, pivoting toward him. "You mean men fool enough."

He hung his head with a sigh. "If you feel that strongly about it, I'll make this my last trip."

"You mean that?" Hope dawned in her mother's eyes as well as Charlotte's heart.

"I do." He pulled Ma to him, resting his chin atop her head.

The tension eased, Charlotte set the telegram aside and dished out the chicken and noodles. It was good her time at her uncle's was nearing an end. With Pa leaving again, she'd be needed here at home.

One thing was certain. They'd all rest easier when he was home for good.

Chad struggled to buckle his saddle bags, filled to overflowing with supplies. In little more than a week he'd be leaving to meet up with the cattle drive. Until then, he had his fair share of getting ready to do. It was going to be close. But now that he could work at it full time, he stood a chance.

That is if he could keep his mind on his work.

Charlotte's unexpected visit had him tied in knots. Despite her often-times self-seeking ways, there was something about her that wouldn't let go of him. He liked to think it was her similarities to Lauren that drew him to her, but it was more than that. She had a hidden nature that seemed to cry out to him, as if the Lord were urging him to delve deeper into this veiled part of her.

Excited shouts sounded down the street from the mercantile. Turning, Chad saw a throng of children standing in a circle in the schoolhouse yard, voices raised. A couple of the students shifted just enough for him to get a glimpse of two boys fighting at the center, bodies intertwined on the ground. Chad mounted and tapped his heels into Buck's sides, urging him to a canter. Miss Hollister appeared in the schoolhouse doorway, eyes widening at sight of the brawl. Hiking her skirt, she skittered down the steps toward the commotion.

Chad reined Buck to a stop and hopped down alongside the crowd of onlookers. He maneuvered his way through them to the feuding boys, one a head taller than the other. Clasping a hand on both of their shoulders, he pried them apart. The older boy yanked himself away and brushed off his soiled clothes, his glare fixed on the smaller child. With a powerful jerk, the younger boy lunged at him. Chad tightened his grip, pulling him back. "Now hold on there, son. What's the trouble?"

The scrappy, blond-haired boy's face pinched in a scowl as he eyed his opponent. The other lad widened his stance, a slight smirk spreading over his lips.

An out-of-breath Miss Hollister barged her way through the crowd of students. She stood, hands on hips, surveying the two boys' torn clothes and soiled faces. "What goes on here?"

The students quieted and shifted their stares to the disgruntled boys. Miss Hollister shook her head. "Honestly. Just days from summer break and you two can't keep from picking at each other?" She pointed toward the schoolhouse. "Inside. Both of you. And if you so much as look at one another, your backsides will pay the price."

Chad worked to hold back a grin as he released his grip on the blond-haired boy. The lad kicked at the ground, head drooped, as he ambled toward the school a few paces behind his opponent.

Miss Hollister motioned for the other students to resume their play. She tugged her bonnet into place, her face softening as she turned to Chad. "Thank you for your assistance, Mr. Avery. It was kind of you to help."

"Not a problem." He mounted, a corner of his mouth lifting. "Don't be too hard on 'em."

A shy grin spread over her lips as she pressed her hands to her cheeks. "I fear you've seen a side of me many don't. I assure you, though, I'm not as harsh as I let on."

"Your secret's safe with me." He nodded toward the younger boy. "Tough little guy, ain't he?"

Miss Hollister followed his gaze. "I suppose he's had to be. Johnny's had a rough go of it, I'm afraid."

At mention of the boy's name, Chad's stomach knotted. He would be named Johnny. What were the chances?

He tipped his hat to her, then pressed a rein against Buck's neck to turn.

She waved. "Thanks again. Oh! You'll join us at our wedding a week from Friday, won't you?"

Chad pulled back on the reins. At the moment, attending a wedding was the furthest thing from his mind. "I'll do my best."

Raw numbness coursed through him as he headed home. In his short life, his son John had shown such zest for living. Given the chance, would he have shared this Johnny's spunk?

Reminders of Chad's loss were everywhere. In the beauty of a sunset like the ones he and Lauren used to sit and gaze at from their front porch. In a grove of purple coneflowers, Lauren's favorite. And in the laughter of a small child.

Would this crushing ache inside him ever end?

Like Job in the Bible, he'd questioned many times why the Lord had taken them, yet never was given a plausible reason. Job hadn't received one either. Not really. God's only answer was that He knew best what Job needed. True, in the end, God had blessed him, but that wasn't likely to happen to Chad, especially since he didn't intend on letting himself get too attached to anyone. It was too risky, the pain too great.

By the time he neared his property, the sun had crested, and Buck was streaked with sweat. Yet, even under the extra load of supplies, the gelding's pace never slowed. He was strong and had the makings of a good cattle horse. A sharp corral dog would be an asset as well. But that could wait until he had his herd settled in.

Chad wiped his brow with his sleeve, his gaze drifting to the front of the cabin. He tensed at sight of the familiar roan horse grazing in the yard. Surely Charlotte wasn't here again. What reason would she have? There was no rain storm to seek shelter from today. He pressed his heels into Buck's sides and urged him faster, breathing easier when he recognized Jed's bulky frame slumped in the porch rocker instead of his spirited daughter's.

Tugging Buck to a stop beside him, Chad leaned on the saddle horn. "This is an unexpected pleasure. Been here long?"

His neighbor pushed his hat back on his head, squinting up at him. "Long enough to make myself at home. Figured you'd be along after while."

A grin pulled at Chad's mouth as he dismounted. "Have you come to lend a hand or escape work at home?"

Instead of his usual chuckle, Jed stood, his expression sobering. "Neither. I've come to ask a favor."

The uncharacteristic solemnness in his friend's tone hinted this was no mere request. Chad could only hope it wouldn't demand too much of his time. But in his heart, he knew he couldn't refuse. "What might that be?"

Jed leaned on the porch rail and stared out into the prairie. "I'm headin' north again. Be leavin' first thing Monday mornin'. May be gone a bit longer this time."

"Sorry to hear it."

Turning toward Chad, Jed cleared his throat. "Clara and the girls are upset at me leavin' again so soon. You bein' our closest neighbor, I wondered if you'd look in on them from time to time."

Chad looped Buck's reins over the railing, unprepared for such a request. He'd not wanted to get involved in anyone's life but his own. When you cared for people, you got hurt. "You know I'll be leaving myself in a little over a week to get my cattle."

"I realize that, but if you'd stop in when you can I'd surely appreciate it."

Chad hesitated and then gave a decided nod. Obviously the matter was of great importance to his friend. What else could he do but agree?

Jed's expression lightened. "I knew I could count on you."

Chad forced a grin, wondering just how he'd manage it without seeming a nuisance. He was barely acquainted with Jed's wife and youngest daughter, and trying his hardest not to become more entangled with Charlotte. But the more he tried to avoid her, the more life seemed to thrust them together.

THE CHURCH BUILDING rang with the final chorus of *Just as I Am*. As the singing came to a close, Pastor Brody motioned the congregation to sit. Charlotte smoothed her dress under her, casting a sideways glance at her father. Tomorrow he'd leave them. What with spending her days with Uncle Joseph, it seemed she'd hardly had time to be with her own father. Now that she'd be home again, he was going away. She could only pray his absence would be short-lived.

The church quieted as Pastor Brody stepped from behind the pulpit, his expression taut. "Before we go, I have a couple of announcements." He paused, clutching his Bible to his chest, eyes panning the congregation. "Last night Ephraim Langston passed away."

A flurry of puzzled expressions and hushed conversations rippled through the congregation. The name Ephraim Langston was unfamiliar to Charlotte, though she recalled hearing the surname Langston somewhere.

Pastor Brody took a step closer, voice raised a notch. "Him being relatively new to the community, many of you may not know him, but his son, Johnny, attends school here in town."

Charlotte straightened. That was it. Johnny Langston, the boy she'd found hiding in her uncle's loft. She clapped a hand to her mouth. Was it his father who'd died?

Her cousin's downcast face assured Charlotte her assumption was correct. The boy's mother had recently died as well, which meant he had no one.

A hint of sadness edged its way into the pastor's voice. "With Mr. Langston's passing, Johnny is left without home or family. I implore each of you to prayerfully consider taking the boy in. Though Mr. Langston didn't attend church services, he was a member of our community. Therefore, I feel it our Christian duty to offer help to this child in need."

Silence blanketed the room. By the looks on people's faces, no one was eager to meet the request. Another mouth to feed meant more work and greater sacrifice for the already hard-pressed families.

Or was it his father's reputation that caused them to shy away?

"On a brighter note," Pastor Brody's voice broke through Charlotte's thoughts. "You're all invited to our wedding a week from this Friday." The announcement received a much more enthusiastic response from the crowd. In characteristic fashion, he took Becky by the hand and strolled with her to the entrance of the church to greet the once again bustling congregation.

Charlotte made her way into the aisle and awaited her turn at greeting. Heaviness pulled at her when she saw no sign of Chad. It had been nearly a week since she'd seen him. She may as well put to rest any hopes of continuing their acquaintance. Obviously he had no room for her in his life. Any camaraderie they may have enjoyed working together at her uncle's had been merely superficial. Norris at least showed interest in her company.

At least he *had*.

She caught a glimpse of him across the room visiting with Lola Brimmer, happy grins lining their faces. Charlotte breathed a soft sigh, envious of their joy. Had her plan worked too well? Whether she wished it or not, had she missed her one chance at a marriage proposal?

He'd had to get out of there. Hearing the boy's tragic loss, today of all days, the date that would have marked his son's third birthday, was almost more than Chad could bear. The memory of it engulfed him like an overwhelming fog.

He slumped forward in his chair and leaned his elbows on his new oak table. How his heart ached for the young boy that bore his son's name. Chad knew what it was to be the sole survivor in a family, left alone without anyone to share life with. To dream dreams with. What a shame it had to happen to one so young.

In time, he'd hoped life without them would get easier. Instead, it seemed to grow harder by the day. He had Charlotte to thank for that, at least in part. Somehow she'd finagled her way into his life, causing him to miss the luxury of a life-long companion all the more.

He shoveled in another bite of beans. The only thing that seemed to help take his mind off his troubles was to stay busy. Maybe once he had his cows to tend things would be better. Yet, even the thought of his cattle farm had lost its appeal. It had been a shared dream, his and Lauren's. Without her, it would merely be a means to make a living.

Look not every man on his own things, but also on the things of others.

The verse of Scripture pressed into Chad's thoughts. The Lord's gentle reminder?

Maybe that's what he needed to settle his loneliness. He'd been a lot better off when he'd been busy helping the Hollisters. There was something healing in giving to others. Maybe Jed's request to keep an eye on his family wouldn't be such a bothersome task after all, but a blessing.

So long as he kept Charlotte at arm's length.

Chapter Eleven

CHARLOTTE STEPPED out onto the porch, milk bucket in hand, and breathed in the early morning air. The rising sun cast amber rays against a blanket of clouds on the horizon. The four days since Pa had left seemed more like four weeks. How she missed his good-natured smile and spry sense of humor. When he'd left, the life had gone out of the place. Still, now that school had let out, she was thankful the daily trips to her uncle's had ended. Even with Pa gone, it was good to be home.

Rubie rose from her resting place and stretched, mouth agape in a lazy yawn. The dog looked a sight, her coat matted with cockle-burs. A trail of muddy paw prints gave clue to her restless night. She'd been out rambling again. The red and white Border collie let out a soft whine, and Charlotte reached to scratch behind her ear. She missed Pa too.

The sound of something pulling through the grass to the west stirred Rubie's attention toward the timberline. Fur bristling, she sounded a warning bark. Charlotte squinted into the mist that hung in the distance. She stiffened at the faint image of a horse and rider edging closer. Who would be out this way so early? Some aimless drifter perhaps?

Or worse yet, a bandit that knew Pa was away?

Thinking it wise to have a rifle in hand, she backed toward the door, but paused as Rubie gave a soft whimper and trotted toward the unknown visitor. Her curiosity roused, Charlotte stared after her. Apparently, Rubie no longer deemed the intruder a threat. Charlotte set her bucket down and brushed a stray strand of hair from her cheek, waiting for the stranger to cross the creek. As he cleared the timberline, her heart quickened.

Chad.

What was he doing here?

His buckskin horse pulled a canvas sled loaded with something heavy. Charlotte cocked her head, squinting up at him as he stopped beside her. "You're out early. What brings you over this way?"

With a tip of his hat, his piercing gray eyes fastened on hers. "I've a problem I'm hoping you can help me with."

"Oh?" She'd taken Chad as the sort to handle any situation. What could she possibly do that he couldn't?

He thumbed over his shoulder at the sled. "I shot myself a couple of deer. Now, I've more meat than one man can manage. Wondered if you'd take some off my hands."

A salty smell wafted up at Charlotte as she craned her neck for a look at the lumps of venison hidden beneath dampened clothes. "Why'd you shoot the second one if you didn't need it?"

The color in his face deepened, and he shrugged. "Shot the first one yesterday, then, this mornin', saw this one standing there beggin' me to pull the trigger. Reckon I couldn't disappoint."

Charlotte arched a brow and rested her hands on her hips. "I've not heard of a deer so eager to wind up in someone's smokehouse."

"Always a first time." The leather saddle creaked under him as he dismounted, a faint smile touching his lips.

She eyed him, curious if the neighborly gesture had originated with him or her father. More than likely Pa had put him up to it, making sure they were provided for.

The door creaked open, and Ma and Esther stepped out onto the porch. Ma's puzzled gaze shifted from the canvas sled to Chad. "What's this?"

Charlotte laced her fingers together behind her back, the corners of her mouth tipping upward. "Mr. Avery brought us some venison."

Ma's eyes flicked from her to Chad, then back again. Charlotte forced the grin from her lips, something in Ma's pointed stare saying she had Norris's interest at heart.

Returning her gaze to Chad, Ma pasted on a smile. "That's right kind of you, Mr. Avery. With Jed gone, it'll come in real handy."

He tilted his hat back on his head and nodded toward the smokehouse. "If it suits you, I'll unload it in there."

Ma gave a decided nod. "Much obliged."

"I'll help." Charlotte stole a glance in Chad's direction, heat burning her cheeks as, for a brief moment, his eyes met hers. Weeks earlier she'd been so irritated at him she'd not wanted a thing to do with him. Now, his presence filled her with strange longing.

Ignoring Ma's watchful gaze, Charlotte snatched up her bucket and started with Chad toward the smokehouse. Rubie trotted after them, nose hovering close to the sled of meat, until Ma's scolding voice called her back.

Charlotte shot a sideways glance at their new neighbor as they walked, his shoulder mere inches from her head. The scent of wood and leather filled her senses. She bit at her lip, searching for something to say. "I-I guess you'll be leaving soon to get your cattle."

He nodded. "In a week."

The wedding was a week away. Would he stay for it? How she longed to feel his arm tucked around her waist once more, though in a more amiable manner than their last dance. "Will you . . . be here for the wedding?"

She reached to unlatch the smokehouse door, tense from his moment of hesitation.

He cleared his throat. "I might."

A slight grin pulled at the corners of Charlotte's lips as she swung the door open. The response, though noncommittal, was enough to give her hope. She helped Chad carry in the venison, intent on finding out more about this thoughtful, yet elusive, man. There had to be more to him than he was telling. "If you've never raised cattle, what was your profession?"

With a shrug, he hung his meat chunk from the rafters, then reached for her smaller one. "Don't know as I had one. I tried my hand at a lot of things."

Charlotte followed him back outside, skirting around a mud hole in her effort to keep pace. His vague answers left her want-ing. "Did you come here out of a sense of adventure? You've nothing or . . . no one tying you to your home in Tennessee?"

His cheek flinched as he lifted two more slabs of venison from the sled. He straightened, and his piercing gray eyes fastened on hers. "My past is my own. I'd rather keep it that way."

Charlotte dropped her gaze to the make-shift sled, Chad's harsh tone slicing through her. Why was it every time she tried to get a glimpse of who he was, he pushed her away? Was there some horrible tragedy or unspeakable wrong marring his past?

Squaring her shoulders, she lifted the final chunk of meat, then started toward the smokehouse. He'd won for now, but he'd soon discover she wasn't one to give up easily.

One way or another, she'd find him out.

RAW NUMBNESS GNAWED at Chad as he rode home. He hadn't meant to hurt Charlotte, only to squelch her curiosity. His memories plagued him enough without being reminded of them. Still, he'd no call to be stern with her. She knew nothing of his hardships. It was unfair to scold her for asking.

But then, maybe it was just as well he'd raised a wall between them. Temptation lurked in Charlotte's limpid green eyes and spirited smile. He'd grown too fond of her. From the start, he'd known it best to keep his distance. Yet try as he may, he found that hard to do.

Something in Charlotte's eyes and voice had hinted she wanted him to stay for the pastor's wedding. Barring all setbacks, if he did stay, he'd still have ample time to make it to Hammett to meet up with the herd. Most likely he'd not see Charlotte again for some time. The thought of leaving her with a wounded spirit didn't set right.

He drew in a breath, his gaze panning the prairie landscape. Maybe he should stay.

Maybe he owed her that much.

CHARLOTTE PAUSED to catch her breath outside Donaldson's Dry Goods Store. The mile and a half trip into town seemed but a short jaunt with her mind so muddled over yesterday's gruff response from Chad. Her initial hurt had dissolved into curiosity after a night's rest and talking it over with the Lord. Why had he grown defensive? What was he hiding?

Most generally, people put up defenses to either hide something they were ashamed of or to protect themselves. In Chad's case, Charlotte believed it to be the latter. He was too giving of a person to possess some sinister secret. He himself had reprimanded her for her rude treatment of others. Only a godly man would care enough to hold someone accountable for their misdeeds.

A door slammed up the street, and a young child emerged from Doc Pruitt's house. He plopped himself down on the ground and cupped his face in his hands. Was he waiting for someone? If so, he didn't look very pleased about it.

But for his combed hair and clean clothing, he resembled the boy she'd found hiding in her uncle's barn. Had the Pruitts been caring for him since his father's death? Charlotte strolled over and squatted down beside him. The glimpse she got of him before he hid his face was enough to assure he was the same boy. The scent of lye soup wafted up at her, though shards of dirt still clung in his fingernails. "Hello, Johnny."

The boy raised his head, eyeing her warily. "How do you know my name?"

"Miss Hollister told me. You and I have met before, remember?"

He gave her a hard look, face pinched in a scowl. "You're the lady in the loft."

"That's right. You gave me quite a start."

"You scare easy." The boy's tone carried an air of annoyance.

She gave a soft chuckle, his rounded face and large blue eyes melting her heart. He was beautiful. "I hardly recognized you all cleaned up. Are you going somewhere?"

He lowered his head and pushed a pebble along the dirt with his toe. "Mr. and Mrs. Crowley's."

"To stay?" The words escaped before Charlotte could stop them. Though she was unfamiliar with Mrs. Crowley, Charlotte knew Ian Crowley to be a stern man with a taste for liquor. The family kept to themselves and never attended church service.

Johnny gave a slow nod.

Charlotte pursed her lips. The Crowleys had a tribe of children of their own. What would they want with Johnny? "You don't seem very happy about it."

His shoulders lifted in a shrug. "Don't guess it matters where I go now that my pa's gone."

Her chest squeezed. The poor little fellow was alone in the world. Here she was feeling sorry for herself doing without her father for a short time. She still had Ma and Esther for companionship. What would it be like to be utterly alone?

A wagon jostled up beside them. Standing, Charlotte recognized Ian Crowley and his wife, Edna, atop the wagon bench, their brood of young children sprawled in the bed, each one a girl. If Charlotte's count was right, Mrs. Crowley held child number eight in her arms. With her hollowed cheeks and drawn expression, the woman appeared decades older than she was.

Mrs. Pruitt joined them, a pleasant smile lining her lips. "Good morning, Charlotte, Mr. and Mrs. Crowley."

Charlotte nodded, a bit nauseous at thought of the boy being handed over to such a clan.

Ignoring Mrs. Pruitt's greeting, Mr. Crowley looked Johnny over, eyes narrowed. "He's a mite scrawnier than what I recall."

The youngster pulled himself to full height, mumbling under his breath. "Ain't scrawny."

With a chuckle, the silver-haired doctor's wife folded her arms across her ample middle and eyed the row of squirmy girls that lined the wagon bed. "Would you . . . care to come in for some coffee before you go?"

"Haven't the time." Mr. Crowley motioned to Johnny. "Well, climb aboard, boy, so we can be on our way."

Johnny kicked at the ground before starting toward the wagon, shoulders slumped. It was all Charlotte could do to watch him go. Surely there was a more suitable home for the youngster.

"Don't forget your things." Mrs. Pruitt trotted to the porch to retrieve a knapsack.

While he waited, Johnny turned to Charlotte, the sadness in his eyes haunting. "Bye, miss."

"Goodbye, Johnny."

Knapsack in hand, the boy climbed the end-gate and slumped into the corner of the wagon bed. The brood of girls stared and poked at each other, giggling.

As they pulled away, Mrs. Pruitt shook her head. "The poor dear. Charles and I would take him in ourselves if we could manage it. Us being older, we just don't have the stamina to keep up with such a lively youngster."

"It was good of you to take him till a home could be found." If one could consider such an option a home.

Mrs. Pruitt brushed a hand over her hair, looking fatigued. "The child needed somewhere to go. We'd heard he was quite a handful, but you know, he never gave a bit of trouble till he found out the Crowleys were coming for him." She hung her head, placing a hand to her cheek. "Grieved is what he was. The whole time."

"How did Mr. and Mrs. Crowley find out about Johnny?"

"Seems Mr. Crowley was Ephraim Langston's best friend. He claimed, with the boy having no living relatives, Johnny's father would want the boy to go to him. Since no one else stepped forward, Pastor Brody had no choice but to agree."

Heaviness tugged at Charlotte's chest. If she were in a position to take Johnny in, she'd do it in a heartbeat. But as things were, she could only hope and pray he'd see happier days.

Chapter Twelve

"I NOW PRONOUNCE you man and wife." The preacher's voice echoed through the packed church building.

Chad gripped his hat in his hand and leaned against the back wall. His and Lauren's wedding hadn't been so well attended. A few friends and family. Nothing fancy. The faded memory came back in a bittersweet rush.

Becky and Matthew Brody clasped hands, eyes fastened on each other as if they alone occupied the room.

"Well, go on. Kiss her." The minister nudged Pastor Brody forward amid snickers from the crowd.

Joyful shouts rang out as the couple sealed their pledge with a tender kiss, touching foreheads before parting.

Chad stared at his boots, more alone in the throng of people than in his own cabin. Maybe he could slip out unnoticed the way he'd come. Charlotte's pleading emerald eyes flashed through his thoughts, chasing away any hopes of leaving.

He'd come this far. He'd stay long enough to make peace with her, then be on his way.

As the Brodys started down the aisle, the onlookers filed out behind. Chad's gaze drifted to the woman in the lace bonnet and jade green and white dress near the front of the church. The becoming dress hung nicely on Charlotte's lean figure. The same dress she'd worn to the homecoming party. Back then, he'd pegged her as a self-centered snob. Now, catching a glimpse of her winsome smile and generous hugs, she seemed a different person, one who'd let go of her insecurities and made a fresh start.

Could he do the same?

She caught him staring, and her smile widened. He tightened his grip on his hat, heat flaming in his cheeks. There was no escape now. She'd be more hurt than ever if he left without a greeting of some sort. He tugged at his collar, itching for the comfort of his buckskins and the solitude of the open prairie. At the least, he'd find the street outside less confining.

Easing into the dispersing crowd, he edged toward the door and the newly married couple. He waited his turn, then stuck out his hand. "The best to you both."

Matthew gave it a firm shake. "Much obliged. See you in church Sunday?"

He shook his head. "I leave for Hammett first thing tomorrow morning to fetch my cattle. It'll be a Sunday or two before I'll be back."

Pastor Brody gave a firm nod. "We'll look for you then."

The new Mrs. Brody tilted her head in a soft smile. A beautiful bride, inside and out. "Thanks for coming, Mr. Avery, and for all your help with the field work."

"You bet."

He donned his hat and started down the steps, thankful to again taste the freedom of the outdoors. Now to make amends with Charlotte. He waited at the corner of the church building, feeling about as out of place as a fox in a barnyard. If only he could speak with her in private, away from the crowd of people. Already they were scuttling about in readiness for the wedding celebration.

At last, Charlotte appeared at the top of the steps, eyes panning the dispersing throng of people. Warmth surged through him when she glanced his way. He peered down at his boots, shaking off the unexpected sensation. Did he feel something for Charlotte? He couldn't.

Wouldn't let himself.

Perhaps he should leave. He turned and started toward Buck.

"Wait!"

The familiar soprano voice froze him in his tracks. Glancing over his shoulder, he saw Charlotte working her way toward him. The curious expression in her eyes, blended with a slight downward curve of her lips, assured him he'd do well to stay put.

She struggled to catch her breath as she came up beside him. "Where are you going?"

"I . . . thought I'd head on back."

"You're not staying for the celebration?"

He squinted against the sun hanging low in the west. "Better not. Gotta get an early start in the mornin'."

"But, I was counting on at least one dance with you . . . after the way our last one ended." Her voice trailed off, and a hint of red shone in her cheeks.

Good sense told him he should leave, but something inside pulled at him to stay. Maybe a dance with Charlotte would settle his conscience.

Then again, it might open his heart to something he would later regret.

CHARLOTTE TAPPED her foot to the music, divvying out cups of cider to red-faced dancers. A blend of fiddle, banjo, and guitar strummed out a lively version of *"Oh! Susanna"*. It seemed the entire countryside had turned out for the outdoor wedding celebration.

She kept a watchful eye on Chad, making certain he'd not ventured from his spot beneath the hickory tree. How she longed for everyone to have their fill of refreshments so she could claim the dance Chad had promised her. Would he tire of waiting?

If only she had more time to spend with him. One dance wasn't much, but it was enough to convince her he thought something of her. Why else would he have changed his mind about leaving? Did she dare to hope he cared for her?

The clear blue sky faded to an amber hue as the sun sank lower on the horizon. The crescent moon shone overhead, its glow aided by the cluster of lanterns strung about. The once full food tables lay bare, pounced upon by a flurry of hungry well-wishers. Even her runny, gooseberry pie had been gobbled up like candy.

Laughter rang out from the group surrounding the bride and groom. A sigh escaped Charlotte as Pastor Brody clasped Becky's hand, his face lit up in a smile. Would anyone ever feel so enamored with her?

A shadow fell across her face as she filled another mug with cider. Glancing up, she startled at Norris standing beside her. She wet her lips and lifted the cider-filled mug. "Would you like some?"

He shook his head, sinking his hands in his pockets. "No thanks. How's about finishin' our dance?"

"Our . . . dance?"

Norris's brow creased. "Don't you remember? Your ankle?"

Charlotte let out a nervous chuckle. "Oh, yes. My ankle." Her gaze flicked to Chad who seemed to be watching with interest. She'd gotten herself in trouble the last time with her pretenses. The truth seemed best if she meant to keep herself out of mischief. "I'm afraid I've promised my first dance to Mr. Avery over there. But if you care to wait, I'll be free a bit later."

Norris's gaze shifted to Chad, then back to her. "Him again? How'd ya get so chummy with him anyway? I've known you for years and you've not so much as offered to save me a dance. Now this guy comes along and you treat him like he's your best fella."

His elevated voice drew the attention of those nearby. Charlotte raised a finger to her lips and pulled him aside, hopeful the music had stifled his words. She cradled a hand on her hip. "Mr. Avery is a friend. I've given my word, and I mean to keep it. If you choose not to wait, I'm sure Miss Brimmer would be more than happy to take my place."

The glow in Norris's orange hair trickled down into his cheeks. "That she would. I've done enough waitin' where you're concerned, Charlotte Stanton. Good day to you."

Charlotte worked to still her quivering hands as she watched him tromp away. Here she'd tried her best to be polite and still ended up losing her temper and causing Norris to lose his.

She glanced to where Chad had stood, her heart sinking at the empty spot beneath the tree. She'd done it again. He'd seen the exchange and been put off. This time, however, it wasn't her fault. At least not entirely.

With a huff, she strolled to her place behind the refreshment table. As she poured another mug of cider, she sensed a presence behind her and turned. Chad's silvery eyes peered down at her. She opened her mouth to speak, to explain what he'd no doubt seen pass between her and Norris. But, he set his hat on the table and clasped her hand in his.

Charlotte stilled at his touch, her heart hammering. Her demeanor softened as he led her amidst the other dancers. She met his gaze, muddled thoughts choking off words. Just who was this man? One instant he was aloof and distant, the next alluring and forceful. He slid his arm around her waist, and they swayed to the soft trill of the mandolin. Heat flared in Charlotte's cheeks under his pointed stare. Was he angry with her again?

She swallowed and willed herself to speak. "I only told him I'd promised you the first dance."

"I figured as much." His gaze trailed past her.

"Surely you can't put the blame on me this time. After all, he's the one who chose to storm off. I told him I'd dance with him later."

"It appears he chose not to wait." He nodded behind her.

Charlotte followed his gaze, her eyes widening when she saw her would-be suitor dancing with Lola Brimmer. Turning, she flashed a wide smile. "Yes. It does."

With a soft sigh, she leaned into Chad's embrace and let the music and his strong arm guide her. Their eyes locked, and a brief smile touched his lips. This dance, so different from their last, was everything Charlotte had hoped for. Despite the mystery shrouding this man, she found herself entranced by his commanding presence.

His hold on her waist shifted as he maneuvered her away from the throng of dancers to the far side of the church building. Charlotte tightened her grip on his shoulder, fearful he intended to leave. As they dipped into the shadows, the music faded and their dance slowed to a mere sway. Chad lifted his gaze to the crescent moon shining overhead, his voice soft and low. "I'm sorry for the way I spoke to you earlier this week. I had no call to be rude."

A hint of moisture formed between their hands as Charlotte's gaze found his. This man. So strong and yet, so gentle. A smile pulled at her lips. "I've been told I ask too many questions."

Especially when she cared deeply for someone and wanted to know more.

A quiet moan expelled from within Chad. "There are parts of my life I'd rather not talk about. Things you're better off not knowing."

Charlotte's mind reeled. Was he some sort of criminal? A shyster, or thief?

Not Chad. He'd not intentionally wrong anyone. Break a

heart perhaps, hers even, but not with evil intent. He didn't have it in him.

She gave his hand a gentle squeeze. "Not now, perhaps, but in time I hope you'll share with me whatever it is that troubles you."

The song ended, and Chad loosened his hold on her waist and offered her his elbow.

Charlotte looped her arm through his and matched his easy stride.

The songs of katydids, crickets, and tree frogs drowned out the sounds of celebration as they strolled further from the gathering. The starry sky and crescent moon lit the wide dirt path, guiding their way to the outskirts of town. Charlotte breathed in the night air, contentment overshadowing her questions. How could she be so peaceful and so unsettled at the same time? She knew so little about this man, and yet had never felt so safe and protected with anyone.

Chad slowed his pace, his rich voice breaking the stillness. "I may not have all the answers, but I couldn't leave without clearing the air between us."

A sense of loss spilled over her. "How long will you be gone?"

"A week. Maybe two."

Her heart sank. Just when they were getting acquainted, he was leaving. But only for a short while. Would he call on her when he returned? Her chin lifted. "You've worked hard to prepare for your cattle. I'm glad for you."

Chad paused, turning toward her. The blue light of evening cast a shadow over his face as he stared down at her. He leaned forward to mere inches from her face, his warm breath caressing her cheeks.

Charlotte edged closer, heart hammering in her chest.

Would he kiss her?

His hand brushed her arm, sending a tingle through her. Her

lips parted as she anticipated his arms encircling her. Instead, he stilled and backed away. "I-I'd better go."

The raspy tone in his voice bordered on frustration. Had she been too willing, too eager? With a nod, she laced her hands together and lowered her gaze, too disheartened for words.

He touched her elbow, pivoting her toward the gathering. "I'll walk you back."

Her chest squeezed, as if some deep sentiment had passed between them, and then vanished like a forgotten dream.

While away, would he miss her?

Something told her she'd miss him. More than she cared to admit.

WHY COULDN'T he have left well enough alone? He should have gone home after the wedding like he'd planned. Chad turned on his cot, visions of Charlotte's moonlit face sapping his sleep. Did she know how close he'd come to kissing her? Was it hurt he'd glimpsed in her eyes when he'd backed away? If he wasn't careful, he'd lose his heart to her.

Or had he already?

He draped his arms behind his head and stared at the darkened rafters. Soon he'd be on his way to Hammett. It was good he was leaving. The time away would help clear his head.

If he stayed, he'd be tempted to see Charlotte again. He pushed the air from his lungs. He couldn't afford to love again. Lauren's memory wouldn't allow for it. He needed to focus on his cattle and the dream he and Lauren had shared. A dream that would soon become a reality.

Chapter Thirteen

CHARLOTTE WANTED TO PINCH HERSELF. Last night's moonlit stroll had left her a bit dazed. The way Chad had leaned into her, then backed away. If only she could have seen his face and caught the expression in his eyes. But like the rest of him, his sudden retreat remained a mystery.

With a sigh, she rose from her three-legged stool and clasped the handle on her bucket of milk. Now, she'd not see nor hear from him for more than a week. Would he let her know when he returned? She leaned against the stall post, hollowness sapping her energy. With the two men she cared for most away, life held little appeal.

She could only pray for their quick and safe return.

Maybe that's why she'd agreed to stay with Uncle Joseph the few days Becky and Pastor Brody were gone on their wedding trip. Esther had offered, but she and her uncle had fallen into a rather comfortable routine, and the extra duties would help take her mind off her loneliness.

A faint "thump" in the corner of the loft drew Charlotte's attention. She tensed and gnawed at her lip. Surely Johnny hadn't run off again. Strolling outside, she turned and flattened herself against the barn timbers, staying hidden as she paused to listen. A faint sigh sounded within.

Charlotte swiveled to stand in the doorway. "Is that you, Johnny?"

The boyish moan followed by a rustling noise all but confirmed her suspicions. She stepped closer and propped her hands on her hips. "You may as well come down. I know you're up there."

Silence.

"Don't make me come up after you."

The boy groaned and stepped into the open. "Ah. What'd ya have ta go and find me for?"

"The question is, what are you doing here? Mr. and Mrs. Crowley will be worried sick."

"No they won't." He hung his head and kicked at the straw, sending several strands sailing to the barn floor. "And you cain't make me go back neither."

She beckoned him with her finger. "Come here."

With slow movements, he climbed down and stood at a distance. At least he wasn't running away. She edged toward him, and he backed into the shadows. "There's no need to be afraid."

He straightened. "I ain't afraid of nothin'."

Charlotte stifled a grin. A large claim for one so young. "Then tell me. Why don't you want to go back to the Crowleys'?"

Johnny rubbed a hand under his nose. "'Cause . . . 'cause I don't like it there."

"Why not?" Closing the gap between them, she could see he was no longer the clean, well-groomed boy he'd been when he'd left Doc and Anabelle Pruitt's home. But then with all those young'uns at the Crowley home, fresh bath water would be hard to come by.

"Jus' don't, that's all." The dim light of the barn hid the boy's face, but there was a tremor in his voice.

Charlotte squatted in front of him and touched a hand to his shoulder. He cringed and veered back. A nauseating thought left Charlotte wishing she'd not found him either. She swallowed down the dryness in her throat. "They haven't hurt you, have they?"

He sniffled, his gaze dropping to his bare feet.

The response was enough to ignite a fire inside her. To harm a child was among the most despicable acts she could imagine. Had Pastor Brody and Becky known such, they'd never have left the boy with the Crowleys. But they were gone to St. Louis on their wedding trip. The boy needed to be kept safe until they returned.

Perhaps Uncle Joseph would let Johnny stay with them. Standing, she blinked back the moisture pooling in her eyes. "Well, you're safe here. Come with me."

The boy's face lifted. "Where?"

"To see my uncle."

Johnny took a step toward her. "Does he live here too?"

With a smile, Charlotte started toward the door. "Oh, I don't live here. I'm just staying with my uncle while his daughter's away. You see he's blind and can't manage on his own."

Johnny fell into stride with her. "But you was here the last time."

She gave a soft chuckle. "I reckon I have been here quite a lot, of late. It almost seems like home."

A cackling hen sounded inside the chicken coop reminding Charlotte she'd not yet turned them out or gathered the eggs. She paused outside the small log structure, her thoughts turning to the setting hen inside. "Ever see a baby chick before it hatched?"

Johnny shook his head, sinking his hands in his pockets.

Motioning for him to stand aside, Charlotte opened the door to the chicken coop. The rooster and several hens fluttered out, leaving a trail of dust and feather-down in their wake. They stepped inside, the air thick with the smell of poultry. One buff hen remained on her nest. She gave a soft cluck as Charlotte reached under her and snatched an egg. Bending down, she coddled it between her fingertips and held it to the stream of light seeping through a hole in the timbers. She glanced at Johnny and then the egg. "Do you see how the lower half of the egg is dark while light shines through the upper portion?"

Johnny scrunched his eyebrows and peered hard at the egg, then gave a slow nod.

"That's the chick growing inside. The mother hen's been keeping the eggs warm for a couple of weeks now. Feel how heavy it is."

The boy's eyes widened as he cupped the warm egg in his outstretched hands.

Charlotte cringed at the red streaks across his wrists. And were those calluses lining his palms? The poor child.

With a self-conscious glare, Johnny gave back the egg and slid his hands in his pockets. "When will it hatch?"

"In a couple of weeks." She slipped the egg back under the mother hen, then turned to Johnny with a weak grin. "There's nothing much cuter than a baby chick."

A horse's whinny sounded in the distance. Charlotte's heart drummed. Was Chad stopping on his way north? She hurried outside and squinted to make out the lone rider to the east. The horse was too dark and the rider too slumped to be Chad.

Johnny stepped to her side. "Who is it?"

"I don't recognize him." Charlotte brushed a wisp of hair from her cheek.

"It's him. Don't let him take me."

"Who? Mr. Crowley?"

In answer, Johnny ducked inside the chicken coop. Charlotte could only pray he hadn't been seen. She took a step forward, chin lifted, pressing down her growing angst. She held nothing but contempt for this man who'd mistreated her young friend.

Ian Crowley halted his horse beside her. His furrowed brow and sunken cheeks mapped out a life devoid of joy. His lips never so much as cracked a smile beneath his thick, salt and pepper mustache. Was his life truly so miserable, or was he simply exhausted from rearing eight children?

Charlotte eased the coop door shut behind her. "What can I do for you Mr. Crowley?"

"I came for the boy."

Charlotte's hopes crumbled. There was no use denying it. He'd, no doubt, seen Johnny. Her gaze flicked to her feet as she worked to still quivering hands. Sending Johnny back with this tyrant was like tossing a rabbit to a wolf. "Johnny's a welcome guest here. We're just now getting acquainted. He'd like to stay a while."

"The boy ran off. He needs taught a lesson."

She squared her shoulders and squinted up at him. "Does your lesson include a thrashing?"

He pinned her to the ground with his pointed stare. "Tain't none of your business, woman."

She sensed the blood drain from her cheeks. The man was intimidating to her. How much more fearsome he must be to the boy. "If you'd not mistreated the lad, he'd not have run off."

A sneer spread across Crowley's face. "Well now, ain't you a feisty one? But you ain't got no say, missy. I took him in, so I reckon he's mine to do with as I please."

The man was deranged, acting as if Johnny were some sort of possession. "If the Brodys had known you'd mistreat Johnny, they never would have let you have him. And I mean to let them know."

The man's eyes narrowed, then he shouted toward the chicken coop. "Get yourself out here, boy, or you and your lady friend will wish you had."

Was that a threat? Charlotte crossed her arms and tapped her heel in the dirt, working to conceal the unsteadiness in her voice. "Stay where you're at, Johnny."

"Don't hurt her. I'll come." The door creaked open, and Johnny stepped from the chicken coop, shoulders hunched.

"I knew you had smarts, boy." Crowley leaned forward in his saddle, brows knit. "Now, git over here."

Johnny stiffened, eyes big as saucers as he stepped toward the man. Charlotte pulled him back, shielding him from the man's harsh stare. "He stays."

Crowley shifted his gaze to Charlotte. "An' I say he goes." He kicked his heels in his horse's flanks, and the bay lunged forward. Prying Johnny from her grasp, Crowley pulled him onto his horse.

Charlotte tugged at Johnny's legs, but released him when she saw his pained expression. She gritted her teeth, propping her hands atop her bonnet. "You'll regret this, Mr. Crowley. As soon as Pastor Brody gets back, expect us on your doorstep."

Crowley sneered down at her. "This boy's got the makings of a right fine worker, and I means t' keep him. No mealy-mouthed preacher or hot-headed female's gonna stop me." He whirled his horse around and sank his heels into its sides. The bay mare blazed off at a full gallop. Johnny peered back over his shoulder at Charlotte, his anguished expression searing her soul.

Like muddied water that had settled, the man's need for Johnny became clear. Mr. Crowley hadn't taken Johnny out of benevolence, but for his own selfish gain. With a houseful of daughters, he needed a stout boy to help with the heavy work.

And to take out his frustrations, it appeared.

Charlotte's chest burned hot. How could she allow Johnny to stay even one night, knowing he'd be abused and taken advantage of?

She could only pray for Pastor Brody's quick return and that Johnny would be spared further hardship.

Chapter Fourteen

SPARKS FLEW as Chad tossed another log on the campfire. Thanks to a successful hunt, there'd be something besides venison jerky tonight. He fastened the skinned rabbit on a spit and positioned it over the flames. Having unsaddled Buck, he spread his bedroll on the ground a safe distance from the fire. Two days journey behind him. He was making good time. If all went well, in another day and a half, he'd be in Hammett. He'd have his thirty head of cattle home within another week.

The evening sky exploded with color as he emptied beans into a skillet and positioned it at the edge of the fire. A twig snapped in the timber behind him. He cocked his muzzleloader and wheeled toward the sound.

"Hold on there, sonny. I mean no harm." A man stepped from the shadows, leading his malnourished, if not mistreated, horse. He raised his hands, slowing his approach. The lower half of the stranger's face was hidden beneath a wiry beard, streaks of gray mingling with shades of brown.

Chad eyed him warily. "State your business."

"Smelled your cookin'. Gets a mite lonesome out here. Wondered if I could share your fire?" He swaggered closer, his worn shirt tight against his bulging stomach. By the looks of him, he hadn't lacked for too many meals.

Chad held his stance. He didn't mind being alone. In fact, he preferred it. The man's dazed eyes and haggard appearance cast an unwelcome light over him. Something deep within Chad told him to send the man packing. But the Good Book said to love the "least of these", and this man certainly qualified for that. Chad lowered his gun. "I reckon there's no harm."

"Much obliged." With a toothy grin, the man dropped his hands to his sides. Once he'd secured his horse to a tree branch, he ambled toward the fire. The smell of liquor hung in the air as he squatted beside Chad. "Where you headed?"

"North. How 'bout yourself?" He'd keep his answers vague. He didn't trust the man.

"Wherever my feet take me, I reckon." The stranger stuck out a hand, the scar on his right temple bulging as he spoke. "Glad t' know you. The name's Rusty Duran."

Chad set his rifle on his far side and shook Duran's hand. "Chad Avery."

The man gave a slow nod and sat back on his haunches. His gaze drifted to the money pouch fastened to Chad's belt, then darted away. Reaching in his pocket, Duran drew out a flask of whiskey. He took a long swig, then pushed the canister at Chad.

With a shake of his head, Chad reached to turn the spit. "Never touch the stuff. And I'd appreciate if you'd lay off it while you're here."

The man's face pinched in a scowl, and he mumbled under his breath as he drew the flask back and screwed on the lid.

The beans began to sizzle, and Chad pulled them from the fire with his neckerchief. Taking a wooden spoon from his pack, he gave the beans a stir. "I've only one set of dishes. Wasn't expecting company."

"No bother. I'll eat whatever's left in the skillet."

Chad pricked at the rabbit with a fork, relieved it was ready to eat. The sooner he was rid of this fellow the better. He pried off a chunk of the meat, and thrust it toward Duran. Hopefully, once his belly was full, he'd leave without further argument.

By the time they'd finished eating, the vibrant sky had faded to deep blue. Chad's patience wore thin as his unwanted companion ran his fingers over the skillet, gleaning every last smidgen of bean sauce. At last, he rubbed his hands on his shirt and raked his sleeve over his mouth. "Much obliged for the vittles."

Nodding, Chad waited for the man to leave. Yet, he gave no indication he was going anywhere.

Instead, he leaned back, patting his ample middle. "No sir. There's nothin' to put a person to sleep faster than a full stomach."

Chad narrowed his eyes. If the stranger was fishing for an invitation to stay the night, he'd not get one. "You've little light left to get where you're going. I'll not detain you any longer."

Duran met Chad's steady gaze. The stranger's nose flared as he slowly rose to his feet. "Well then, as you say, I'd best be off."

Chad watched him leave, listening until the sound of his horse's hooves faded in the distance. Only then did he settle back down before the fire. He yawned, drinking in the sounds of nightlife, the hoot of an owl and the drone of insects. The dishes could wait. Lying back on his make-shift bed, he pillowed his head on his saddle and stared up into the starry sky. He draped his loaded rifle across his chest, resting his hands atop it. As peaceful as the night seemed, it was never without its dangers.

CHARLOTTE PACED the floor of her uncle's cabin, unable to get Johnny off her mind. In a sense, he was proving a fitting distraction for her while Chad and Pa were away. She had to do something. It would be days before the Brodys returned from their trip.

"You keep that up and you'll wear a trench in the floorboards."

Her uncle's voice brought her pacing to a halt. She melted into a chair and stared into the glowing embers in the fireplace. "I'm sorry, but I can't keep from worrying about Johnny. He's in harm's way every hour he's with that brute."

Uncle Joseph settled deeper in his rocker. "From what you say, you've cause for concern, but no problem was ever solved by worrying. You'd do better to spend your energies praying."

Charlotte heaved a quiet sigh. Uncle Joseph was right. Worrying accomplished nothing. There wasn't a blessed thing she could do to free Johnny from the man's clutches. To try was pure foolishness. Leaving it in the Lord's hands was a much better option, yet everything in her longed to bash a skillet over the man's head and steal Johnny away.

Darkness cloaked the cabin as twilight banished the last smidgen of daylight from the sky. She reached to turn up the wick on the lantern. Ma and Esther would be headed for bed soon. As should she. Charlotte found herself missing them. It seemed strange to spend nights here as well as days, and yet it gave her a sense of what it would be to run her own household.

When Chad returned, would their budding relationship blossom into more or fade like the setting sun? Would he ever open his heart to her? She knew him to be a man of faith and integrity, but there were still so many unanswered questions, so much she needed and wanted to know.

Her gaze drifted to the open window and to the stars spreading over the night sky. She always prayed better in nature. Somehow the Lord just seemed closer at hand. "I think I'll go outside a bit."

Her uncle gave a slow nod, not seeming to care if she stayed or went.

The chirp of insects filled the night air, their melodious songs calming her restless spirit as she stepped onto the porch. She lifted her face to the sky, breathing in the coolness of the evening. The last starry sky she'd gazed into she'd shared with Chad. Was he enjoying a similar view under prairie skies? Was her father?

She felt a bit like Martha in the Bible, her heart troubled by many things. It was time to lay her worries to rest, here in the presence of Almighty God.

Lord, I need Your peace. Watch over Johnny until something can be done to get him to a safe place. He's endured so much at such a tender age. Incite someone to open their heart to him. Give him a place where he can be loved and cared for. Keep Chad safe as he travels and give him a willingness to open his heart. And please watch over Pa while he's away. Bring them both home very soon.

She smiled to herself, feeling the first sense of peace she'd had in some time. Uncle Joseph was right. A few moments with the Lord was worth more than decades of worry.

If only she could hold onto this peace in days to come.

SOMETHING WASN'T RIGHT. It was too still. Chad shifted in his saddle, the leather creaking under him as he tugged Buck to a stop. Last night's encounter with Duran had him on edge. Thankfully it would be his last night out before reaching his destination.

Chad cocked his head, listening for some unknown sound.

Nothing.

Still, he couldn't shake the feeling he was being followed.

Dark shadows fell over the prairie as the sun dipped below the horizon. If he didn't make camp soon, it would be too dark to gather firewood. But then, if he was being tailed, he wouldn't want much of a fire anyway. Buck snorted and shook his head. The smell of sweat wafted up as Chad leaned to pat the horse's neck. He'd pushed the gelding hard today. Too hard maybe. But there was a limit to how far either of them could go.

He reined Buck to an open area at the edge of the timber near a creek. A soft breeze cooled his damp skin as he dismounted. He rubbed the back of his neck, bone weary after the long day's travel. The sooner he got some shuteye, the sooner he could get moving again. If all went well, he'd be in Hammett by noon tomorrow. None too soon for his liking. He should have a few hours to rest up before the herd arrived. He raised his arm and took a whiff. The first order of business would be to get himself a bath.

He loosened the cinch and slid the saddle from Buck, giving him a firm pat on the rump. The horse lowered his head and shook out his damp coat. Chad took a tin of oats from his saddlebag and offered a handful to Buck. A well-deserved reward for a hard day's work. With a nicker, the horse nibbled at the grain until Chad's palm was licked clean.

Rifle in hand, Chad led him to the creek for a drink. The horse pawed at the water, forcing Chad further upstream. He bent to refill his canteen, then splashed cool water on his face, keeping a watchful eye on the darkening timber. If someone were to ambush him, the woods would be a prime place to do it. He loosened the leather cord that tied the money pouch to his belt and slipped it inside his shirt. This close to his dream, he couldn't afford to let his guard down.

He trudged back to camp and tied Buck at the edge of the timber without so much as gathering a stick. He'd forgo a fire tonight altogether. Reaching in his saddlebag, he took out a strip of venison jerky. Good thing he'd packed plenty. He bit off a piece of the tough meat and chewed it as he untied his bedroll. Tomorrow he'd buy himself a plate of fried chicken or a beef steak, but for now, at least he had something to fill his belly.

He spread his blanket on the ground beside his saddle. He choked down another wad of jerky, then took a swig from his canteen. A near half-moon cradled low in the sky, shedding little light on the ever-darkening prairie. With a yawn, Chad settled back on his makeshift bed, rifle in hand. As tired as he was, he could easily sleep through till morning.

A TUG on his shirt roused Chad. His eyes bobbed open and shut. The spattering of stars overhead shed little light on the black night. Boots scuffed on the ground beside him. Something blocked the starlight over him. He blinked, tried to focus. Was he dreaming?

But then the darkness moved.

He reached for his rifle.

It was gone.

His coin pouch jingled.

"Hey!" He lunged forward and clasped the man's sleeve. In the dim light, Chad caught a glimpse of a wiry beard and the whites of eyes. The stench of whiskey filled his nostrils as the figure above him pulled back.

A strong blow struck Chad's jaw.

Another stabbing pain shot through his right temple. Then, coldness washed over him as everything faded to black.

Chapter Fifteen

CHAD WOKE WITH A START. He cringed and raised a hand to his throbbing forehead. A stiff welt lined his temple. He glanced at his blood-stained fingertips. What had happened? The last thing he remembered was taking a blow to the jaw and another to his head. Who'd done this?

He sat up, squinting against the morning light. How long had he lain there? Several hours at least. The sun was well above the horizon. A sudden thought sent a tremor rippling through him. One touch of his buckskin shirt confirmed his fears.

He'd been robbed.

He ran a hand over his jaw. It was all coming back now. The shadowy figure leaning over him in the night. The beard and smell of whiskey.

Duran.

He must have doubled back. Chad balled his fists, seething inwardly. Well, he wouldn't get away with it. His and Lauren's life's savings was in that pouch.

Light-headed, Chad reached to steady himself against his saddle. Instead, he fell back, his hand meeting with the ground.

His eyes narrowed at sight of the empty spot where his saddle had been. That low-down thief had taken his saddle.

Buck.

His gaze darted to the timberline, eyes panning in all directions. With an outraged growl, he kicked at the ground with the heel of his boot. No one stole his horse and saddle and got away with it. He'd track Duran down if it was the last thing he did.

There was no time to lose. Duran had several hours lead as it was. Rising to his feet, Chad pitched forward, steadying himself before he fell. How could he track someone when he could barely stand?

Lord, help me.

His shoulders lifted when he spied his rifle and saddle bags several yards to his left. Duran had either been too drunk or in too big of hurry to be thorough. His carelessness would be his undoing. Chad pressed a hand to his temple. The cattle would have to wait. First he had to find Duran. Somehow he'd catch up with the no-good varmint, even on foot.

As he packed up his bedroll, something fell from his blanket. Two silver coins, shining in the morning sun. He picked them up and rolled them over in his palm. They must have fallen out in the scuffle. With a sigh, he sunk them in his pocket. They wouldn't buy cattle, but at least he wasn't penniless.

Blood trickled down the side of Chad's face as he reached for his hat. He loosened his neckerchief and fastened it around his forehead, then set his hat gently over top. Retrieving his saddle bags, he hefted them over his shoulder. With a sigh, he took out a strip of venison jerky. He'd not rest until he had his money back — and his horse.

He clutched his rifle, searching the ground for clues. Knowing which direction Chad was headed, it sufficed to say Duran would go any way but north. Chad scoured the area for tracks until he found a fresh trail leading west. That figured. His friend Rusty was trekking toward the Illinois River. If he wasn't stopped, he'd hold up at some river town until he'd gambled away every last penny.

Chad stumbled forward, then paused. A rustling noise, too big for a squirrel or bird, came from the timber behind him. He cocked his rifle and squinted into the underbrush, taking a slow blink to clear his vision. A soft whinny sounded a few yards in. Training his eyes in the direction of the sound, he caught sight of Duran's malnourished horse among the underbrush. So, Duran had abandoned his nag in exchange for Buck. Fortunately for Chad, the four-legged beast hadn't strayed far.

Lowering his gun, Chad stepped toward the horse, its long, thin neck a mass of tangled mane and scars. It lunged sideways as he neared. Chad slowly reached out his arm, his voice soft and low. "Whoa now. I won't hurt ya none."

Though she stilled, the horse's black eyes tracked his every move. Ever so gently, Chad ran a hand down the mare's neck and onto her bony withers. Ribs protruded from her sides, and her flesh quivered at his touch as he reached to straighten the cocked saddle. One could often tell the character of a man by his horse. That being the case, he should have guessed from the start Duran was up to no good.

Chad took up the reins and led her to an open area. She arched her head toward him as he tightened the cinch. Positioning one hand on the horn, the other on the cantle, he placed his foot in the stirrup. It seemed almost cruel to mount her. But he had no choice. The poor thing was better than no horse at all. He patted her scarred neck. "Don't worry. You get me where I'm goin', and I'll see to it you're never mistreated again."

The horse gave a soft nicker. Heaving himself up, Chad swung his leg over her. The horse's back swayed downward as Chad eased into the saddle. He'd walk from time to time to give her a rest. But the Lord seemed to be smiling on him in his misfortune. He had a gun, a horse — so to speak — and a trail to follow. All he needed now was the self-restraint not to put a plug in Duran on sight.

"WE HAVE to get Johnny out of there. It's not safe." Charlotte hated to bother the Brodys with her troubles the moment they returned home, but she refused to make light of her young friend's predicament.

Pastor Brody set his travel bags on the floor of the cabin and lifted a hand to still her. "Hold on now. What's the trouble?"

Charlotte eased back and took a deep breath. "I found Johnny in the barn loft again. He had marks on his wrists and I'm certain bruises elsewhere. He needs out of there."

Pastor Brody's brow creased. "You saw the bruises?"

"No. But Johnny cringed when I touched him. I know he's being mistreated."

Pastor Brody rubbed a hand over his chin. "Did the boy say he'd been mistreated?"

"Not in words, but I could read it on his face. Mr. Crowley merely wants him for a work hand." Charlotte swallowed the dryness in her throat, irritated by the calmness in Pastor Brody's tone.

He and Becky shared a weary look. Did they think Charlotte was making this up or were they too travel-worn to care? Had she waited all this time for nothing?

Becky gave her father a hug, then turned to her husband. "Isn't there somewhere else the child could stay, Matthew?"

"Mr. Crowley was a close friend to Johnny's father. I'm afraid, with no other known relatives, he's first in line. So long as he wishes him to stay."

Charlotte took a step forward, a hint of urgency lining her

words. "But if he abuses the boy, Johnny could be taken from him, right?"

"If there's proof."

The pastor's pointed words only made Charlotte more determined. "What about you two? You'd make fine parents for Johnny."

Her cousin's cheeks pinked. "Thank you, Charlotte but . . ." She shot a desperate glance at her husband.

He stepped behind her and placed his hands on her shoulders. "We could, but we've only just married. We're not quite ready to rear a seven-year-old."

He planted a kiss on Becky's cheek, then turned to Charlotte. "We'll stay here tonight, and I'll be sure to check on Johnny first thing tomorrow."

Charlotte squared her shoulders. "Then I'll meet you at the edge of Crowley's property an hour past sunrise." Without allowing time to argue, she nodded goodbye and slipped outside.

She drew in a breath, forcing herself to calm. Hopefully tomorrow Johnny would be free of Mr. Crowley. But where would he go? What if no one was willing to take him in? She could only pray someone would have the gumption to step forward and give the boy a home.

One side of her mouth hinged upward. Maybe, given the right persuasion, Ma and Pa would be willing. But first, Pa had to return. Her mother would never agree to such an arrangement without his consent.

As she mounted, her thoughts shifted to Chad. Was there a chance he'd be back? Though he'd not yet been gone a week, perhaps she should swing by for a look. Reining Willow westward, Charlotte sensed her hopefulness growing. She knew little of the love between a man and a woman. She'd not loved a man other than her father. Yet, if the flurry inside her as she neared Chad's place were any indication, she loved him already.

At least she believed him the sort of man she *could* love.

Charlotte pulled back on the reins as his cabin came into view and searched the pasture for signs of cattle. Instead, an empty, grass-covered meadow stared back at her. She chewed at her lip, her spirits plummeting. No sense going any closer. He wasn't there.

The old place looked a bit more kept since she'd last seen it. Chad's imprints were everywhere. In the new shingles on the cabin roof, in the zigzag of hewn timbers fencing off the yard, and in the freshly worked field to the cabin's east.

She smiled. His dream of a cattle farm was taking shape. She only hoped she'd have the opportunity to be a part of it.

CHAD SQUATTED at the edge of the dusty trail, trying to decipher the myriad of hoof-prints lining the path. Which way now? West to Colby, or East to Rosewood? Up to this point, there'd been visible signs to follow, broken branches, distinct hoof-prints, and an occasional tuft of Buck's coat caught on twigs or brambles. But how could he pick out a set of tracks along the well-traveled road?

Instinct told him to veer west, toward Colby. The river town would be just the sort Duran would be looking for to make use of his ill-gotten gain. Yet west would take Chad farther from his cattle.

And his dream.

The image of Charlotte's jade eyes staring up at him blurred his thoughts. What sort of man would she think him if he returned empty-handed? But then, why should it matter? They were friends at best. Nothing more.

He gripped a handful of the gritty dirt and tossed it into the breeze. Even friends needed to own each other's respect.

He stood and brushed off his hands, seething inwardly. A lesser man might string Duran up from the nearest tree for his thievery. He'd be satisfied with retrieving what he'd lost, and seeing Duran behind bars.

Mounting, Chad gave the weary mare a firm pat on the neck, steering her toward Colby. "Well, girl, let's go find your owner." With a tap of his heels, he tightened his grip on the reins, praying his instincts were right.

Chapter Sixteen

CHARLOTTE'S STOMACH clenched as the Crowleys' ramshackle homestead came into view. She'd thought Chad's place looked bad before he'd made repairs. This cabin wasn't fit for chickens, with rags for a window, rotting timbers, and very little chinking to shut out daylight.

She spotted Pastor Brody standing, hat in hand, beneath the shade of a shag-bark hickory up ahead. She spurred Willow forward until she came up beside him. "Thanks for waiting."

He greeted her with a weak smile, hinting he was eager to get this unpleasant task over with. Donning his hat, he nodded toward the run-down cabin. "Do you see the boy?"

Charlotte followed his gaze to the cluster of young children darting around the dilapidated shack as though in a game of tag. From what she could tell, all the youngsters wore gunnysack frocks, not trousers. "Hard to tell, but I don't think so."

She'd not seen or heard a word about how Johnny was faring in nearly a week. It had taken all her willpower not to come for him herself. But after Ian Crowley's stern reaction, she'd thought better of it. Surely, with Pastor Brody along, they'd have no trouble freeing Johnny from this brute of a man.

A shadowy figure peeked from behind the rag curtain and then disappeared as they started toward the cabin. Were they being watched?

As they neared, the children stopped their play, smiles fading. Charlotte halted Willow beside them, and they stared up at her and the pastor with wide eyes and smudged faces. As feared, Johnny wasn't among them. Sadness rippled through Charlotte as she took in the girls' tangled hair and tattered clothing. Did their parents give so little thought to even their own children?

Pastor Brody sat forward in his saddle, smiling down at them. "Is your ma or pa at home?"

The youngest girl, looking to be no more than three, twirled a finger through her ratted hair. "Ma is."

Her older pig-tailed sister nudged her with her elbow, at which the younger child scrunched her face and rubbed her arm.

Charlotte tried to squelch the urgency in her voice. "Could we speak with her, please? We'd like to see Johnny."

The four urchins exchanged glances, then skittered off to the woodshed.

With a shake of her head, Charlotte dismounted. She sensed eyes upon her, not only from behind the woodshed, but also from inside the cabin. She shared a disgruntled look with Pastor Brody and followed him to the rickety porch, careful to avoid the abundance of holes in the planks. A light rap on the door produced a child's soft whimper, but nothing more. Pastor Brody knocked a second time, then stood back and listened for movement within.

Nothing.

Charlotte hung her head. Obviously they weren't going to make this easy. She raised her hand to the door and rapped harder, her patience wearing thin. "You may as well open up, Mrs. Crowley. We know you're in there."

A pause, then soft footsteps approached the door. The latch lifted. Charlotte took a step back as the door creaked open. Mrs.

Crowley peered out at them like a mouse from its hole. "Yes? What is it?"

Charlotte craned her neck for a look inside the cabin, a putrid smell wafting out at her. "Where's Johnny?"

Pastor Brody placed a restraining hand on her arm, drawing her back. With a smile, he nodded to Mrs. Crowley, still half hidden behind the door. "Good day, ma'am. We've come to pay Johnny a visit. Is he about?"

The woman's sunken cheeks flinched. "He . . . he's around."

Charlotte wet her lips. Something in the woman's voice didn't set right. "May we see him?"

Mrs. Crowley ran a hand over her unkempt hair and dropped her gaze to the floorboards. "He ain't here just now."

Pastor Brody shifted his feet, edging closer. "May I ask where he is?"

"He . . . uh . . ." A tiny hand from within the cabin latched onto the edge of the door, stealing Mrs. Crowley's attention. With a loud grunt, the unseen child pulled the door wider and smiled out at them through tear-stained cheeks. Mrs. Crowley gave a disgruntled grin, joggling the near naked tot on her bony hip. Her dress sagged against her thin frame as yet another young child came from behind to clutch her leg.

Charlotte's heart sank. How could Johnny possibly get even a smidgen of the attention he needed amid such a tribe of children? She cleared her throat, fixing her gaze on the woman. "You were saying?"

Mrs. Crowley's face flushed, and her eyes darted from Charlotte to the child at her feet. "He and Ian have gone to . . . fetch some game." Her hand shook as she brushed a strand of hair from the toddler's face.

Charlotte's eyes narrowed. Something wasn't right.

Pastor Brody seemed to sense her unease. "When do you expect them back?"

The woman fidgeted with a thread on her homespun dress.

"Not for some time, I 'spect." She gave a nervous laugh, eyes trained on the child beneath her. "May even be toward evenin'."

"Well, I reckon we'll just wait here till they get back." Charlotte crossed her arms in front of her, shooting Pastor Brody a sideways glance.

His eyes widened as if not fully sharing her conviction.

Mrs. Crowley pitched forward, her expression sobering. "Oh, no need for that."

"You go on about your business. We won't be a bother." Certain they wouldn't get an invitation to wait inside, Charlotte plopped down on the porch bench.

The lean woman's mouth twitched, but she gave no response.

Pastor Brody eyed Charlotte as if trying to determine if she were bluffing or in earnest. If he wished to leave, she'd not stop him. But regardless of the pastor's intentions, she was staying put until she saw Johnny. Finally, he eased down on the opposite side of the bench. No doubt he'd much rather be writing a sermon or keeping company with his beloved than whittling away his time alongside her.

A faint smile tugged at Charlotte's lips. By the wearied look on both his and Mrs. Crowley's faces, her threat seemed to be working. She fanned herself with her hand, wishing for a stiff breeze. The semi-shade of the meager porch roof did little to shield against the swelling heat.

Charlotte tugged at her dress sleeves. "Mind if we borrow a pail to water ourselves and our horses?"

Mrs. Crowley shook her head and pointed a shaky finger toward the barn. "Bucket's inside the door." With that, she and her young ones slunk back inside the shack and bolted the door.

Pastor Brody started to rise. "I'll get it."

Charlotte shook her head. "Don't bother. I'd rather you stay and keep an eye on things."

Standing, she squinted against the hot sun. With quick strides, she made her way to the barn and pried the weathered door from its resting place. She stepped inside, giving her eyes time to adjust to the dim interior. No bucket.

Dust streamed in the shafts of sunlight that shone through generous gaps in the crude timbered walls. Though vacant of animals, the shabbily built structure reeked of rotten grain, filth, and manure. Charlotte held her breath as she stepped over broken boards, mislaid tools, and busted feed sacks in search of a bucket. She spied it overturned outside an open stall. Items were strewn about the place with no semblance of order. Ian Crowley was a sluggard if ever there was one. No wonder he wanted Johnny's help.

Inhaling a short breath, Charlotte hurried over and snatched up the pail. A frayed bit of cloth lay to the side. As she bent to pick it up, her stomach knotted. The material resembled the shirt Johnny had worn.

A damp, stickiness cooled her fingertips. She held the frayed cloth in a stream of sunlight, noting the red stain that marred its center.

Blood?

She clutched the rag to her chest, eyes searching the straw-covered floor. There. Another drop of blood. And another. Heart pounding, she followed the trail into the open stall. An overturned stool, clumps of straw, and a wadded blanket hinted of a scuffle. Charlotte bit her lip, swallowing down the grittiness in her throat.

Her thirst forgotten, she tossed the bucket aside and clung to the rag. If something had happened to Johnny, she aimed to find out what. Her face flamed as she traipsed across the cluttered floor and sprinted outside.

Pastor Brody stood at her approach. "What is it?"

"I found this in the barn. It looks like a piece of Johnny's shirt." Fighting tears, she thrust the scrap of material toward him.

Without waiting for Pastor Brody to respond, she banged on the door. "Open up in there."

A moment later, the door eased open. Mrs. Crowley peeked from behind it, eyes downcast.

Charlotte pushed the door wider, holding up the stained cloth. "Where's Johnny? The truth this time."

The woman's lips curved downward. "He's . . . run away."

The blood drained from Charlotte's cheeks. "When?"

"This morning, after Ian . . ." Mrs. Crowley's voice cracked, and she fumbled for words.

Charlotte tensed, moving within inches of the woman's face. "After he what?"

Mrs. Crowley's face pinched as she slumped forward. "Struck him."

Charlotte clapped a hand over her mouth, tears stinging her eyes. This was her fault. She'd allowed Johnny to stay, knowing the sort of man Mr. Crowley was.

Turning, she clasped Pastor Brody by the arm. "We have to find him."

Chapter Seventeen

LONG SHADOWS CLOAKED Chad's path as he rode into the town of Colby. He'd slept little the past forty-eight hours. Nothing sounded better than a warm bath, a soft bed, and a quiet room to rest.

But first, he had a score to settle.

He scanned the line of horses tethered on either side of the street. Was Buck among them? In the dim light of dusk, their darkened coats all looked alike. If Duran was here, finding him might take some doing. Every river town Chad had passed through boomed more under cover of night than brightness of day.

He dismounted and looped the reins over the hitching post, then strolled along the wooden planks outside the long row of storefronts. The mercantiles, feed stores, and cobblers had closed their doors for the night. In their stead, lantern glow shone from the windows of numerous gambling halls, hotels, and restaurants. Piano music poured from a saloon up ahead, along with peals of laughter and heated men's voices. Not the type of establishment he'd want to set foot in, but most likely the type where he'd find Duran.

With a determined stride, Chad pressed forward, his boots clicking against the creaky boardwalk. As he neared, a man staggered out, a half-empty bottle in his hand. He fell against Chad, mumbling to himself, his words slurred beyond distinction. Chad pulled the man to his feet. The stranger wagged his head side to side and blinked. He stared up at Chad with bloodshot eyes and brushed a hand down his buckskin shirt. "Surry big fella. Where's my . . . hor-se?"

The stench of liquor on the man's breath forced Chad back a step. "What's he look like?"

"Shh! Not he. Shhee!" The man hiccupped, drool trailing from one side of his mouth. His whiskered face scrunched. "She'z white with bul-ack s-pots." With the final word, he spewed saliva, spraying the side of Chad's face.

He wiped his cheek in disgust, eyes searching the row of horses at his back. Heat burned his chest. He had no time for this nonsense. At last, he spied a pinto a few yards to their left. Placing a supportive arm around the man, Chad walked him to the front of the plump horse. "This her?"

The man leaned in closer, squeezing out another long blink. He smiled and fell forward, clinging to the horse's neck. "Lu-cy Belle." The horse edged back, shifting on her hooves.

With a firm hand, Chad pried him from around the horse's neck and hoisted him into the saddle.

The man slumped forward, releasing a horrendous belch.

Chad breathed a long sigh. If he hadn't already vowed to keep from liquor, the state of this man would have been enough to convince him. Handing him the reins, he fastened the man's other hand to the saddle horn. "You make it home okay?"

The man waved his hand through the air, eyes drooping as he leaned into the saddle horn. "Shore. Shore. Lucy Belle knows."

"Keep your seat, old feller." Chad gave the horse a firm slap on the rump, sending her on her way. No doubt this wasn't the first time she'd ushered her master home. With a shake of his head, Chad made his way back to the saloon. As he pushed on the swinging, double doors a sharp whinny sounded from across the street. He paused, the tone so familiar he knew at once who it belonged to.

He stepped away from the doors and edged back into the street, eyes searching. "Buck?"

A soft whinny sliced the humid night air. Chad squinted through the darkness until he saw a horse head arched toward him. His heart pumped faster. So he'd guessed right.

Duran *was* here.

He crossed the street and slid a hand over the animal's smooth coat. "Well, ain't you a sight for sore eyes." With a soft nicker, Buck nuzzled his nose against Chad. He rubbed a hand over the horse's face and down his chest and legs, grateful he was still in one piece. Otherwise, things might not have fared so well for Duran once he found him. How grateful Chad was the Lord had led him here and that the old drunken codger had lured him back into the street.

With a pat of Buck's neck, Chad's gaze settled on the gambling hall before him. Any further reunion would have to wait. He had business inside first. Squaring his shoulders, he skirted around the hitching post and pushed through the double doors. Rows of plush tables lined the interior, flanked by noisy patrons. Workers spun wheels and shouted out numbers, resulting in disgruntled moans or shouts of joy from onlookers. Chad's eyes narrowed as he scanned the large room. No sign of his friend Rusty.

A woman in a low-cut dress laced with frills approached, her oval face splashed with color and hemmed by raven-black hair. In her hands she carried a tray of empty glasses, traces of liquor lining their bottoms. She flashed a stunning smile as she neared, her eyes canvassing him head to toe. "Come on in, handsome, and try your luck."

He dropped his gaze, heat rising in his cheeks. The woman's dress left little to the imagination. "I'm looking for someone."

She leaned in closer, her voice alluring. "Will I do, sugar?"

He shook his head, unable to meet her probing eyes. "No ma'am. I mean, I'm searching for a man by the name of Rusty Duran. Red hair, wiry beard, scar on his right temple. Came into some money a couple days back. Ever see him?"

She gave a quick huff. "Figures you'd be all business. We get all sorts here, sweetie. Doesn't sound familiar, but have a look around, if you like."

"Thank you, ma'am." He tipped his hat and took a step forward only to have her shoulder brush against him.

Her dark eyes met his. "And when you're finished, look me up."

He turned away face aflame, feeling a bit like Joseph in the clutches of Potiphar's wife. Temptation lurked within these walls. The sooner he found Duran and lit out of here the better.

A piano at the far wall plunked out *Oh Susanna* as Chad ambled about the room studying the patrons. A red-haired man resembling Duran from the back struck up a hearty laugh as he raked in a pile of colored chips. Chad's heart hammered as he worked his way around to the man's front. With a closer glimpse, Chad's shoulders sagged. Not him. What he needed was a lead of some sort from someone who kept a watchful eye on the place.

A brawny bartender stood drying glasses behind a lengthy counter, his upper lip hidden beneath a long mustache. His close-set eyes perused the row of customers at the counter. Chad pursed his lips. Maybe this fellow would know something. With Duran's love of whiskey, he wouldn't pass up a chance to indulge himself. Or had he taken up with one of the ladies and wouldn't emerge till morning light? Chad rubbed the bridge of his nose, eyes stinging for lack of sleep. He couldn't hold out much longer.

Stepping to the counter, he nudged his way to an empty spot

and nodded to the muscular bartender. The man's balding head was fringed on the sides by wavy, brown hair and thick side-burns. His somber expression remained unchanged as he moved toward Chad. "What's your pleasure?"

"I'm looking for a fellow. Medium build, red hair and beard, and a scar on his right temple. Wondered if you might have seen him?"

The man spread his hands out on the counter with a scowl, his beady, dark eyes fixed on Chad. "Look, mister, that describes any number of men in this place. Now, if you ain't gonna order somethin', move and make room for a paying customer."

Chad took one of his two remaining coins from his pocket and slapped it down on the counter. He leaned forward, voice low, eyes intent on the burly man. "The fella I'm looking for stole my horse and my life savings. Now, I know he's in here. My horse is tied out front. He's got a taste for whiskey and may be throwing around money that ain't his. Now, if I was a betting man, I'd pull odds you've laid eyes on him sometime today."

The barkeeper held his stare. By the looks of him, he could have bested Chad with one hand tied behind his back.

Chad's throat tightened as he swallowed down an unwelcome lump, yet he refused to back down. His future was at stake. If this man wouldn't help him, he'd find someone who would.

At last, the man stood erect and slid the coin into his vest pocket. With a curt nod, he motioned toward the far corner of the room. "Most likely the man you're looking for is over there. But I ain't so sure you'll recover your purse. He's been rather loose with his money."

Chad followed the bartender's gaze to a man slouched over a table, empty but for a couple of drained whiskey bottles and a toppled glass. Nodding his thanks, Chad pivoted. Eagerness washed over him as he meandered through the throng of people. He strained to decipher the slumped-over figure ahead of him, but the man's face remained hidden beneath his arms. Was it truly Duran, or another lookalike? If it was him, he'd splurged on new boots and a fancy set of store-bought clothing. A knot balled in Chad's middle. Was he too late?

Stepping up beside him, Chad nudged the man's shoulder. No response. Out colder than a bear in winter. He tilted the man's head to one side, seething inwardly at sight of the diagonal scar on his right temple. With renewed vigor, Chad gripped the hair at the back of Duran's head and pulled him to a sitting position. Duran dangled like a puppet in Chad's grasp, completely wasted in a drunken stupor. Chad clenched his jaw, shamelessly searching the man's pockets. On his third try, his hand fastened around a soft, leather pouch. Pulling it out, he broke into a cold sweat as his fingers squeezed the familiar money bag, its contents having shriveled to near nothing. He sunk the purse back in the man's pocket as proof.

With a groan, Chad turned loose of Duran, letting him fall back to the table. Chad dropped down in a chair and raked a hand over his face. In two days' time, his life savings had been chiseled away, his dream vanishing with it.

Now what was he to do?

Chapter Eighteen

PART THREE · UNCERTAINTIES

Late June, 1855

THE SUN DIPPED low on the horizon as Charlotte led Willow into the barn. She bowed her head, heart-sick at having to give up the search for Johnny. But with little daylight left, she'd do better to get a night's rest and start fresh in the morning.

Weariness tore at her, both soul and body, as she unsaddled Willow. Sweat streamed down the horse's middle where the blanket and cinch had hugged. Charlotte set the saddle over the side of the stall, then led the horse out into the pasture. Freed of her burden, Willow dropped to the ground, rolling in the gold-stemmed prairie grass. A well-deserved end to a long day.

With the bridle looped over her shoulder, Charlotte trudged back to the barn. She and Pastor Brody had spanned the country-side to no avail. They must've hit every homestead west of Miller Creek asking people to be on the lookout. How far could the boy have gone? Or was he simply hiding out somewhere? As resourceful as he was, he might stay hidden for days.

Pastor Brody had agreed to head out again first thing in the morning. They needed to find Johnny before Ian Crowley did.

Or had he already?

Charlotte clenched her teeth, fighting back tears as she hung the bridle on its peg. If anything had happened to the boy, she'd not forgive herself.

The scent of hay and straw stirred a striking notion inside her. Surely Johnny wouldn't have hidden himself away in the Hollisters' loft again. Not after Ian Crowley had found him on the premises once before. But then his young mind might not think so logically. Might he even try to seek her out as a safe haven? He had no one else.

A nervous tingle ripped through her. She had half a mind to go have a look. Yet the lantern light inside the cabin and thoughts of food and sleep called to her. Neither she nor Willow had the energy or fortitude to set out again tonight. And neither, she reasoned, would Ian Crowley. More than likely he'd be sacked out on his bed with a full belly about now, leaving his frail wife to do the chores and tend to their horde of children.

She drew a weary breath. At first morning light, she'd set out for her uncle's place.

CHAD PLUNGED Duran's head in the water trough, holding him there to the count of three. Angry, muffled sounds bubbled from the water, the man's arms flailing under Chad's firm grip. He clenched his jaw. Vengeance belonged to the Lord, but surely He wouldn't mind Chad squaring things up a bit.

The ornery thief deserved to be wide awake to greet the sheriff.

Ignoring the handful of snickering onlookers, Chad heaved Duran from the trough. He gulped for air, eyes bulging. Streams of water gushed from his hair and beard, drenching his front. "Listen, fella I . . ." he sputtered.

"Save it for the sheriff." Chad took up his rifle and gave the man a shove forward, keeping the gun trained on his back.

Duran staggered out into the darkened street, hands in the air.

Maneuvering around the horses on the far side of the street, Duran stumbled onto the wooden walkway. Chad prodded him along, growing more agitated with each click of the man's boots. Boots Chad had paid for. He'd passed the sheriff's office on the way in. Hopefully someone would still be there. If not, exhausted as he was, he'd have no choice but to gag and tie the critter to a chair in his hotel room for the night.

As they neared the small jail, Chad drew a satisfied breath at the sight of lantern light filtering through the curtained window. He jabbed the rifle barrel between Duran's shoulder blades, and nudged him toward the door. "Open it."

With a disgruntled scowl, Duran twisted the latch, and the door creaked open. Cigar smoke wafted from within as the door widened, revealing an overweight deputy, his legs propped on a cluttered oak desk. As they entered, he lowered his feet and stamped out his cigar. His dark eyes shifted from Duran to Chad. "What's the trouble?"

Lowering his rifle, Chad met the deputy's steady gaze. "Name's Chad Avery. This man waylaid me a couple nights ago and stole my horse and cattle money."

Duran's head shifted side to side, a nervous groan escaping his throat. "N-no. That ain't so. The man's crazy. He attacked me for no reason and shoved my head in a horse trough." He tugged at his soaked shirt, edging away from Chad.

The oversized deputy pursed his lips, tugging at his britches. "Well now, seein' as it's one man's word against the other, I 'spect I'll have to hold you both till the Sheriff comes."

A wry grin spread over Duran's face. The man was lower than a thieving snake.

Widening his stance, Chad propped his rifle in front of him

and leaned on its barrel. "The whiskey on the man's breath and the new clothes were bought with my money."

The deputy sniffed at Duran, eyeing him head to toe. "Does look a mite suspicious."

Duran wet his lips, shifting his feet. "N-now I won me the money for these here clothes over there at that gamblin' hall."

Chad narrowed his eyes. "The bartender tells a different tale."

The color drained from Duran's cheeks as his head drooped forward.

"If you'll check the inside pocket of his shirt, you'll find a pouch with the initials CLA." Thankfully, he'd thought to return the purse.

The deputy moved toward Duran and thrust a hand inside his shirt. As he drew out the leather pouch and examined the burned-on letters, his eyes widened. "What's the L for?"

Chad swallowed down the ache inside him. "My wife, Lauren."

With a nod, the over-sized deputy tossed it at Chad. "That's proof enough for me. And the sheriff. Come along feller." He gripped Duran's arm and tugged him toward the cell.

"Hold up there." Edging forward, Chad gestured toward the prisoner. "I'll take those boots and clothes, seein' as my money paid for 'em."

The deputy's mouth twisted in a sideways smirk. "Sounds fair enough."

Duran's eyes grew round as silver dollars. "You cain't leave me in just my underclothes."

The deputy tightened his grip. "Drop 'em, or I'll do it for you."

A groan sounded from Duran as he jerked his arm from the deputy's grasp. He tugged off his boots and tossed them toward Chad. Loosening his suspenders, he lowered his britches, then unbuttoned his shirt. Stripped of his clothing, and apparently his pride, he shuffled his way into the cell.

A sense of satisfaction welled in Chad as the deputy clanged the iron door shut behind Duran. Yet, as Chad gathered up his things, it seemed a hollow victory. He'd brought the man to justice, but not in time to recover his losses. After all he'd been through, was he to return home empty-handed?

He nodded his thanks to the deputy and strode out into the dark night. He fingered the depleted pouch tied to his belt. Might as well splurge and get himself that hotel and bath. It wasn't enough to do much else with. A restful night would give him time to pray and sort through the situation. The Lord had brought him this far. Where to go from here was the question.

Would Charlotte be disappointed if he returned without his cattle? But then, why should it matter? The cattle ranch was his and Lauren's dream. Yet, it was Charlotte's face that preyed on his thoughts. Somehow he couldn't bear to let her down.

Tightening his grip on the boots, he clutched the clothes under his arm and headed deeper into town. There was nothing to consider. After a good night's rest, he'd set out to catch up with the cattle drive.

Somehow — some way — he'd get his herd.

Chapter Nineteen

CHARLOTTE SHIFTED in the leather saddle and rubbed her thigh, sore from all the excess riding. The morning's coolness was a welcome relief after yesterday's scorching heat. The sun had barely risen when she'd left home. Ma's disgruntled complaints of her being gone too much lent to the fact she was fretting over not hearing from Pa but once since he'd left home — a short note telling them he'd arrived safely. Esther too seemed a bit put out for being burdened with most of the chores. Once Johnny was found, Charlotte would make it up to them.

All appeared quiet at her uncle's cabin. The horses in the pasture and the wagon outside assured he and the Brodys had yet to move into their place near town. What a shame the homestead would soon sit empty. Yet, pastoring the church would prove near impossible living so far out.

Charlotte caught sight of Pastor Brody emerging from the cabin and called to him. He turned toward her, a wide smile on his face. "I was just on my way to see you."

She stopped Willow beside him, baffled by his cheery mood. There could be only one reason. She drew in a hasty breath. "Has Johnny been found?"

At his reassuring nod, joy trickled through her like fresh spring water on a summer day.

"Miss Charlotte!"

The child's voice pulled her attention to the cabin. "Johnny!" Moisture stung her eyes as she dismounted and stooped to greet the boy running toward her. He stopped short of hugging her, looking clean, though a mite thin and worn. Charlotte's heart caught in her throat at sight of the bruise lining his jaw. "Are you all right?"

"I reckon." He squinted up at her. "Where was ya? I came here lookin' for ya."

She grinned, brushing a hand over his sleeve. "I was out searching for you. Then I went home. This is my uncle's place, remember?"

His face scrunched. "Oh yeah."

"Are you hurt? I found blood in Mr. Crowley's barn."

Johnny sniffled, wiping his nose with his sleeve. "I bit him."

Charlotte smothered a grin. "You bit Mr. Crowley?"

He nodded, head tilting downward. "He hit me again, so I bit him."

"Oh, Johnny. I'm so sorry."

He clutched her dress sleeve, gazing up at her. "Don't let him take me again, Miss Charlotte. I'll do anything ya ask."

Tears welled in Charlotte's eyes, and she pulled him to her, raking a hand over his hair.

"You're safe now, Johnny. I promise. You'll never have to go there again."

"So, are you gonna be my new ma?"

Charlotte chuckled at Johnny's question, snugging her arms tighter to his sides as they swayed to the rhythm of Willow's steady gait. "More like your older sister."

That was if Ma would allow it.

No doubt, when Pa returned, he would take to Johnny like sugar molasses. It was Ma they'd have to persuade.

Johnny smiled back at her. "Do you have any brothers?"

"No. Just a younger sister. Esther." She let him help hold the reins, mentally trying to decipher the best approach to present Johnny to Ma.

"Girls again. How old is she?"

"Soon to be sixteen."

Johnny's shoulders sagged. "Not much good to have sisters too old to play with."

Charlotte shook her head, unable to hold back a grin. If Johnny were allowed to stay with them, he'd certainly spice up the place.

He leaned against her. "You like me, don't ya, Miss Charlotte?"

"Sure I do."

"You think your ma and pa and sister will like me?"

She rested her cheek against his blond hair. "Oh, Pa and Esther are easy. It's Ma we'll have to win over."

They rode in silence for a time, then Johnny breathed a loud sigh. "What'll happen if they don't want me?"

Charlotte's heart melted at his straight-forward question. Johnny'd been through so much already. Could he withstand any more heartbreak? "Well, I'm sure either the Brodys or the Pruitts would take you in until a proper home could be found." Even as she said the words her stomach knotted. She was making presumptions she ought not to make. Besides, she and Johnny belonged together. Her heart had sensed it from the start.

Their cabin came into view, and she breathed a silent prayer asking the Lord's wisdom in her approach. Johnny deserved a family who loved him, one that would look after him and teach him the Lord's ways. He had a good heart. All he needed was a chance.

As they neared, Charlotte noticed several wagons and horses gathered. One looked to be the Brimmers', another the Albrechts', their neighbors to the south. Even Doc and Anabelle Pruitt's rig was there.

Heaviness weighed on Charlotte's chest. Had something happened?

The door to the cabin opened and the Brimmers and Albrechts emerged, the womenfolk dabbing their eyes with hankies as they made their way to their wagons. She watched for signs of her mother or Esther, but the cabin remained cloaked in silence.

"Who are them folks?"

Charlotte hadn't the breath to answer. Instead she took the reins from Johnny and kicked her heels in Willow's flanks. Her heart drummed in her ears as she halted the horse before the cabin. She gave Johnny a hand down, then slipped to the ground. Taking the boy by the shoulders, she looked him in the eye. "Stay here, Johnny."

With a nod, he sunk down onto the porch step, seeming to sense something was amiss.

Soft whimpers and murmured voices filtered through the open window. Charlotte drew in a breath and pulled on the door latch, prompting silence within the cabin. As the door swung open, all eyes pivoted in her direction. Doc Pruitt stood at the window sill, a pained expression creasing his brow. Mrs. Pruitt sat on the hearth, poker in hand as though getting set to stir hot embers for a fire.

Yet it was Esther's and Ma's bloodshot eyes and tear-stained cheeks that held Charlotte's attention. Her mother gripped a piece of paper in shaky hands. Charlotte grew cold. Something terrible had happened. Had Pa been injured?

She fled to her mother's side. "What is it? Has something happened to Pa?"

At her question, silent tears streamed down Ma's cheeks. With a trembling hand, she slid the telegram toward Charlotte.

Charlotte hesitated, then took it from her. Like forbidden fruit, the words pulled her eyes toward them. With shallow breaths she strung them together, trying to make sense of them.

WE REGRET TO INFORM YOU YOUR HUSBAND, JED STANTON, DIED IN A LOGGING ACCIDENT THIS 22ND DAY OF JUNE, EIGHTEEN HUNDRED AND FIFTY-FIVE. HIS BELONGINGS ARE BEING SHIPPED. DEEPEST REGARDS. BENJAMIN S. CRAIG LOGGING MANAGER

Numbness coursed through Charlotte as she dropped into a chair. She tossed the cold, lifeless letter aside and leaned over the table, covering her face with her hands.

A soft hand touched her shoulder. "I'm so sorry, my dear." It was Mrs. Pruitt's voice.

Charlotte kept her face hidden, attempting to block out every remnant of the horrific news. Her father meant everything to her. And being sorry could never bring him back.

CHARLOTTE PLOPPED down on the creek bank and plucked a prairie grass stem. The cabin had become like a crypt. She'd had to escape. Hours had ticked by without so much as a word being spoken. Thankfully, the Pruitts had agreed to take Johnny with them. This was no time to broach the topic of him staying. Already she'd glimpsed the agony her hurt was causing him. Still grieving the loss of his own father, there was no need for him to shoulder her burden as well.

She tossed the grass stem aside and leaned back against the rough bark of a white oak, its lofty branches sprawled out above her.

It was so hard to believe her father was gone. Even now, after he'd been away for weeks, she could envision his infectious smile and hear his hearty laugh. How he'd pampered her. She'd been so jealous for his attention, especially where her cousin Becky was concerned. The memory of it gnawed at her. Becky had lost both her mother and sister, and yet all Charlotte had thought of was herself. How petty she'd been not to sense her cousin's anguished loss.

Charlotte hung her head and wrapped her arms around her legs. Now Pa was gone. Her loving, joyful father, who'd doted on her and always knew just how to coax her out of a loathsome mood, was dead. Never again would she feel his warm embrace or enjoy the pleasure of his company.

"Charlotte?"

Her head lifted at the sound of her cousin's voice. Turning, she saw a wagon parked outside the cabin in the distance, and Becky walking toward her. Charlotte stood, reading the emotion in her cousin's sapphire eyes. She knew exactly what Charlotte was going through. She'd been there.

As she neared, Becky opened her arms, no hint of animosity, only compassion and sorrow. "We came as soon as we heard."

Charlotte choked back sobs as she fell into her cousin's embrace. She didn't deserve her pity. She'd done nothing but add to her cousin's grief. Why had it taken another tragedy for her to understand the devastating loss Becky had endured?

All their past grievances seemed to melt away as they clung to each other, their cries intermingling. At last, Charlotte pulled away and wiped the tears from her eyes. "I've been so awful to you. Can you forgive me?"

A weak smile broke through Becky's tears. She raised a hand to Charlotte's cheek, wiping moisture away with her thumb. "I already have."

With a nod, Charlotte leaned back into Becky, soaking in the comfort of her words. Pastor Brody had indeed married the right woman. Her cousin was the epitome of a pastor's wife, full of grace and good deeds. The two of them making amends would have pleased Pa. Somehow Charlotte sensed he knew, that the Lord would grant him that.

Her thoughts fled to Chad. She'd barely had time to think of him with Johnny's troubles and now her father's untimely death. Pa had taken to Chad from the start. Her friend would be heart-sore over the news. Surely by now he'd be on his way home.

She could only pray he was faring better than she.

Chapter Twenty

BUCK'S HOOVES clomped along the near vacant street of Hammett, the town where Chad was to have met the cattle drive. Thanks to his thieving friend Rusty Duran, he was several days overdue. He peered over his shoulder at Duran's sorrel horse tethered on behind. At least he had a bit of compensation for his loss. Given time and better treatment, the broken-down mare might just make a good cattle horse.

A chorus of *Amazing Grace* wafted from the windows of a church building up ahead, a cluster of buggies and carriages fringing its foundation. Sunday morning. The only time river towns ground to a lull. Chad reached for his pocket watch. 11:20 a.m. The service would be all but over. His second week in a row missing worship. Surely the Lord would forgive his negligence, given his circumstances and all the time he'd spent praying in the saddle.

If things had gone as planned, he'd have been halfway home by now. Instead, most likely he'd have to traipse further north with the few coins in his pouch, and a belly full of hope. But what did it matter? He'd no one to track him down if he went missing.

Except maybe Charlotte.

His chest tightened. The way those emerald eyes of hers had shone up at him the night before he left. Would she be missing him? The thought sparked both pleasure and unease. He shook the thought away, determined to stay focused.

The Illinois River came into full view, its vast waters glistening in the sunlight as he meandered further through town. A pair of ferryboats lay idle along the water's edge. A drowsy fisherman sat propped up against a block on the closer one, hat pulled down over his face. Chad stepped out away from the buildings, eyes panning the open spaces beyond. Could the herd still be loitering on the outskirts of town? It wasn't likely they'd stall their trip north for one man's sake, but it didn't hurt to check.

He dismounted and led the horses to the edge of the water for a drink, eyeing the sleeping man. "Mornin'." His loud greeting drifted over the water like a canyon echo.

The fisherman nudged his hat from over his eyes and squinted up at Chad. With a slight nod, he straightened and tugged at his line.

"Did a herd of cattle cross over here recently?"

The man scratched his whiskered cheek and pointed over his shoulder, his voice a lazy drawl. "Day before yesterday, heading north to Chicago."

"Much obliged." Chad tipped his hat and mounted. Now that he knew they'd moved on, the sooner he started after them the better. Shouldn't be hard tracking a thousand head of cattle. He only hoped once he found them, the cattle-master would accept his proposition.

WAS THIS IT? Charlotte stared down at the opened package in her lap containing a worn hat with a pocket watch and half-filled money bag tucked inside. Was this all that remained of her beloved father?

She leaned back on the bench outside the post office and ran her fingertips over the rim of the upside-down hat, noting the sweat-stain at its center. Should she be surprised? Pa wasn't a man who held to possessions. Instead he'd taken pride in hard work, his faith, and his family.

Taking out the watch and money bag, she noticed a folded paper with the words: **To the family of Jed Stanton** written across its back. With quivering hands, she lifted it out and broke its wax seal. As she opened it, a small piece of paper floated to the ground. The official looking document landed on its back, concealing its contents. Charlotte turned it over and saw it was a bank note made out to her mother. Moisture pooled in Charlotte's eyes. The ninety-five dollars was an exorbitant amount for a horse and three week's pay. Yet, it had cost her father his life. The emptiness of it sheared Charlotte's soul.

She glanced at the folded paper that had housed the note, and drew a hand to her mouth. Barely legible and in her father's handwriting, the words, I LOVE YOU decorated the lower left portion of the page. Tears stung her eyes, and she blinked them away. Had he used his final strength to scribble the note? She drew the paper to her chest, the message from her father far more valuable than the bank note which accompanied it.

She swiped away tears with the back of her hand, half agitated and half relieved that Ma had ordered her to fetch the package. In the four days since the awful news had arrived, not once had Ma left the cabin. She'd shooed away visitors and done little to improve her appearance. Even much of the cooking and cleaning had been left to Charlotte and Esther, not to mention the chores. How would she respond when Charlotte returned with the packet of her father's things? Would it throw her mother into a worse state?

Ma and Esther were the fragile ones. Pa had always told

Charlotte she was the one with "grit". Unfortunately that "grit" often got her into trouble, as it had with Becky.

And a time or two with Chad.

Maybe that's why she and Pa had shared such a close bond. They'd admired each other's spunk. Most likely that was why she'd taken to Johnny, too. It had taken a lot of gumption for a youngster his age to fight off Ian Crowley.

Charlotte gave a low sigh. Pa would have loved the boy as his own.

Chad was a different sort. It wasn't spunk he possessed, but quiet strength and a deep sense of character. How she longed for him to return. She could shoulder her loss a bit better with a strong arm to lean on. By now, he should be home. Why had she not heard from him?

Did he know about Pa? If she didn't hear from him in a few days, she'd venture over his way.

She gathered up her father's things and strapped them in her saddle bag. While in town, she really should stop by and see Johnny. But she didn't have the heart to face him just yet, knowing he couldn't go with her. Taking in a young boy was the furthest thing from Ma's mind at the moment. What poor timing it had been for them. At least Charlotte had the peace of mind in knowing he was being well taken care of. Pastor Brody had stopped by earlier in the week to assure her that he and Becky had offered to take over for the Pruitts and look after Johnny as long as needed.

The problem was, she had no idea when or if that time would come.

CHAD WHISTLED UNDER HIS BREATH. The sea of cattle looked as numerous at the Israelites coming out of Egypt. The air was strong with the scent of livestock. Brash bellows sounded from the cattle as they trekked over the unbroken prairie. The handful of men stationed around the herd prodded the cattle along at a steady pace, coaxing stragglers into position. At the rear, in a swirl of dust, a younger man worked to corral the spare horses.

Spurring Buck to a trot, Chad fell in alongside the gangly youth. "I'm looking for Pete Callaway."

With a glance in his direction, the boy pointed out ahead of them. "That's my Pa. You'll find him at the lead."

Nodding, Chad cut a wide berth around the herd and made his way to the front, gleaning curious stares from the weary cattle drovers as he passed. A chuck-wagon clanked along the worn path that cut across the vast terrain. Chad strained to spot the cattle master and spied him a short distance behind the wagon. With a tap of his heels, he reined Buck in the man's direction.

The cowboy turned, his sun-leathered skin adding years to his face. A layer of dust on his light brown hair made his age hard to distinguish, but his muscles held firm beneath his shirt. His horse kept pace as Chad wedged Buck in beside him, Duran's horse tied on behind. Chad leaned to the side, raising his voice over the tromping cattle. "You Pete Callaway?"

The man's steely brown eyes washed over Chad. "I am."

"Name's Chad Avery. I was supposed to have met up with you back in Hammett, but was waylaid and robbed before I could get there."

The man rested a gloved hand atop his saddle horn, staring out in front of him. "Sorry to hear it."

"I've not much money left for cattle, maybe three or four head, but I was wondering if we could work out some sort of deal."

They followed the chuck wagon across a narrow stream, then Mr. Callaway threw his hand up to halt the group while the cattle spread out for a drink. He pushed his hat back on his head and squinted over at Chad. "What'd you have in mind?"

Chad wet his lips, meeting the man's steady gaze. "Could you use another cow hand to see you through to Chicago?"

The cattle master rubbed a hand over his stubbled chin. "Lost a flank man a ways back, so I reckon I could . . . if'n he was the right sort of fellow."

"I'd earn my keep." And hopefully enough money to buy some of his herd.

One side of the man's mouth lifted in a half grin. "Drivin' cattle's no picnic, son. It's hard ridin' sun up till sun down."

Chad squared his shoulders. "I'm up to the task."

Mr. Callaway stared back in silence as though sizing him up. "You look sturdy enough, all right, but you'll need chaps and a change of clothes and boots."

"Got the clothes and boots right here." Chad reached a hand back on his saddle bag. Duran's extravagance would come in handy after all.

The man sat forward in his saddle, gazing out over the herd. "Tell you what. We've several cows that have calved and can't keep up. You go the rest of the way with us, and I'll let you have your pick of five cows with suckling calves, in addition to those you pay for."

Chad extended a hand. "You've got a deal."

Mr. Callaway gave it a firm shake, then gestured toward the wagon. "Cookie over there can set you up with a pair of chaps. When you're ready come pick your cattle. I've a friend who lives a half-mile back. Tell him Pete sent you, and he'll house 'em till you return."

With a tip of his hat, Chad pressed his heels in Buck's side. As he trotted toward the chuck wagon, his lips edged upward in a grin. Calves quickly grew into cows. Humble beginnings or not, he'd have his herd.

Chapter Twenty-One

CHAD DISMOUNTED and leaned to stretch the kinks from his back. After a full day in the saddle, it was a pleasure to stand. Fatigue pulled at his muscles. Herding cattle was rough work, but not much harder than chasing after a fugitive horse thief. He patted Buck's sweat-stained neck. Poor fellow had put in a day in this sweltering heat. Even now, with the sun dipping low on the horizon, the humid air hung like a fog. Tomorrow he'd allow Buck the day off and give Duran's horse a turn. But then, he couldn't keep referring to her as Duran's horse. She was his now. Already, the sorrel mare had wedged a soft spot on his heart. He'd call her Tag, short for Tag-along.

A strong hand gripped his shoulder, and he turned to find Pete Callaway standing before him. The man's leathery skin creased as the corners of his mouth lifted. "You done good today, Avery."

Chad returned a brisk nod. "Thank you, sir."

With a slap on Chad's back, the trail boss lumbered away. Years in the saddle had left his legs slightly bowed, yet there was a youthful spring in his step as he sauntered on, pausing to speak to each drover as he passed. Like a beloved captain with his crew, he seemed in good standing with the men.

Chad loosened the cinch and slid the blanket and saddle off Buck. Heat radiated from the sweat-drenched blanket, coating Chad's arms with hair as he carried the saddle to an open spot in the glow of the campfire. The young man to his left nodded as Chad dropped down beside him. The lanky fellow's chiseled jaw held at least two days' growth of stubble, but his mouth wore a pleasant grin. "You did all right out there, mister. Ever herd cattle b'fore?"

Chad grinned. "Not near so many."

The young man removed his hat, revealing a full head of wavy, brown hair. He wiped his damp forehead with his sleeve, then leaned forward and offered Chad his hand. "Name's Stewart Brant. My friends call me Stew."

Chad took his hand, surprised at his firm grip. "Glad t' know you. Chad Avery."

With a nod, Stew unpacked his bedroll and gathered up his tin cup, plate, and fork.

Unaccustomed to the stiff chaps, Chad tugged at the leather straps that held them in place. "How long you been with this outfit?"

"Going on three years now."

Chad arched a brow. "Must've started young."

Stew clutched his utensils and pivoted on his knees toward Chad. "I left home at seventeen. Pete started me out as wrangler, lookin' after the spare horses. I worked my way up to swing man from there."

Dropping his chaps in a heap beside him, Chad gestured toward the trail master. "He seems well liked."

"Pete's a good man. Been more like a father to me than my own." Stew rose to his feet. "Better collect your things and get in line before Cookie runs out of vittles." He bent over, cupping a hand to his mouth. "Not that you'd miss much."

The scent of chili wafted from a large kettle atop the fire where Cookie was busy divvying out scoopfuls to the line of waiting men. The wiry fellow seemed full of grit and vinegar as he darted this way and that, mumbling under his breath at one man's complaint about his food.

Chad unrolled his pack and gathered up his things before joining Stew at the back of the line. No one else bothered speaking to him, but instead offered a quick nod or ignored him altogether. Stew nudged Cookie's arm as he reached for his plate. "Take it easy on my friend Chad here. His stomach's not used to your grub."

Cookie's clouded eyes narrowed. "May just be this new fella has a taste for my chow."

He eyed Chad warily, plopping a scoopful of chili into his mug and sliding a generous chunk of cornbread on his plate. "Don't pay him no never mind. They'd be hard pressed to get by without me, the whole lot of 'em."

A mix of grumbles and chuckles erupted from the men. Chad gave the aproned cook a nod as he passed by and headed back to his spot on the ground.

He sensed Stew's eyes upon him as he scooped up his first bite of chili. After working the fiery concoction around in his mouth, he swallowed it down. Instantly, a burning sensation pricked his tongue and trailed down his throat. Eyes watering, he groped for his canteen to the snickers of those around him.

Stew clapped him on the back as he choked down a mouthful of water. "Got the bite of a rattler, don't it?"

Chad wagged his head side to side, his mouth slowly losing its sting. "I reckon it takes some gettin' used to." A bit hoarse, he choked down the burning in his throat.

"It'll get better, once Cookie kills off your taste buds." Stew's final words rolled out in a loud banter.

The runt of a cook wheeled toward Stew, fire in his eyes as he chopped the air with his ladle. "You mind your manners, young pup, or I'll serve you from the slop bucket from here on."

Chuckles rang out from the other men. Even Pete wore a grin as he propped himself against the wagon wheel. The busyness of the day forgotten, it was plain the feisty cook made for great sport in the leisure of mealtime.

Stew's shoulders shook in laughter as he dumped his chili onto his cornbread. "Ah, it's fun to get a rise out of ol' Cookie, but he's right. They don't come any better. We couldn't manage without him."

A rumble erupted from Chad's stomach, urging him to try the food again. Mimicking Stew's example, Chad poured the chili over his cornbread. As hungry as he was, he needed something in his belly. Venturing a small bite, he swallowed it down with greater ease. Hopefully breakfast would prove less intimidating.

When he'd finished, he rinsed off his plate and mug and poured himself some coffee. Stillness settled over the camp as several of the men bedded down for the night, while others went to take their turn guarding the cattle.

Stew tugged at his boots. "Better get some shut-eye. Boss says we've got the two o'clock watch."

Chad nodded, then drained his cup. He set aside his hat and boots and lay back on his blanket, taking a deep breath. A spattering of stars shone down on him in the twilight. Crickets chirped in the undergrowth as a cowboy's low song sounded on the far side of the herd. The cattle seemed to calm, lulled by the soothing sounds of nightlife and the ever darkening prairie.

Stew turned to Chad in a whisper. "Where do you hail from, Avery?"

"Tennessee. But for the past few months, I've made my home near the town of Miller Creek, Illinois."

"When I ain't cattle droving, I hang my hat in a little town called Taylor Springs, Missouri. Ever hear of it?"

"Nope."

Stew shifted on his blanket. "You gotta girl waiting for you back home, Avery?"

Chad bent his legs at the knee, his mind racing back to the night of the reception. His stomach clenched as a vision of Charlotte swirled through his head, blended with an image of Lauren. Was it the downed chili or his muddled thoughts that suddenly made him queasy? "Can't say I do."

Stew locked his hands behind his head, a silly grin playing on his lips. "Well, I do. Miss Delta Fanning. Purtiest gal west of the Mississippi." He turned on his side. "You ain't never had a girl to call your own?"

With a sigh, Chad choked down the lump in his throat. "Had a wife. She died a while back."

His young friend's head lifted. "Oh, sorry. Tough break. But I reckon in time, young as you are, the Lord'll send you another."

Chad fell quiet, listening to the crackle of the fire as he stared up into the starry sky. He had to admit, the thought of having someone like Charlotte waiting for him wasn't unpleasant. But it wasn't to be. Not now.

Not ever.

He'd lost one wife. He couldn't bear the thought of losing another.

"THE WAGON'S READY." Charlotte stood in the doorway of the cabin half afraid Ma would change her mind. Not thinking it proper to leave their mother alone in her fragile state, she and Esther had missed last Sunday's church service. Now, after over a week of seclusion, a bit of coaxing had persuaded Ma to at least don her Sunday dress.

Her mother's mouth worked back and forth as though attempting to form words, but none came. Instead, she gradually lifted herself out of the rocker and strode toward the door. Charlotte shared a hopeful glance with Esther. Pa's passing had drawn the very life from their mother. This was the first smidgen of hope they had to cling to.

Esther placed a hand on Ma's shoulder. "I'll fetch the Bible."

Ma gave no indication she'd heard as she retrieved her bonnet from the peg at the side of the door and slid it on her head. Charlotte took her arm as she stepped outside and helped her onto the wagon. A pang of soreness shot through Charlotte's lower back. In years past, she'd done her best to avoid laborsome tasks like hitching the team to the wagon. She'd taken for granted all the heavy work her father had shouldered. Now it would fall to her and Esther.

The thought made her crave her father's presence all the more.

When Esther joined them, Charlotte took up the reins and snapped them across the horses' rumps. Unaccustomed to the harness or pull of the wagon, Willow jerked forward, throwing Charlotte back. She fought to keep her hold on the reins, wishing Pa's horse had been returned rather than sold. Willow wasn't suited for heavy work, and neither was she.

The usual half-hour trip into town seemed more a day's journey with the mismatched team and Charlotte's less than masterful skill at the reins. It was with relief that Miller Creek came into view. Charlotte's stomach clenched at sight of the spattering of people headed inside the church building. How would Ma handle the attention they were sure to garner? With her refusing any sort of visitors, many still hadn't had the opportunity to pay their respects. Charlotte wasn't certain she herself would be ready to face a crowd of people.

Hopes of seeing Chad there spurred her on.

She reined the horses to an empty spot amid the gathering of wagons and buggies. With a steadying breath, she set the brake. Until this moment, she'd not ventured a look in her mother's direction. Silence had become the norm since the news of her father's death. But now, Charlotte glimpsed the nervous wringing of Ma's hands in her lap and the stern set of her jaw. Coming had taken a great deal of resolve.

Esther slid a hand atop Ma's. "Ready?"

She gave a slow nod, and latched onto Esther's hand. Music poured from within as they climbed the steps to the church building. Their tardiness would only draw more unwanted attention.

As they entered, Charlotte ventured a look at the back bench where Chad usually sat. Coldness spilled over her at its vacantness. More than two weeks had passed. What could be keeping him? Worry coiled its way to her heart, pressing in on her. If something had happened to him, it would be more than she could bear.

Lord, bring him back safely.

A blend of faint smiles and mournful expressions greeted them as they made their way to their usual spot mid-way down the aisle. Charlotte smoothed her skirt under her, the bench seeming far too spacious. Johnny waved to her from the front pew, and she mustered a weak grin. Could he read the sorrow on her face? He tugged at Becky's arm, and she leaned for him to whisper in her ear. At her nod, Johnny sprung to his feet and made his way back.

"Miss Becky says I can sit with you." Charlotte wrapped her arm around him, and he leaned into her, his boyish tone standing out over the voices of the congregation.

The thoughtful gesture warmed her wounded soul, easing some of the void left by her father's absence. The service passed in a blur, Charlotte's mind too distracted to catch much of the message. Not until Pastor Brody mentioned her father's name did he gain her full attention. "Our thoughts and prayers are with you as you mourn his passing. He'll be sorely missed."

Charlotte bowed her head, unable to front the onslaught of stares trained in their direction. Though well meaning, the attention was more than any of them wished for or needed. It would be weeks, months, possibly even years before they'd recover their loss. Without something substantial to finalize their good-byes, it still seemed Pa was merely off on one of his jaunts. It was hard to fathom he'd not be returning.

As Pastor Brody stirred the congregation to their feet, John-ny's hand latched onto Charlotte's. She gave his fingers a gentle squeeze, thankful for his touch. When the song ended, she slid down onto the bench and peered into Johnny's pale, blue eyes. How she'd missed him. "How have you been, Johnny?"

One shoulder bobbed. "All right, I reckon."

"I'm sorry things didn't work out the way we hoped." Char-lotte swallowed down the ache inside her. She'd not only lost her father but Johnny as well. Pasting on a weak smile, she brushed a hand through his blond hair. "How do you like the Brodys?"

"They're right nice folks, but when can I stay with you?"

The question seared Charlotte's soul. She'd love nothing more than to take the boy home with them now, but as things were, it wasn't possible. "Not for a while, I'm afraid. We've some things to sort out first."

Johnny's face lost its shine. "Is it 'cause your Pa died?"

"Sort of." Charlotte cast a glance over her shoulder, surprised to see her mother and Esther had ventured off, Esther to a circle of friends, her mother to the far corner of the room, seemingly swathed in deep conversation with the town banker, Mr. Garri-son. Charlotte let her stare linger on the two. Odd Ma would be so chatty with him when she'd barely spoken to anyone for more than a week. Surely they weren't discussing her father's bank note here at church.

Johnny's loud huff pulled her attention back to him. Moisture shown in his rounded eyes. "Must be, too, 'cause your ma don't want me."

The youngster was more perceptive than she'd given him credit. She gave a quiet sigh, smoothing his hair with her hand. "I think it's more she doesn't know you. Give it time."

Her heart melted as he leaned into her. It would take some smooth talk to persuade her mother to take the boy in. Without Pa to back her up, chances seemed pretty grim. She could only pray someone else would find it in their heart to give the boy a home.

Chapter Twenty-Two

"I'm selling the place."

Charlotte dropped her spoon in her bowl, her mother's sudden declaration tying her in knots. "What? Why?"

Ma rested her hands in her lap, her drawn expression pulling tighter. "I can't stay. There's too much of your Pa here."

"But that's just why we should stay. This place was his livelihood." Charlotte cast an unsettled glance at Esther, hoping she would aid her argument. Instead, her sister sat in long-faced silence, too compliant to balk against Ma's wishes, though her downcast expression hinted she was no more eager to leave than Charlotte.

"Soon as things are settled, we'll move." The quiver in Ma's voice implied she'd struggled in reaching the decision. Had that been the cause of her long silence? Had she been plotting and planning how to go about it from the start?

"Where will we go?" Esther's soft tone lacked the fight Charlotte's wielded. Her sister was likely to go along with Ma's wishes no matter how inconvenient.

Ma wet her lips, lifting her eyes, but not quite meeting either daughter's gaze. "East. To Ohio. I have relatives there."

An invisible hand clutched Charlotte's throat, choking off her air. She struggled to hold back the rush of heat burning her throat. She couldn't leave. This was their home. All her memories of her father were here. She couldn't just run off to some unknown place, especially without knowing what had happened to Chad. Neither would it be right to abandon Johnny.

She slumped back in her chair. If she stayed, Ma and Esther would manage quite well without her. With Esther's amiable personality, she was certain to garner friends and suitors wherever she went. Not so Charlotte. She belonged here. Somehow she'd manage on her own.

Squaring her shoulders, she lifted her chin. "You and Esther can go, but I'm staying."

Ma shot her a hard look. "You will go. I tell you I'm selling the cabin, the land, everything. I spoke with Mr. Garrison about it yesterday. He assured me we'll have no trouble selling the place." The words spilled out in a powerful gush as though the week of pent up silence had bolstered strength within.

Charlotte tensed. So that's why they were so steeped in conversation. Well, Ma could sell the land, but Charlotte wasn't budging. She stood, fists clenched. "I'm staying."

Amid her mother's protests, she turned and fled from the cabin. She brushed back tears as she snatched up Willow's bridle and traipsed toward the pasture. She had to find Chad. He'd know what to do.

She could only pray he'd give her a more solid reason to stay.

AN EERIE SENSATION pulsed through Charlotte as she neared the pasture surrounding Chad's ramshackle cabin. Instead of cattle milling about within the zigzag fence, tall grass swayed in the hot breeze. His fields and yard lay overgrown with weeds, the place looking as vacant as it had on her last visit. The tightness in her stomach propelled her forward, demanding a closer look.

Heaviness settled over her as she reined Willow toward the broken-down cabin. Why hadn't Chad returned? Her mind whirled with possibilities, none of them good. A covey of quail sprung up from the ground beside her, startling Willow. Her heart at her throat, Charlotte struggled to keep her seat as the horse veered sideways. "Whoa, girl," she soothed, patting her on the neck.

Her eyes shifted to the lonesome cabin. What other surprises awaited her here?

A ground squirrel scurried across the porch and sped away into a hole in the ground as Charlotte tugged Willow to a halt outside the cabin. A trail of chaff littered the entryway, hinting of the animal's persistent visits, the lack of boot prints evidence that Chad was not at home.

Charlotte dismounted and looped the reins around the porch rail and strode toward the cabin. Her chest tightened as she brushed cobwebs from the door frame. As certain as she was the cabin was vacant it just didn't seem proper to barge in unannounced. She lifted a hand to the door and gave it a soft rap. To no surprise, her knock met with silence. Gripping the latch-string, she swallowed down the dryness in her throat. With a tug, the door creaked open.

A stale, ashy smell poured from within. Craning her neck, she peered around the near empty cabin, its poorly chinked walls letting in ample streams of sunlight. Did she have a right to go where she hadn't been invited? It seemed intrusive. She stepped inside, heart pounding. The table her uncle had made rested at the room's center, coated with a thin layer of dust. So little else. A chair before the fireplace. A small kettle hanging from a crane over the ashes. A few dishes scattered about. Was this all he had? Or had he taken most of his belongings with him?

A brown and white photograph, alone on the dusty fireplace

mantel, caught her eye. She edged closer, her gaze transfixed on the tiny images of a raven-haired woman and a young child. Who was it? Not once had he owned up to having any relations.

Snatching the photo from the mantel, Charlotte stared into the dark eyes of the woman. So beautiful. And the child. His lop-sided grin reminded Charlotte so much of Chad. Could it be his sister and nephew? Or someone dearer still? She flipped it over, eyes searching. Her heart caught in her throat at sight of the inscription engraved on the back.

To my dearest Chad, on our Third Anniversary.

A cold sweat trickled through Charlotte. Chad married?

Fearful her trembling hands could no longer keep a grasp on the photograph, she set it back on the mantel. Was this why he hadn't returned? Had he rejoined his family?

She dropped to the fireplace chair in a heap, jaw clenched. No wonder he'd been so elusive about his past. And all this time, she'd been convinced he thought something of her.

Had everything about him been a lie?

She sunk her face in her hands, trying to stem the tears that threatened to fall. Now what was she to do? She had half a mind to run and hide in her uncle's barn loft the way Johnny had. The one person she thought she could count on had let her down.

The no-count varmint! Had she seen the last of him?

One thing was certain, if he did return, he had a lot of explaining to do.

CHAD LET OUT A WHISTLE, prodding the group of Hereford cattle into a pen at the Lake Shore Stock Yard. Some of them would be lucky enough to be sold or transported elsewhere. Yet, the putrid smell of freshly tanned hides reminded him others wouldn't be so fortunate. A worker slammed the wooden gate shut behind them. Unaccustomed to the smaller confines of the pen, the cattle bawled and trampled each other in their quest for freedom. Gazing out at the endless array of towering buildings and smoke-stacks, Chad could understand their urgency to escape. It was stifling just to look at the place. The city reeked of constraint, its only redeeming quality being the wide river that flowed through its midst.

Chad removed his hat and raked a sleeve over his sweaty brow. He raised his canteen to his lips, letting some of the water trickle onto his chin and down his neck. Eight grueling days in the blistering heat was enough cowboying for him. He'd kept his bargain.

Time to head home.

Stew rode up beside him and motioned for him to follow. Chad reined Buck away from the pens to a quieter open area where the other workers had gathered. The weary men — most of whom had been on the trail for weeks without a break — collapsed under a shade tree or loitered at the back of the chuck wagon where Pete sat at a table, divvying out wages.

Chad dismounted and rubbed a gloved hand down Buck's sweaty neck. The horse would need a night's rest before heading back. So would he and Tag.

Stew ambled up beside Chad and nudged him with his elbow. "Best get in line for our pay. I know a good eatin' place that puts ol' Cookie's grub t' shame."

"My pay's waiting for me back toward Hammett." Chad stripped off his gloves and slipped them in his saddlebag.

"Oh yeah. Your herd." Stew scratched his chin, then cuffed Chad on the shoulder. "Well, come along anyway. My treat."

With a nod, Chad strode with him to the back of the line. When Stew's turn came, the drive master nodded his thanks, tossed him a bag of coins and crossed him off his list. Turning to Chad, Pete's dark eyes creased. "Sorry I've none for you, Avery, but I reckon you've earned your wages in cattle."

"Yes, sir." Chad straightened, widening his stance.

"You gonna stick around a few days before you head out?"

"No, sir. I figure on leaving at first light."

The edges of Callaway's mouth lifted. "Well then, son, you may make out better than the rest." He leaned back in his chair, nodding toward the other men. "The whole lot of 'em is liable to spend most of what they've earned before they leave town."

Stew jingled his money pouch. "Not me, boss. I've a gal back at Taylor Springs expectin' me to bring home something to show for my time away."

Pete gave a slight nod, his gaze still fixed on Chad. Reaching in his pocket, he pulled out a coin and rolled it across the table at him. "Get yourself a good sleep. It's a long ride home."

Chad gripped the silver dollar between his fingertips, his lips hinging upward. "Much obliged."

The drive master leaned forward and thrust out his palm. "You're right good help, Avery. If you're ever out my way and in need of a job, look me up."

He sank the coin in his pocket, then gave Callaway's hand a firm shake. "Will do."

As he turned to go, Chad donned his hat, a jumble of emotions coursing through him. Tomorrow he'd be heading home to collect his herd and begin the venture he and Lauren had dreamed of. Hollowness tugged at his heart. Somehow, now that it was within reach, it seemed empty without someone to share it with.

A gal back home. Stew's words echoed through his mind. Would Charlotte be glad to see him? Was she fretting over his delay?

Suddenly, getting back home couldn't come soon enough.

Chapter Twenty-Three

LAST WEEK'S silence had been bearable. Now, a dense strain accompanied it, making the confines of the cabin almost stifling. Seated at the table, Charlotte pored over the notes Pa had made about payments due for the seed he'd planted that spring. His bank note would cover the cost and more besides. But who could harvest the crop? She certainly couldn't tackle the job herself.

She'd held fast to her insistence on staying behind, and after numerous skirmishes, Ma had finally seceded on the issue. But having her way had come at the cost of her mother's blessing.

Ma bided her time piddling about the cabin, gathering up what few items they possessed into crates. Esther had ridden Willow into town on some unknown venture, leaving the two of them behind to sulk. Ma had every right to be concerned. Expenses out east would be greater than here on the prairie. She and Esther would need the money from the selling of their land to live on. If Charlotte stayed behind, she'd have no place to live and no means to provide for herself.

What would she do?

There was the teaching job at the school, but she hadn't the will or the patience to endure it. Still, somehow there must be a way for her to go it alone.

Surely the Lord would make a way.

THE RAP on the door came unexpected. Though, by the look on Esther's face, she seemed none too surprised. Not more than an hour ago she herself had arrived home, but neither Charlotte nor Ma had questioned what she'd been up to. Nor had she offered to say.

But something told Charlotte they were about to find out.

Ma pulled back the curtain for a peek, then, without a word, went to open the door.

"How are you, Aunt Clara?"

At Becky's gentle voice, Charlotte craned her neck for a look, hoping Johnny had finagled his way into a visit. Instead, Becky ushered Uncle Joseph in, with no sign of either Pastor Brody or Johnny.

"As well as can be, I suppose," came Ma's downhearted reply. "What brings you out our way?"

"We have something we'd like to run by all of you, Charlotte in particular." Though her uncle's demeanor bore a friendly air, it also carried a business-like nature.

Charlotte swiveled toward them. Why had she been singled out? Whatever the reason, they had her full attention.

The room quieted as Becky helped her father to a chair. He laid his cane across his lap and cleared his throat. "Esther informed us of your plans to sell the place and move out east."

Ma wrung her hands as she eased into her rocker by the fireplace. "Yes. Mr. Garrison has someone interested in buying the place. We'll be leaving as soon as arrangements can be made."

Uncle Joseph gave a brisk nod. "She also told us Charlotte isn't of a mind to go."

Esther averted her eyes from Ma's questioning stare, one that asked why she'd taken it upon herself to air their family matters. Charlotte, on the other hand, warmed inside that her younger sister thought enough of her to plead her cause.

Ma cast a weary glance at Charlotte, then returned her gaze to their visitors. "It's her intention to stay behind, though I strongly disapprove."

Charlotte bit her tongue to keep from jumping to her defense. This was her homeland. Where she belonged. She had every right to want to stay.

Uncle Joseph sat forward in his chair. "What if she was to have a place to live and income to sustain her?"

Charlotte's heart pumped harder as she tried to decipher her uncle's meaning. Was he insinuating she live with him and the Brodys and be his personal caregiver? Although she and Becky had made amends, would it be wise for them to live under the same roof?

She waited for her mother's response, still intent on the decision being her own.

Ma swept a strand of hair from her forehead. "Well, I don't know. I suppose it would settle some of my concerns. What are you proposing, Joseph?"

He shifted in Charlotte's direction, his unseeing eyes turned downward. "Matthew's ministry demands he live close to town, so Becky and I have no use of our place. With Meg and Melissa's graves there, we don't wish to sell it, and we don't like the thought of it sittin' empty. So, we were wondering if, in exchange for keeping the place up and a share of the crop, Charlotte would live there."

A smile touched Charlotte's lips, but she willed it away, expecting Ma to shoot down the idea with a resonate 'no'. Instead her only response was a raised brow.

Hope stirred within Charlotte. In her time caring for her uncle, she'd grown fond of the place and the thought of tending her own home. For the first time, it seemed a real possibility, the answer to her prayers. "It's a wonderful solution. I'd have a place to live, something to occupy me and earn my keep."

"It's a kind offer, Joseph, but it's so far out. I'm not certain it's wise for a woman alone."

Becky placed a hand on Ma's arm. "We'd check in with her from time to time, and we've already asked Mr. Avery to help harvest the crops."

Charlotte melted back in her chair, her enthusiasm waning. Before her recent discovery, she'd have relished the idea of having Chad as her closest neighbor. But now, the thought was like rubbing dirt in an open wound. Should she warn them, that if her guess proved right, he may not even return?

She clamped her lips tighter. No. The news might have a negative bearing on her uncle's offer to let her stay. Her mother seemed to waver, then gave a consenting nod.

Lacing her hands together, Charlotte mouthed a "thank you" to Esther. Her sister smiled a half-smile that seemed to teeter between joy and sorrow. She'd risked Ma's wrath for Charlotte's sake, a selfless act she wouldn't soon forget.

What she did hope to forget was that she'd ever laid eyes on her handsome neighbor, Chad Avery.

Chapter Twenty-Four

"Sure you won't change your mind?"

Johnny peered up at Charlotte, as though fearful she would consent to the request. Yet, Ma's pleading words did little to stymie Charlotte's determination to stay behind. She leaned to give her mother a kiss on the cheek. "I'm sure."

Ma's blue eyes flinched. "If you should change your mind, just send word, and I'll forward you the funds. We'll let you know where we are once we reach Cincinnati."

Charlotte gave a decisive nod, finding it hard to imagine she'd ever see the need to leave the prairie. Though she had to admit, staying behind had lost some of its appeal. The image of the photo of the woman and child atop Chad's mantel still burned in her chest.

"You will at least let us hear from you from time to time." Her mother's words seemed more statement than question.

Charlotte managed a slight grin. "I promise."

Ma held out her hand to let Pastor Brody help her onto the wagon seat. The man's gracious offer to see her mother and Esther to Peru to catch the canal boat to Chicago was a double blessing. It would spare Charlotte having to listen to her mother's constant attempts to persuade her to leave and would also give her an opportunity to spend time with Johnny.

In response to the boy's pleas, Becky had offered to let him spend the week with Charlotte, to which she'd heartily agreed. Johnny's presence would help stem the ache of loneliness that was certain to accompany Ma and Esther's absence, and would also help divert her mind from Chad.

Esther stepped up beside her and reached for a hug. "I'll miss you."

"And I you." Charlotte leaned into her sister's warm embrace. Now that they were parting, a sense of loss enveloped Charlotte. Pa's passing had somehow deepened the bond between them, their past differences forgotten.

"Thanks for what you did." Charlotte's voice was a whisper in her sister's ear.

Esther gave her a gentle squeeze, then released her with a teary smile. "Come see us."

"You do the same." The finality of their leaving rippled through Charlotte. With Esther's sixteenth birthday just days away, she would spend it in route to Cincinnati. The next time Charlotte saw her sister, she would likely be a grown woman, refined by city living.

Heaviness pulled at Charlotte's chest. In the handful of times they were likely to visit each other over the years, would their reunions be joyful ones or plagued with unfamiliarity?

As Esther moved to say her goodbyes to Becky and Uncle Joseph, Charlotte placed an arm around Johnny's shoulders. He leaned into her, seeming content just to be near her. Would that he could stay with her always. Yet, he needed the love of both a mother and a father.

Something she alone couldn't give.

RUBIE GAVE a soft whine and stared back at the cabin in the distance. Charlotte pulled Willow to a stop beside her, casting a wistful glance at the homestead where she'd grown up. Memories of her childhood, of her father, lingered everywhere — in the patched barn roof, in the field of ripening corn out back, and in the worn path to the pasture. How many times had she walked with him along that familiar trail to bring in the horses or simply enjoy the view? How she longed to hear his gentle voice, see his mischievous smile, and laugh at his clever wit.

But he was gone now, along with her mother and sister.

A sense of aloneness washed over Charlotte. For the first time, she understood her mother's qualms about staying. Pa's absence cried out from every hewn log, every tool laid silent. Soon strangers would sleep in their beds and eat at their table, not knowing the joys and sorrows that had transpired there before them. As promised, Ma had sold everything, even the animals, save Willow, Rubie, and ol' Nell, their cow. Ma had taken nothing but the essentials, not even Pa's hat or pocket watch, both of which remained tucked inside Charlotte's saddle bags.

Ma wished to make a fresh start of things, to forget. But was leaving the answer?

Not for Charlotte.

She held tighter to the young boy snugged against her in the saddle. Even he would leave her in a matter of days.

"You all right, Miss Charlotte?"

"Just saying my goodbyes." With a sigh, she reined Willow toward her uncle's place, her new home, Nell tied on behind. Rubie tore herself from her spot to traipse along beside them.

Johnny leaned into Charlotte, toying with the reins. "Are you sad?"

The boy's perceptiveness never ceased to amaze her. "A bit."

"I was sad when my Pa died. Mama too."

The moment of silence was swallowed up in Willow's gaited

stride. At last, Johnny craned his neck to gaze up at Charlotte, his pale blue eyes shining. "I reckon we're both by ourselves now, ain't we?"

The truth of his words sliced through her, and she struggled to bolster words of encouragement. "Well now, I don't know. You've got the Brodys."

Johnny's head drooped downward. "Ain't the same. They're just keepin' me temporary 'cause I ain't got nowhere else."

He was right. It wasn't the same. They weren't family, and it wasn't a real home. Not yet anyway. Charlotte leaned her cheek against his blond hair. "I'm sure the Lord has some place real special in mind for you. Anyway, that's my prayer for you."

Johnny quieted, his only movement the gentle working of his fingers up and down the leather reins, a sure sign something was stirring inside that sweet blond head of his.

Charlotte could only pray the Lord would soon answer her prayers.

CHAD CIRCLED his small herd into a cove along the tree-lined creek at the far edge of his property. The tired animals lumbered to the stream for a drink, the heat having taken a toll on them. The young calves traipsed in belly-deep after their mothers, touching their noses to the rippling water and wagging their heads. Eight cows and five calves. Not much of a herd.

But it was a start.

Chad dismounted and let the horses drink while he filled his canteen. The trip hadn't turned out the way he'd hoped. But it was over now. He was finally home.

With a cleansing breath, he glanced over the acres of prairie grass. The land was his. The cattle were here. So, why this unquenchable longing for more?

Hollowness pulled at his chest. If only Lauren were here to

greet him. She'd have given him a hero's welcome. Could he dare to hope Charlotte would? He shouldn't. He had no right. Yet, the gleam in her emerald eyes the night before he'd left had seared his heart, weakening his resolve. He'd determined to live out his days alone.

Now, he wasn't so sure.

A dream wasn't truly a dream unless there was someone to share it with. Was he being fair to himself, to Charlotte, not to give them a chance? He had to admit, being near her dredged up feelings he'd thought were lost to him. Given time, could he open his heart to her? Lauren's image seemed to fade as he warmed to the thought.

Removing his hat, he raked a sleeve over his sweaty brow, hope rising in his heart. Tomorrow he'd pay Charlotte a visit to let her know he was back and see where the Lord led.

Chapter Twenty-Five

EARLY MORNING LIGHT seeped through the cabin window, waking Charlotte from her night's rest. Despite the strange bed and the unsettled thoughts churning inside her, she'd slept soundly. She opened her eyes, a smile touching her lips at sight of the small boy curled up on the far side of the bed. Sometime in the night he'd abandoned the loft and taken up residence beside her, still dressed in his clothes, his lengthy blond hair draped over his face.

The poor child had been through so much. How he must long for a family to call his own. Only weeks ago Charlotte thought it might be her family that could fill that void.

She breathed a quiet sigh. How quickly things change.

The boy stirred and sat up, rubbing his eyes. They widened as he saw Charlotte staring up at him. Hopping to his feet, Johnny slid his hands in his pockets. "I wasn't scared or nothin'. I came to ask for a drink and fell asleep."

Charlotte smiled at his boyish pride and motioned toward the fireplace. "Well now, I do recall we left a bucketful of creek water alongside the hearth last night.

A sheepish grin spread over his face. "I reckon so."

Charlotte held back a chuckle as he trotted off to the front of the cabin. She'd had no cause to laugh or even smile in weeks. Johnny's company was as refreshing as a mid-summer rain. Rising, she changed from her nightgown into her calico and pinned her braided hair into a roll. When she rounded the corner of the fireplace, Johnny stood nose pressed to the window pane.

His head veered toward her as she leaned to stoke the fire-place embers. "Rubie looks lonesome."

Charlotte's chest clenched. He was right. Rubie missed her early morning romps with Pa. "Why don't you keep her company while I get breakfast?"

Without a word, Johnny scooted out the door. The fire stoked, Charlotte moved to the window and caught a glimpse of the boy and dog darting around the yard, circling the outbuild-ings. Rubie's playful yips alongside Johnny's giggles lightened Charlotte's mood. The boy had made her first night and day alone tolerable. How lonesome it would be when he left.

Turning, she strode to the hearth and slid the skillet from its peg. Being with Johnny was much more enticing than cooking. Uncle Joseph had been thoughtful enough to leave a few of his chickens, including the setting hen. Fresh eggs and milk would be just the thing.

Cackles blended with Rubie's more vigorous barks outside the cabin. Charlotte dropped her skillet and rushed outside in time to see Johnny squatted before the open door of the hen house, hands on head, a flurry of feathers settling over him. The sparse flock of chickens stood scattered about, feathers ruffled as they scratched at the dirt outside the coop.

Hurrying over, Charlotte took Johnny by the hand, unsure who'd been startled most.

He stood, big blue eyes staring up at her. "I only wanted to see if the eggs had hatched."

With a chuckle, Charlotte led him inside the chicken coup.

The buff-colored hen squawked, but didn't offer to peck when she reached under her. Warmth enveloped Charlotte's hand as she lifted the mother hen and surveyed the nest of eggs. How many days had she been on the nest now? Nineteen? Twenty?

She held one up against a stream of sunlight, viewing the growing chick within. "It won't be long now. Another day or two at most."

"I ain't never seen baby chicks freshly hatched."

The excitement in Johnny's voice wound its way inside Charlotte. He smiled up at her, his expression full of wonder. She brushed a hand over his wayward bangs. The youngster had finagled his way into her heart much like Chad, which left her with one searing notion.

When Johnny left, would he too break her heart?

Something wasn't right. Where was Jed's livestock? The place looked near deserted.

Chad tapped Buck's flanks with his heels, spurring him into a slow canter. Movement at the front of the cabin pulled his attention to the slender, silvery-headed man tramping toward the wagon out front. A mismatched team of horses, one black the other white, stood at its head. Surely the man was a relative of the Stantons, though Chad denoted no resemblance to either Jed or Clara. Venturing closer, Chad caught the man's eye as he lifted a crate from the back of the wagon. The unknown man paused, his expression a mixture of welcome and suspicion.

As he neared, Chad gave a slight nod. "Mornin'. Are the Stantons at home?"

The stranger tightened his hold on the crate, brow creased. At last, his expression eased. "You mean the previous owners. My wife and I own the place now."

Chad's mind reeled. The Stantons, previous owners? It didn't make sense. What could have possessed them to sell their farm? Had they traveled north to be with Jed? "Do you happen to know where I could find them?"

"I'm afraid you've missed them. I believe they've moved eastward."

"East?" Chad fought the urge to question the stranger further. What had happened? He'd been gone less than a month. How could so much change in such a short time? Jed wasn't even due back from up north yet. Visions of Charlotte rippled through him. Had he lost her before he'd even had a chance to know her?

"Sorry to have bothered you." With a tip of his hat, Chad reined Buck toward town. A visit to the Brodys would clear things up.

But something told him he wouldn't like what they had to say.

"I DON'T WANT NO BATH." Johnny crossed his arms in front of him, lower lip extended.

Taking up a bar of lye soap, Charlotte tested the tub of water with her finger. "Didn't the Brodys make you wash?"

"They let me wash up in the crick same as I always do."

Charlotte stared at him wide-eyed. "Haven't you ever had a real bath?"

The boy's face pinched in a scowl. "What fer? Crick water does just fine."

"Well, it's about time you found out what warm water and soap are."

"Uh-uh."

Johnny made a dash for the door, and Charlotte caught him by the sleeve. "Either you chuck those clothes and hop in, or I'll do it for you."

A look of horror shrouded his smudged face as he clutched the front of his shirt. "And I thought you was a nice lady."

"Oh, I am. So nice in fact that once you're clean, I'll whack the hair from over your eyes so you can see." Charlotte worked to mask a smile as the boy covered his head with his hands.

She reached for the milk bucket and placed a hand on her hip, willing herself to sound firm. "Just toss your clothes out on the porch, and I'll wash 'em up soon as I finish milking Nell."

His eyes widened. "But what'll I wear?"

"Have you no spare set of clothes?"

He scuffed his toe against the puncheon floorboard, head drooped. "Just the Sunday ones Mr. and Mrs. Brody bought me, but I don't like 'em."

Charlotte nodded. "Oh. I see. Well, maybe I can find something for you to put on while I trim your hair. The breeze and sunlight should dry your clothes in no time."

She made her way to the back of the cabin and rummaged through her things until she'd found her spare nightgown. As small as the boy was, a gunny sack might suit him just as well. A trip into town was a definite must sometime during the week. Clutching the gown in her hand, she started toward Johnny.

His eyes flickered at her approach. "I ain't wearin' no woman's clothes."

"It won't be for long. And I'll be too busy cutting your hair to notice what you're wearing."

His lips skewed downward.

Charlotte bent to his eye level. "No one will see. I promise."

He cocked his head to one side, eyes narrowed. "Better hurry with my clothes."

Straightening, she draped the gown over the back of a chair, then fetched a linen towel. "When I get back, I expect to find you sparkling from head to toe."

He heaved a soft sigh. "Yes'm."

Scooping up her bucket, she pivoted toward the door. She

swung it open, then paused, a smile playing on her lips as she peered back at him. "Don't forget to scrub behind your ears."

He balled his fists, a look of defiance in his eyes.

With a smile, she pulled the door shut behind her before he resorted to throwing soap.

CHARLOTTE SNIPPED another generous amount of Johnny's damp hair with the shears. He sat poised on a stool, nightshirt pulled over his legs, bare feet propped on the warm hearth. With every snip, he cringed and scrunched his neck lower into his shoulders.

She nudged his head forward. "It'd be easier on us both if you quit your slouching and hold still."

He gave a loud huff and sat up straighter. "How much longer?"

"Just a few more snips." She finished leveling off his bangs, then stood back to survey her handiwork. Her lips lifted in a grin as she set the shears on the table. He looked like a different child. "My, what a handsome boy you are all spruced up."

His rounded face glowed pink. "Am not."

"See for yourself." She held a small hand mirror up to his face.

His pale blue eyes sparked as he stared at his reflection, shifting his head side to side. "Don't look like me."

"Well it is, sure as rain."

A smile lit his face as his gaze shifted back and forth between the mirror and Charlotte. "I reckon cleanin' up now and then ain't so bad."

She shook her head, reaching for the broom and dust pan. "If you can tear yourself away, I'll have you sweep the floor while I check to see if your clothes are dry."

"Even if they ain't, bring 'em just the same. Wet britches

beat none at all." He hopped to his feet, tugging at the over-sized nightshirt.

Charlotte's heart warmed at the image of the red-faced boy struggling to retain his dignity. No doubt about it, he'd stolen her heart.

By the week's end, it would tear her apart to see him go.

Chapter Twenty-Six

THE NEWS HIT Chad like a punch in the gut. He propped one boot up on the porch step, letting Mrs. Brody's words sink in. Jed Stanton, dead? It was hard to fathom the spirited, burly fellow was gone. Though Chad hadn't known him well, what he'd seen of him he'd liked and admired. His heart ached for the man's family. Charlotte especially. Would Chad ever have the chance to tell her how sorry he was?

If anyone understood loss, he did.

"Sorry to hear that." Chad twisted his hat in his hands, the words catching in his throat. "And Mrs. Stanton and her daughters? Word has it they moved out east."

Mrs. Brody gave a slight nod. "Yes. To Cincinnati."

"All but Charlotte, she stayed behind."

At Joseph Hollister's words, Chad's face lifted, along with his spirits. "Then she hadn't left."

"What's that, Mr. Avery?"

Had he spoken the words or merely surmised them? The curious gleam in Mrs. Brody's eye suggested he'd at least mumbled them. He cleared his throat. "Do you know where I might find Miss Stanton?"

Joseph shifted in his chair. "Sure can. She's staying out at our old place. We had no need of it, and she needed somewhere to go. Seemed just the solution."

With a nod, Chad donned his hat. "Much obliged."

He mounted Buck, his mind in a whirl. No doubt Charlotte was still grieving her father's passing. Could she manage on her own so far out? He'd heard tell Illinois winters could be downright brutal. Why had she chosen to stay?

Might it have something to do with him?

With a tip of his hat, he reined Buck toward the mercantile. Soon as he rounded up his supplies, he intended to find out.

"MISS CHARLOTTE, COME QUICK!" Johnny's loud peal held an air of urgency.

Charlotte tugged the dry bed sheet from the clothes line and dropped it in the basket. What had the boy gotten himself into now? He'd only gone to gather the eggs.

A sudden thought shot a chill down her spine. Just yesterday she'd found a snake skin near the garden. Snakes were known to slither their way inside outbuildings and curl up in the least likely places. Had one found its way into the hen house?

Worse yet, could it be a timber rattler or a copperhead?

Hiking her skirt, she ran toward the front of the cabin. A second earnest plea from Johnny propelled her on, until she stopped breathless before the open hen house door.

Johnny's somber gaze remained fixed on the hen-covered nest before him. Nothing seemed amiss, outside of the boy's solemn state.

Charlotte swallowed the dryness in her throat, struggling to catch her breath. "What is it? What's wrong?"

He knit his brows as he gestured toward the nest. "She's gone and squished her eggs. See?"

Drawing a hurried breath, Charlotte stepped closer and peered at the disgruntled mother hen. Bits of eggshell lay strewn about the nest, and toward the back, a tiny, orange foot poked from beneath ruffled feathers. A corner of Charlotte's mouth lifted as she edged closer, placing an arm about Johnny's shoulders. "She's not squished them. They've hatched."

The hen gave a warning squawk as Charlotte nudged her to one side.

Johnny leaned over the nest, eyes widening at sight of seven fuzzy, mustard-colored chicks, their downy feathers still damp. His gaze shifted between Charlotte and the chicks. Red seeped into his cheeks as he kicked at the straw-covered floor. He shrugged his shoulders. "I figured as much."

Charlotte suppressed a grin as she scooped one of the drier chicks up in her palm, ignoring the mother hen's gentle peck. "Wanna hold him?"

Johnny's embarrassment vanished as he nodded and cupped his hands out in front of him. The newly-hatched chick peeped as the boy rubbed his finger down its back. "Sure is soft."

He smiled up at Charlotte, his innocence melting her heart. The Lord had certainly blessed her by sending Johnny. With Pa gone, Ma and Esther away, and Chad's image tarnished, the boy was all she had. How she would cherish every moment until he, too, would leave her.

"Who's that?" Johnny's boyish voice sounded beside Charlotte.

She leaned on her potato fork and peered in the direction he was pointing. Sight of the buckskin-clad rider coming toward them sent a tremor through her. Then he'd returned after all. "I-I believe it's my neighbor, Mr. Avery."

Ducking her face beneath her bonnet, she propped her foot

on the wooden fork and pushed it deeper into the soil. For weeks, she'd longed for Chad's return. Now, his presence only twisted her in knots.

Johnny tugged at the fold of her skirt. "Ain't ya gonna go greet him?"

Charlotte stilled. Obviously, the boy wasn't going to let her ignore the unwanted guest. With a sigh, she left her tool and stepped over the rows of shriveled potato plants. She glanced up just in time to see Chad raise a gloved hand in greeting.

Charlotte's throat thickened, and she struggled to swallow. He was even more handsome than she recalled, with his broad shoulders and sun-tanned face. Setting her jaw, she determined to hold to her resolve. She had nothing but contempt for a man who'd leave his family and pretend they didn't exist.

Worse yet, lead her to believe he cared for her.

With a tip of his hat, Chad halted his horse at the edge of the garden, his gaze fixed firmly on her face. "Afternoon."

She squared her shoulders, forcing herself to meet his stare. "Mr. Avery." Her cordial words were laced with formality, the weeks apart and her unwanted discovery weaving a thread of awkwardness between them.

"Thought I'd run by and see how you're doing."

Her upper lip stiffened. "We're managing."

His silvery eyes softened. "Mrs. Brody told me about your father. I'm sorry."

"Thank you." She brushed a strand of hair from her cheek, trying to stem the flow of emotions his words initiated.

Johnny came and stood beside her, and she placed an arm around his shoulders.

Chad's gaze shifted to the boy. "Who's your helper?"

"Johnny Langston. He's staying with me a few days."

Venturing a step forward, Johnny squinted up at Chad. "I know you. You're that fella what busted up my fight at school a few weeks back."

Chad tilted his hat back with his thumb. "Reckon I was."

"You know each other?" The words flew from Charlotte before she could stop them.

"Just seen him the one time." Johnny kept his eyes riveted on Chad.

Charlotte wet her lips, shifting her gaze back to Chad. "When'd you get back?"

"Night before last. Not as soon as I'd hoped."

For a long moment, his eyes held Charlotte's, seeming to bore right through her. Tightness gripped her middle. Should she speak what was burning on her tongue to say?

She cleared her throat. "Sort of wondered if you'd come back at all." She glanced at her feet, the words trickling out in almost a whisper.

A slight chuckle rose from Chad. "Why wouldn't I?"

The image of the dark-haired woman and child raced to the forefront of Charlotte's mind. Eyes narrowing, she again met his stare. "I can think of two very good reasons."

He sat taller in the saddle. "Don't rightly know what those might be. I had every intention of returning."

Tenderness lined his words, further confounding Charlotte. Was he really so deceptive, or just plain oblivious to her meaning? "Then what kept you?"

"I got waylaid."

Charlotte rocked back on her heels, nearly swallowing her tongue at the words. Was he in earnest or jesting?

He watched her, seeming to guess her uncertainty. "A fella jumped me in the night, stole my savings, and spent most of it before I could catch up with him. I had to help run the herd to earn back some cattle."

Charlotte's heart sank. Chad's cattle meant everything to him. How she longed to speak words of comfort, but she held back, unwilling to let go of her angst. His misfortune didn't erase the fact that he'd deceived her.

Before she could give any sort of response, Johnny blurted, "Are you a cattleman?"

Chad seemed to have won the boy's admiration without even trying, as he had her father's. Hers too.

For a time.

Chad nodded to the boy. "I aim to be, if the Lord sees fit to grow my thirteen head."

Johnny stood taller, puffing out his small chest. "I'm gonna be a cattleman too."

A grin broke out on Chad's face. "Is that so?"

"Yes s'r. Soon as I'm able, I'm gonna learn to rope and ride."

"Well now, I may just have to hire you on, someday."

"Really?" Johnny stared up at Charlotte, beaming ear to ear.

She raked a hand through his blond hair. "That's a long way off, I'm afraid."

Johnny's face lost its smile. Shoving his hands in his pockets, he kicked at the ground.

Chad leaned forward, resting his forearm across the saddle horn. "Oh, I don't know. I've five young calves in need of branding. Once I get things set, I'll need a steady hand to hold the iron. You might be just the man for the job. That is, if Miss Stanton gives the okay."

Johnny tugged at her sleeve, peering up at her. "Could I, Miss Charlotte?"

"I don't know, Johnny." She looked into the boy's pleading face, his pale blue eyes sparkling with enthusiasm. Despite every intention of wanting to squelch any further association with her wayward neighbor, something deep inside kept her from mustering the word "no". Instead, her eyes flickered and fell to the soil beneath her. Would Johnny even be with her by the time Chad got around to it? "We'll see."

"Thanks, Miss Charlotte." Johnny's arms encircled her waist. Apparently, he'd taken her maybe for a yes.

She heaved a sigh and rested her hand on the boy's back. How could she deny Johnny the only true eagerness he'd shown?

She sensed Chad's eyes upon her, yet refused to meet his gaze. He'd caused her enough heartache, with his winsome smile, alluring promises, and hidden past. If the opportunity presented itself, she'd see to it Johnny got his chance to help. Even go with him. But she didn't have to like it.

And afterward, she'd end things for good.

Chapter Twenty-Seven

"Women."

Chad shook his head, hammering the wooden peg into place. He'd been foolish to think Charlotte cared for him. Or that he could open his heart again.

Why, she even seemed irritated to see him.

He reached in his pocket for another nail. Was she put out at him for causing her worry? Surely she could understand the delay wasn't his fault.

Clenching his jaw, he wiped sweat from his brow. Let her think what she wanted. He had more important matters to tend to. Like finishing this chute.

One by one, he pounded in the remaining nails. There was something therapeutic in swinging a mallet. Nothing like a bit of manual labor to clear the head.

When he'd driven in the last peg, he took a swig from his canteen and stared out at his herd. Coming home hadn't turned out as he'd hoped. But like all the other disappointments in his life, with the Lord's help, he'd press on and make the best of things. He'd worked hard for what he had, and he'd not allow a moody female to squelch his dreams.

He swung the chute doors open and shut to test them. With a satisfied nod, he tied them shut. One step closer to staking claim on his herd.

Reaching for the branding iron, he leaned against the rail fence. He ran his fingertips over the smooth iron tip welded in a circle with a J at its center. All that remained was to stoke a fire and herd the cattle into the corral. This chute would simplify things. Still, branding was sure to prove a challenge. Hank Brimmer had agreed to help tackle the handful of cows. Johnny could help with the calves another day.

Chad heaved a tired sigh. He shouldn't have promised the boy he'd let him help. The thought of facing Charlotte again filled his stomach with lead. He had no cause to feel guilty. Whatever had put her out of sorts, was her doing. Not his.

At least not intentionally.

He raked a hand over his face. Jed would have been a great help, had he been here. Chad ached knowing the grief Charlotte must be going through. A feeling he knew all too well. Maybe that was part of her problem. But if so, why had she directed her angst at him?

One thing was certain. His instincts had been right all along. He was better off alone.

A horse's canter pulled Chad's attention to the worn path. He slipped out the gate, then strode to meet his neighbor to the east.

Hank slowed his mount, sending a cloud of dust drifting toward Chad. The stout man, hair flecked with gray, eyed the newly constructed chute. "Looks like you're set."

"Just finished." Chad brushed off his trousers and extended a hand in welcome.

With a firm shake, Hank glanced over the small herd. "You're in need of a bull, ain't you?"

"Soon as I can afford one."

"I've a young Hereford bull I'm looking to sell. Might be just what you're needing."

Chad tugged at his gloves. "I'm afraid at this point I've no means to buy one."

Hank scratched at his jaw. "Now, hold up. I'm willin' to give a person a fair shake. I've some odd jobs I could use a spare set of hands with. As handy as you are, it might just be we could strike some sort of bargain."

"Sounds good. Can't grow a herd without a bull."

"That's certain." With a chuckle, Hank dismounted. "Well, then. Let's get to work. Ida wants me home in good time." He leaned sideways in his saddle, his voice softening. "My daughter Lola's beau is comin' for supper. Seems a right nice boy. Name's Norris Pickford. Ever met him?"

Chad's mind drifted back to the night Charlotte had cheated Norris out of a dance. "I believe I have."

It appeared Charlotte had succeeded in sending her would-be suitor into the arms of another. Now it was him she was pushing away. She was a hard one to figure. Yet, maybe something good had come of her conniving scheme for Norris and Miss Brimmer.

But if Charlotte didn't watch it, she'd end up as lonely as he was.

THE CHURCH QUIETED as Pastor Brody took his place at the pulpit.

A knocking noise sounded under the pew next to Charlotte, generating stares from the family in front of her and Johnny. She placed a hand on the boy's knee to calm his swinging leg.

With a frown, he stilled his foot and tugged at his new Sunday shirt collar. Unaccustomed to the confines of church clothing and routines, the rigidness seemed to stifle Johnny's active spirit. Charlotte smiled at him, thankful for his company in her otherwise empty pew. Had Ma and Esther arrived in

Cincinnati? More than likely they were attending some fancy church service in some grand building. Her heart ached for news of their journey.

Her week with Johnny had passed in a flurry. After the service, he'd return to the Brodys. The unpleasant thought filled her with longing. Would it really be so wrong for her to take him in on a permanent basis? No one could love him more than she did. Still, in her heart she knew it best he have the influence of a father. At eighteen, she could hardly qualify as mother, let alone both parents.

At least they'd not heard any more from Chad Avery. Now she'd not have to worry about going with Johnny to brand calves. The Brodys could have that privilege. Being near Chad could only bring her more heartache.

Opening his Bible, Pastor Brody glanced over the congregation, brown eyes dancing. "We've a fine crowd today. I'm pleased you've all come. Now, if you'd please turn your Bibles to the Gospel of John, chapter eight, we'll tackle the issue of accountability."

Never one to mince words, Pastor Brody's sermons were generally concise and to the point. Well worth the five-mile trip into town. That he'd chosen to give up his circuit to settle with Becky in Miller Creek was truly a blessing.

Charlotte held her Bible toward Johnny, letting him help find the place. She ran her fingertip along the thin page, pausing at the start of the chapter. Johnny bent his head down, silently attempting to sound out some of the words.

Pastor Brody stepped to the side of the pulpit, Bible in hand. "How should we respond when a brother or sister is openly involved in sin?"

The question sharpened Charlotte's senses, capturing her full attention. Was Mr. Avery listening? Tilting her head to the side, her eyes sought him out. There he sat, in his usual spot on the back bench. Charlotte arched a brow. Perhaps the sermon would convict him of his wrongdoing.

His eyes veered toward her, and she snapped her head forward.

"What does it mean to hold someone accountable? Does it mean we're to chide and find fault with one another?" Pastor Brody's dark eyes panned the crowd. "Brothers and sisters, as Christians, we have a responsibility to each other. Not in a condemning way, but out of love and with a spirit of humility.

"In chapter eight of John's Gospel, we see a woman caught in adultery brought to Jesus by the Pharisees. In their subtle way, the Pharisees tried to trap Jesus into a wrong motive or action, knowing that, by law, the woman deserved to die." Pastor Brody held up his Bible, face shrouded with emotion. "Yet, rather than condemn her, we read in verse seven, he told her accusers, 'He that is without sin among you, let him first cast a stone at her.'"

Silence cloaked the building, in the wake of his fervent words. Even Johnny stared wide-eyed at Pastor Brody. Becky gazed up at him from the front pew, face full of pride and affection. They truly made the perfect couple.

A pang of regret shot through Charlotte. Would she ever know such love? She'd tasted of it with Chad, only to glean disappointment.

Pastor Brody clenched his fist, then extended his arm in a throwing motion. "From the oldest to the youngest, they dropped their stones and left, leaving Jesus alone with the woman. He said to her, verse ten, 'Woman, where are thine accusers? Hath no man condemned thee?'

'No man, Lord,' she said. And Jesus said unto her, 'Neither do I condemn thee; go, and sin no more.'"

He stepped closer to the pews, voice softening. "Jesus, the Son of God, the sinless man, did not condemn this sinful woman. Instead he exposed her sin for what it was, and lovingly instructed her to change."

He paused, striding back to the pulpit. "Proverbs 27 verse 17 tells us 'As iron sharpeneth iron; so a man sharpeneth the countenance of his friend.' As Christians then, it's our duty, not to condemn others for their sin, but to help them rise above it. To draw them out away from wrongdoing and restore them to more Christ-like ways."

Charlotte's stomach tensed, the pointed words searing her soul. Had she condemned Chad without so much as lifting a finger to steer him in the right direction? If so, she was no better than the Pharisees.

Her mind raced back to the night Chad had pulled her away to dance, to spare Becky more of her insolent remarks. *Iron sharpeneth iron.* Hadn't he done that very thing? Confronted her sin and set her on a better path? He'd proven a friend in time of need. Should she do any less for him?

She bowed her head, sensing the paleness in her cheeks. *Lord, forgive my condemning attitude. Give me courage to speak words of truth into the lives of others, yet in a humble way.*

She felt a tug on her sleeve and opened her eyes. Johnny stretched his mouth toward her ear, and in a whisper asked, "Are you sleeping?"

A hint of a smile touched her lips. Bending toward him, she shook her head and answered softly, "Praying."

With a nod, he paused, then spoke again. "How much longer?"

"Not long."

With a huff, Johnny sat back, toying with the buttons on his shirt. Charlotte gave him a pat on the leg. As long as he was with the Brodys, he'd have to get used to preaching. In time, hopefully his heart would be touched by the Gospel message.

As the sermon came to a close, the congregation stood for the final hymn. Charlotte peered over her shoulder at Chad, this time meeting his gaze before turning away. Would he accept an attempt to confront him about his past? He was a good man.

Too good to squander his life away.

She could only pray for the right chance to approach him and that the Lord would give grace for Chad to listen to what she had to say.

"Good news."

The sparkle in her cousin's expression aroused Charlotte's curiosity. She could do with a bit of good news.

Becky pulled her and Johnny aside, letting the remaining congregation file past. "We may have a home for Johnny."

The words hung in the air like an unpleasant odor. Charlotte pasted on a smile, pretending what she didn't feel. "That's wonderful, isn't it Johnny?"

With a shrug, Johnny stared at his shoes.

"The family is new to the area. They live over towards Palmer and would like to come meet Johnny later in the week."

Palmer lay several miles to the east, too far to expect to see much of Johnny. If any. Charlotte gave a slow nod, reminding herself the arrangement would be for the best, though the ache inside her compelled her to deny it. "You said family. Have they other children?"

"Yes. Three daughters, the oldest age nine and twin girls that just turned five."

Johnny's face contorted as if he'd swallowed an onion. "No boys?"

Becky bent to his eye level. "That's where you come in. Mrs. Flynn can no longer have children, and they'd dearly love to have a son."

Johnny slid his hand into Charlotte's, the color draining from his cheeks. "Is it all right I stay with Miss Charlotte till they come?"

"If that's what you both want."

Johnny's pale blue eyes found Charlotte's. "Could I?"

Her chest tightened. A few more days with him would only make saying goodbye more difficult. Yet, she hadn't the heart to refuse. "All right, Johnny."

Becky straightened, the enthusiasm fleeing from her expression. "I thought you'd be overjoyed."

Forcing a smile, Charlotte squeezed Johnny's hand, and he leaned into her. "We are. Just weren't expecting it so soon."

Her grin returning, Becky touched a hand to Johnny's shoulder. "Well, you have a few days to let it sink in. Matthew and I will bring the Flynns by mid-week."

With weighted steps Charlotte and Johnny made their way outside the church building. Try as she may, Charlotte couldn't rid herself of the dread of passing Johnny off to strangers. As if that wasn't bad enough, as they downed the church steps, she noticed Chad Avery standing alongside Willow. She slowed her pace, watching him run a hand down her horse's neck, oblivious to their approach. What was he doing here? Ever the first one out the door, he was usually on his way home by now. Not once had he stayed to greet her or anyone else.

"Hey, there's Mr. Avery!" Excitement oozed in Johnny's voice. He slid his hand loose of her grasp and ran to meet Chad.

Charlotte hesitated, then strolled after him, arriving just in time to see them strike hands. Johnny turned toward her, his dismal expression transformed into a beaming grin. "Mr. Avery wants my help with his calves tomorrow. Can we go?"

Charlotte swallowed the lump in her throat. She wavered between her need to distance herself and the need to confront him. Would this be her chance? "I suppose so."

She shifted her gaze from Johnny to Chad, his face more somber than their last meeting. Had he, too, been convicted?

It appeared she was about to find out.

Chapter Twenty-Eight

CHAD STOOPED to stoke the fire, making certain it was hot for the branding iron. Lifting his gaze eastward, his eyes searched the tree-line for signs of Charlotte and the boy.

Nothing.

He wet his lips, half dreading having asked them. Would he regret them coming?

He stood and fastened on his chaps, extra protection for when he wrestled the calves. The restless calves paced in the pen, bawling to their mothers in the pasture beyond. The anxious cows stood lined along the fence row, answering back, their loud bellows cutting through the humid air. Separating them had proven quite a challenge. He dreaded when the calves would be of weaning age, and he'd have to separate them all over again.

A faint movement in the distance caught his eye. They were coming.

Right on time.

Better get the branding iron heating. He snatched it up and plunged the tip in the center of the red-hot coals. The hotter the better.

Turning, he peered out at the approaching horse and riders.

His stomach tightened at sight of Charlotte's slender frame atop the sturdy roan mare. Her bonnet flipped upward in the breeze, exposing her smooth, sun-kissed face fringed by a halo of crimson locks. Try as he may, he couldn't pry his eyes from her face.

Twice he'd caught her glancing back at him during yesterday's church service, her puzzled expression masking her thoughts. What was he to think of her, stiff as a broom at times and at others soft as feather down? What went on behind those limpid green eyes?

With effort, he pulled his hat down over his face, obscuring his view of her. The sooner this was over with the better.

THE MORNING BREEZE toyed with Charlotte's bonnet. She tugged it back into place, gnawing at the inner lining of her cheek. Chad had seen them coming. Stared even. His eyes upon her, even from a distance, caused her heart rate to quicken. Standing tall and sure, he looked every inch a cattleman in his loose linen shirt, suspenders, chaps, hat, and bandanna.

A disturbingly handsome one at that.

Warmth flooded her cheeks, and she tamped down the angst brewing inside her. She was here for two purposes and two alone — for Johnny's sake, and to follow through with the mission the Lord had placed on her heart.

She squared her shoulders. At first opportunity, she'd do her best to bring Chad to his senses.

Johnny squirmed in the saddle, oozing with excitement. "There's the calves."

With a tap of her heels, Charlotte urged Willow to a slow trot. No sense prolonging things.

At their approach, Chad sauntered toward them. His gaze swept past Charlotte to the boy. "You all set?"

"Sure am." Faster than a frog leaping to shore, Johnny swung his leg over Willow and slid to the ground.

Before Charlotte could object, strong hands encircled her waist, gently pulling her from Willow's back. The act left her breathless, and she fought to speak. "Thank you."

Chad tipped his hat, still not meeting her gaze.

Heat spread down her neck and into her chest. The man's southern roots evidently ran deep, revealing themselves in courteous ways. Something inside her wished his gesture was more than mere politeness.

She gnawed at her lip. She had no right to wish such. He was a married man, after all. And she intended to see he did right by his family.

Chad tugged at his gloves and, with a nod, started toward the corral.

Johnny scurried ahead and thrust his face through a gap in the timber rails, eyes glued to the fidgety, young calves. "Only five?"

"That's it." Chad stepped up beside him, propping his boot on the rail fence.

Positioning herself on the far side of Johnny, Charlotte glanced over the small cluster of Hereford calves. "They're fine looking ones."

Chad clapped his gloved hands together. "Well, let's find out how tough they are." He turned to Johnny. "Do you have gloves?"

Johnny's eyes fled from Chad's hands to his own. The youngster shook his head, his countenance waning. "No, sir."

Bending down, Chad clasped a hand to Johnny's shoulder. "Maybe if you ask real nice, Miss Stanton will grab the extra pair out of my saddle bag."

The boy's face lifted. He turned to Charlotte, eyes pleading. "Would you, Miss Charlotte?"

She nodded. May as well make herself useful. For the time

being, all she could do was stand back and watch . . . and wait for her chance to voice her grievances to Chad. The way Johnny had latched onto him, it might prove a real challenge to speak privately with Chad.

Retrieving the gloves from Chad's saddlebag, she turned back to the pair of would-be cattlemen. They'd slipped inside the corral and looked to be discussing their plan of action. Chad talking and motioning with his hands. Johnny listening and nodding.

Charlotte's heart clenched. To see Chad so at ease with the boy was proof he had the makings of a good father. What could have enticed him to abandon his own son?

Pushing her way through the corral gate, she stepped to Johnny.

A huge smile lined his lips as he took the gloves from her. "Thanks."

The large, leather gloves swallowed his hands as he slipped them on. He frowned, watching hollow finger sleeves sway back and forth as he flexed his fingers. "They're too big."

Chad gave him a light cuff on the back. "No matter. Just so they protect you from the heat of the iron."

Iron sharpeneth iron. A chill ran through Charlotte. Would the Lord protect her and Chad from being burnt by the heat of confrontation?

Together, Chad and Johnny strolled to the fire at the center of the corral. The frightened calves darted back and forth along the far side, their calls more frantic.

Charlotte leaned against the outer fence, listening to Chad's instructions in case Johnny ran into trouble.

Chad drew the iron from the fire, exposing its red-hot tip. "Once I've brought down the calf, you bring the branding iron and press the emblem against his upper thigh and count five."

Johnny scrunched his forehead, his expression wavering. "Ain't we gonna use that there chute?"

Chad shook his head, plunging the iron back into the coals. "Not for the calves. It'll be easier to drop 'em out here in the open than try to drive 'em in." Straightening, he brushed off his chaps. "All set?"

With a nod, Johnny took his place beside the fire.

Chad edged toward the group of huddled calves, his gaze fixed on the largest one. Two quick strides forward and he was on it. The other calves scattered as the cornered calf let out a distress call. The mother cow answered back, trotting along the fence line.

In one smooth motion, Chad twisted the calf to the ground and held it in place. "Now, Johnny!"

A look of urgency lined the boy's face as he pulled the iron from the fire and rushed over. The calf kicked his hind leg, keeping Johnny at bay. Chad tried to pin the calf's leg down with his knee, but couldn't manage both the front and back end.

Johnny drew back, panic in his eyes, as the calf continued to kick and squirm. "I can't get close."

Charlotte leaned forward, her heart drumming in her chest. She had to do something. Slipping inside the corral, she hiked her skirt and ran to them. "What can I do?"

A look of gratitude washed over Chad. "Can you pen his back leg down?"

She squatted, struggling to get a grip on the calf's ankle. With a quick thrust, she took hold of it with both hands. The frazzled calf jerked her back and forth. Bracing her feet, she was finally able to extend the leg out and hold it in place. "Go, Johnny."

With steady hands, Johnny pressed the hot iron against the calf's thigh. A sizzling sound accompanied the smell of singed hair as the boy counted out the allotted seconds. As he pulled back, Charlotte's hands slipped, and she fell back with a "humph".

Loosening his grip on the calf, Chad leapt to her side. "Are you hurt?"

She took the hand he offered, brushing off the back of her dress as he helped her up. "Other than a few bruises, just my pride."

Johnny returned the branding iron to the fire and rushed back, a huge grin on his face. "Boy, Miss Charlotte. You pitched in like a real cattlewoman."

She chuckled, warmth shrouding her face. "Was there a choice?"

Chad's lips hinged upward. "Sorry about that. Reckon this is more a three-person job. I can wait and have Hank Brimmer help, if you'd rather."

Johnny lunged forward. "No. The others are smaller. You'll help, won't you, Miss Charlotte?"

She brushed a loose strand of hair from her forehead. "Might as well, now that I know what I'm in for."

Chad's face softened in a grin, a slight dimple in one cheek. "Well, all right then. Let's give it another go."

CHARLOTTE SPRAWLED in a chair on Chad's cabin porch, muscles aching. She'd need a wagon load of liniment tonight. Yet, the look of gratitude on Chad's face had made it all worthwhile. Loosening her bonnet, the cooling breeze teased her sweat-dampened hair. She'd thought farming was hard work. But, if today was any sort of indicator, tending cattle appeared even more rigorous.

Chad and Johnny's voices drifted to her from inside the corral. Neither could get enough of the cattle, it seemed. A corner of her mouth lifted. She'd never seen Johnny so taken with anything, or anyone. The way he clung to Chad, when would she ever find opportunity to approach him about his negligence to his family?

"A circle with a J. Is that what your ranch will be called? The Circle J?" Johnny's high-pitched voice cut through the stillness.

"Yep." Chad's rich tone carried more joy than usual.

"What's it stand for?"

Enticed by the youngster's question, Charlotte listened more closely.

"The circle represents the unending love of Christ."

"Huh. Miss Charlotte's been learnin' me about Him." Johnny's voice lifted. "What about the J?"

Charlotte cocked her ear to hear the softened tones.

Chad cleared his throat. "It stands for . . . John."

John? Charlotte leaned forward in her chair, ears intent on the conversation. Had she heard him right? Surely it wasn't her Johnny he'd named his ranch after. They hardly knew each other. Who was John?

"You named it after me?" The boy's voice rang with honor and disbelief.

A long moment lapsed before Chad answered, his voice much deeper. "No, my son, John."

The blood drained from Charlotte's face. So, her suspicions were right. He did have a family tucked away back in Tennessee. Yet, she found it hard to believe such a kind, God-fearing man would abandon his wife and child.

"You have a son? Where is he?"

Charlotte's hands gripped the edges of the chair, turning her knuckles white as she strained to hear Chad's reply. Would he divulge the truth to the boy when he'd kept it hidden from her?

Even at a distance, she could hear Chad heave a long sigh. "He died a little over a year ago, along with his mother."

Charlotte sucked in a breath, Chad's words searing her very soul. They were . . . dead? Tears welled in her eyes as she melted back in her chair.

Father, forgive me.

Chapter Twenty-Nine

With a final pound of his mallet, Chad sat back on his haunches. That'd do it. The patched roof looked nearly as good as new, but for the lighter shade of the fresh clapboard shingles. He wiped his brow with his sleeve. The warm afternoon working for Hank Brimmer had passed in a hurry. Time to head home. He clenched his jaw.

With the exception of a short detour.

Until now he'd put it out of his mind. Put Charlotte out of his mind. But now the thought of her washed over him like a spring storm. She'd pitched in yesterday like a seasoned cattlewoman. He scrubbed a hand over his face. Why couldn't he simply get her out of his thoughts for good?

Tossing his mallet to the ground, he climbed from the ladder.

Mr. Brimmer limped over to him. "You done a fine job, son. Much obliged."

"Glad to help." Chad brushed off his trousers and retrieved his fallen mallet.

"I could do it myself. But Ida insists, at my age, I should keep both feet on the ground."

The corner of Chad's mouth lifted. "Well, I appreciate the

labor in exchange for your bull. Never could have afforded him otherwise."

"Works well both ways, I 'spect."

Chad slipped his mallet in his saddlebag. "Same time tomorrow?"

Hank dipped a hand in his pocket, squinting against the glow of the ebbing sun. "If you're able."

With a nod, Chad extended his hand. "See you then."

Mr. Brimmer gave Chad's hand a firm shake. "Ida'd be more than happy to serve you a bite before you go."

The thought of a home-cooked meal made Chad's mouth water. But if he delayed, there'd be no time to stop by Charlotte's. "Maybe another time."

The older man lifted his hat. "A good evening to you, then."

Chad mounted and reined Buck toward the trail. The quiet, mile-and-a-half trek to Charlotte's would bring a welcome change from the steady pounding of the mallet. Yet as he rode away, turbulent thoughts crushed any hopes of a peaceful trip.

When she'd arrived at his place yesterday, Charlotte had been colder than December snow. By the time she'd left with Johnny, her composure had softened considerably. Though she'd refused to make eye contact, her cheeks had flamed red, and her jade eyes had teemed with moisture. Had he done something to upset her?

It seemed that's all he'd done since he'd returned.

He reached in his pocket and clutched the carving in his palm, running his fingers over its smooth surface. His chest tightened. Seeing Charlotte again was the last thing he needed right now. Yet the boy deserved some sort of reward for their help. If it took fronting Charlotte again, so be it.

Chad dropped the carving back in his pocket, his spirits sinking with it. He'd keep the visit short and to the point. Anything else and, more than likely, he'd find himself wishing he'd not stopped at all.

CHARLOTTE SHIFTED, trying to find a comfortable position in the porch rocker. But the bruises on her backside made it impossible. She leaned to one side, cupping her chin in her hand. She didn't deserve comfort, not after the wrongs she'd imposed on Chad. Moisture pooled in her eyes, and she blinked it away. How she'd misjudged the man. All this time he'd carried the burden of his loss, never once hinting of his pain.

She draped an arm around her middle to ward off the growing tension inside her. "'Twas only by God's grace she'd been spared the indignity of injuring Chad further . . . and making a total fool of herself in the process. Even so, she'd given him plenty of indications she wasn't pleased with him. How wrong she'd been. It seemed, without even trying, his very nature exposed her weaknesses.

Only a godly man could do that.

Johnny sprinted up beside her, blue eyes shining. "Chickens are all shut up for the night. Sure are growin'."

She smiled at him, his carefree expression, for the moment, chasing away her regrets. She raked a hand over his straight, blond locks. How dear he'd become to her. If only they could be together always. But it wasn't to be. He had a new life awaiting him in Palmer with a ready-made family. What could she offer him that they couldn't?

Rising, she took the dishpan from beside the chair and pitched the soiled water over the porch rail. The faint clomping of hooves drew her attention northward. A shadowy figure emerged in the pink glow of evening, edging closer to the cabin.

Johnny trailed along beside her. "Who is it?"

"I'm not sure." She strained to distinguish who it might be.

Her breath caught in her throat at recognition of the buckskin gelding and the broad-shouldered man in a fringed shirt. Heat rose in her cheeks as she gnawed at her lower lip. How could she face him? She'd contemplated a hundred ways how to undo her misjudgment. Nothing seemed enough.

"It's Mr. Avery!" A smile lit Johnny's face as he jogged down the porch steps to greet him.

Charlotte dug her fingers into the porch rail. She couldn't face him. Not tonight. Not with her nerves shot and looking a mess. She tossed the empty pan into the rocker and brushed stray wisps of hair from her forehead. There was no time to mend her appearance. He was a mere stone's throw away.

She squared her shoulders, swallowing the dryness in her throat. *Lord, help me.*

With a deep breath, she clasped trembling hands behind her and downed the porch steps.

Chad tipped his hat and eased forward in his saddle as he brought his horse to a stop. "Evenin'."

She stood beside Johnny, mustering the courage to meet his gaze. "Good evening, Mr. Avery."

His gray eyes seemed to penetrate her thoughts. Did he glimpse her longing to make things right?

"My apologies for stopping so late."

"It's no bother." She edged closer, brushing hair from her cheek. If not for her unkempt appearance, his visit would have been most welcome.

Indeed, it was anyway.

His gaze shifted to Johnny. "How are you, boy?"

"Good." The obvious bond between them was unmistakable. Did Johnny remind him of the son he'd lost? Such a tragedy, that someone like Chad, who had so much to give, had been stripped of his family.

Charlotte's stomach churned. Even more tragic was the shameful way she'd treated him.

Dismounting, Chad pulled something from his pocket. "I'm a bit short on money, but I wanted to give you a little something for your time yesterday." He stretched his arm out toward Johnny.

The boy cupped his hands, eyes wide as Chad dropped the object into his awaiting palms. He gripped the piece between his fingers and held it up. "Look, Miss Charlotte. It's the Circle J."

Charlotte bent over for a closer look at the carved replica of the image of Chad's brand. "It's a wonderful gift."

"Thanks, Mr. Avery. Since it's mine, can the J stand for me?"

With a wink, Chad gave the boy's hair a tousle. "Why not? You earned it."

Johnny cocked his head to one side, his smile fading. "What about Miss Charlotte? She helped too."

Charlotte's face flamed hot. She had the bruises to prove it.

Chad scratched at his cheek, glancing in her direction. "I reckon she did at that."

"I don't need anything. Really."

"I'll give it some thought." His gaze fell away, a somber tone marring his voice. Turning, he strode to his horse.

Charlotte took a shallow breath, plagued with a sense of loss at his leaving so soon. Her mind grappled for something to say. How she longed to ease not only the pain she'd caused him, but his loneliness as well. "Chad?"

He pivoted sideways, the evening shadows shrouding his features. "Yes?"

"We've some stew left. You're welcome to it." She pointed over her shoulder, a bit too much enthusiasm in her voice.

He gave his horse a pat on the neck. "Much obliged, but I best be gettin' home."

Though he had every right to leave, how she longed for him to stay, and for the first time, she could fully admit why.

She needed him.

Chapter Thirty

CHARLOTTE SET a steamy plate of cornbread and sausage in front of Johnny and another for herself and took a seat across from him. The young boy leaned over the table, chin resting on his arms, his pale blue eyes glazed over. She reached to clasp his hand for prayer, a gesture they had begun on his last visit. "What is it?"

He shrugged. "Nothin'."

With a soft sigh, Charlotte bowed her head. She knew what was troubling him. Mid-week had arrived, and with it the reality that he would soon be leaving, a time for which neither seemed ready.

The prayer said, their meal had barely begun when the clatter of a buggy cut through the stillness. Charlotte lowered her fork, then stood and glanced out the curtained window.

"Is it them?" Apprehension lined Johnny's usual cheerful tone.

Charlotte could only nod, her emotions choking off her words. A tremor of mixed feelings washed through her. Was letting Johnny leave the right thing for him?

For her?

Johnny stared up at her, unspoken angst seeming to edge out his joy.

Forcing a smile, Charlotte touched a finger to his nose and motioned him to follow.

The buggy rolled to a stop as they stepped out onto the porch. Charlotte's gaze was drawn to the rather short, plump couple riding in back, their eyes fixed on Johnny. The woman leaned to whisper something in the man's ear, to which he gave a pronounced nod.

With a tip of his hat, Pastor Brody loosened his hold on the reins. "Charlotte, Johnny. I'd like you to meet Mr. and Mrs. Flynn."

Charlotte gave a slow nod and tightened her hold on Johnny's shoulders. The couple looked pleasant enough, if not for their pointed stares. That they weren't from the area was plain. The man's rounded hat and striped suit pegged him as a big city man, his wife's pale complexion beneath her parasol hinted she'd never seen a day's work. Hair, the same orange tint as Norris Pickford's, framed both their rounded faces.

"Come closer, me boy. Let us have a look at you." Mr. Flynn tapped a stick on the side of the rig, a thick accent in his tone.

Johnny's mouth twisted, and he peered up at Charlotte. With a nod, she nudged him forward. This hurt her every bit as much as it did him.

He edged forward, chin to his chest, toes scuffing the ground.

Not offering to step from the carriage, Mr. Flynn leaned for a closer look. "What be your age, youngster?"

"Seven," came Johnny's barely audible reply.

"That blondish hair tis likely to stand out as not our own." Mr. Flynn said with a chuckle, more to his wife than to anyone.

"Aye. It 'tis." She gave her parasol a twirl. "But, my, won't the girls think him grand?"

"Ah, they will at that." The man shook with laughter. "What

says you about coming to stay with me-self and Mrs. Flynn, young Johnny?"

With a shrug, Johnny squinted up at them. "For how long?"

Mrs. Flynn's face cracked a wide smile. "Why, for always. We'd be your new parents."

He kicked his heel into the dirt, not giving a reply.

Charlotte tensed. Was it her, or did Johnny seem less than thrilled by the prospect? She fought the urge to pull him back and tell the Flynns he already had a home. Selfish or not, she wanted her own happiness as well as Johnny's. Anymore, she didn't know that she could be content without him. Yet, she couldn't bring herself to squelch his future with a well-to-do family. Out here, he'd have no children to play with, no father's influence, and no means for schooling, other than what she could manage. His staying would put him at an utter disadvantage.

The boy's mouth worked side to side. Once again he stared up at Charlotte. "Is it what you want, Miss Charlotte?"

She cleared her throat, choking down the unsteadiness in her voice. "I believe it's for the best."

Johnny fell silent, face pinched. At last his head lifted. "All right. I'll go."

"That a boy. Go get your things, and we'll be on our way."

"I need t' finish my lunch first." Turning, Johnny skittered off to the cabin.

Torn between staying or joining Johnny, Charlotte's curiosity won out. She needed to know more about this odd-sounding couple who planned to take Johnny into their home. He'd had one unpleasant experience, not to mention a less than ideal home situation with his father. She couldn't abide letting him endure another.

"Pastor Brody tells me you're new to these parts." Charlotte looped her arms in front of her, hoping to bait the couple into divulging more information.

"Aye, lassie. We've come to the quaint village of Palmer to escape the rigors of city life."

Mr. Flynn's answer did little to stymie her inquisitiveness. "Where exactly do you hail from?"

"The grand city of Dublin."

"Ireland?" Up to this point, Pastor Brody had remained quiet. Now he turned for a look at the couple behind him, eyes wide.

"Aye. But that was before me children arrived. More recently, we've resided in Pennsylvania."

Equally as stunned, Charlotte ventured yet another inquiry. "How is it you've come to Illinois?"

"We've missed the openness of our homeland," inserted Mrs. Flynn, her voice fluctuating as she spoke. "Although, we've come to find this place a smidgen less, shall we say, refined?"

Before anyone could respond, the cabin door hinged open and a sour-faced Johnny strolled onto the porch, satchel in hand.

Mr. Flynn motioned to him with his stick. "Come, laddie, don't be just standing there, we've miles to journey and the girls to gather from their sitter."

Johnny sauntered toward the awaiting carriage, face downcast. Heartbroken, Charlotte met him halfway and squatted in front of him. Johnny's eyes pooled over. "Do I gotta go? I won't ever see you."

Everything in her wanted to say "no". Instead, she reached to hug him, wiping a tear from her cheek as his small fingers latched around her neck. "I'll come visit you. I promise."

With a sniffle, Johnny leaned his head on her shoulder. "I'll miss you."

"Me too." Charlotte lifted her eyes heavenward, willing back tears as she gave him a final squeeze. She released her hold and kissed his blond hair. "Time to go."

With a sigh, his warm arms slid from around her neck. Forcing a grin, she clasped his hand in hers and started with him toward the carriage. At their approach, smiles generated on Mr.

and Mrs. Flynn's faces. Charlotte shifted her gaze to the distant timber, swallowing down the tightness in her throat. Why could she not rejoice with them? Was it Johnny's less than enthusiastic response or her own misgivings?

As the carriage pulled away, dense stillness fell over her. Like a proud prisoner about to be executed, Johnny held his head high, lips pursed, wedged between the chattering Flynns. Given time, would he become so enamored with this unique couple and their daughters that he'd forget all about her? If nothing more, it would be a fresh start for him.

A real family.

Yet, somehow the thought didn't soothe the pang of loss taking root within her.

CHAD PLUCKED a head of wheat and rubbed it in his palm to separate the grain from the chaff. He picked up one of the tiny grains and bit into it. Much harder than the last time he'd checked. Come week's end, it would be ready for harvest.

The sun dipped below the horizon as he trudged toward the cabin, muscles aching. Thankfully, Mrs. Brimmer had insisted he stay for supper, else he would've had to resort to beans or venison jerky yet again. This weekend, he'd take the opportunity to do a bit of hunting and restock his dwindling supply of meat. But for now, all he wanted was a good night's rest.

In the cabin, Chad tugged off his boots and flopped back on his cot. Folding his arms over his chest, he blew out a puff of air. What a day he'd put in. Everything from patching shingles to fixing fence to chopping and hauling wood. Not to mention his responsibilities to his own place. How did he intend to keep up?

A slight smile touched his lips. It would be worth it all when he brought home Mr. Brimmer's fine Hereford bull. Within a year, his herd would nearly double.

He glanced around the darkened cabin. Moon-glow filtered through gaps in the log walls. In no time, August would be here, then September. Cold weather would soon be nipping at his heels. There was still much to do before his old broken-down cabin would be set for winter. The barn and lean-to as well. There'd be wheat to harvest, straw and hay to gather, and later corn to pick. Not to mention his obligation to harvest the Hollisters' wheat. It, too, would soon be ripe.

A nervous twang worked through his middle. Would Charlotte offer to help as she had with planting? She'd been more her old self when he'd stopped by earlier in the week. More the woman he'd envisioned coming home to.

What had changed?

He punched at his feather pillow. It didn't matter. There could be no future for them. He'd tried moving forward. And look where it'd gotten him — more heartache.

With a yawn, he turned on his side. He was too tired to think about it. If Charlotte wanted to help bundle wheat, he'd not turn her down. But it would be neighbor helping neighbor.

Nothing more.

"Yes, I believe a letter arrived for you just yesterday."

Mrs. Chaney's pleasant news stirred Charlotte to the first bit of enthusiasm she'd experienced in days. Without Johnny's company, the pang of loneliness had seeped into her spirit like poison. She shifted her weight to the balls of her feet, craning her neck as the postmistress thumbed through the stack of letters.

"Ah, here we are," Mrs. Chaney announced, pulling out a folded letter sealed with candle wax.

Taking it from her, Charlotte glanced over the lettering at the upper left, the corners of her mouth tipping upward. "Thank you." She pivoted toward the door and pried the seal open with her fingertip.

"Say, did you hear the news?"

In her eagerness to open her letter, Charlotte had half a mind to ignore the postmistress' fetish for town gossip and hurry on. Instead, she slowed her pace, but continued to edge toward the door. "I'm certain I haven't."

The woman drew in a breath, softening her voice. "Young Lola Brimmer's run off with that Pickford fella and gotten herself hitched."

Charlotte jolted to a stop at the woman's words and retraced her steps. "Norris Pickford?"

Mrs. Chaney bobbed her head, her loose roll of chestnut hair bouncing with each nod. "That's the one."

"When?"

"Yesterday. Gus delivered the telegram to the Brimmers just this morning."

A rash of emotions coursed through Charlotte — shock, amazement, even an element of envy. Not that she wished to be in Lola's place, but how wonderful it would be to know someone loved her enough to sweep her away to become his bride.

If it be the right someone.

The postmistress shook her head. "I hate to think what her folks have to say."

Heat blossomed in Charlotte's cheeks. She nearly felt responsible. Who would have thought her scheme would work? Had he married Lola out of love or spite? Little more than a month had passed since her last conversation with him. Charlotte could only hope poor Lola hadn't paid the consequences for her rebuff.

She turned to go, her enthusiasm waning. "Thank you, Mrs. Chaney."

Pushing through the door, she opened the letter, instantly recognizing Esther's penmanship.

Dear Charlotte,

I pray this letter finds you well. Our trip was long and uneventful. It's so good to be in one place again, though it in no way feels like home. The riverboat ride left us both queasy, and Ma a bit irritable, but was more tolerable than the jolting coach ride. My, what a different world Cincinnati is from the open prairie, buildings snugged together like geese in flight. We've found a place to stay until more permanent arrangements can be made. Will let you know when we get settled. How are things at Miller Creek? I'm homesick for news of the prairie.

Miss you. Come visit us.

Esther

Charlotte ran her fingertips over the letters, savoring each precious word. Until this moment she hadn't realized how much she'd missed them. Pa would dislike that the family had been rent apart. If she were ever to see her mother and sister again, she'd have the unpleasant task of making the long journey east.

Refolding the letter, she heaved a quiet sigh. Everyone dear to her had left. First her father, then Ma and Esther. Now Johnny.

Even Chad seemed to have distanced himself.

A sickened feeling churned inside her. She'd willingly given up a future with Norris. Had she missed her chance with Chad as well?

Chapter Thirty-One

PART FOUR · REVELATIONS

Late July, 1855

THE WARMTH of the late morning sun seeped through Charlotte's plaid, calico dress and bonnet. She wiped her brow, wishing for a stiffer breeze. The constant scraping of the cradle scythe ahead kept her ever aware of Chad's presence. Yet his continued silence pricked at her like a cocklebur tucked beneath her sleeve. Was he so intent on his work he gave no thought to words? Or had he tired of her changeable disposition?

Gathering a bundle of toppled wheat stalks, she tied them together with twine and took a sweeping glance over what remained of the five-acre patch. Their hours of labor had made only a large dent in the plot of golden grain. It would take much of the week to finish.

She ventured a peek in Chad's direction, noting his firm muscles beneath his fitted shirt. He grew more handsome each time she saw him. What a fine husband and father he must have made, with his strong, yet gentle demeanor. Had his wife worked alongside him too? She was so beautiful. It must have broken his heart to lose her . . . along with his young son. Would he ever share what had happened?

A sigh escaped her. Most likely not. He'd said little more than a polite hello since he'd arrived. Barely even looked at her. Did he intend to shun her the entire time?

She clenched her jaw, gathering another armload of wheat. If silence was what he wished, she could oblige.

She snatched a piece of twine from her bag and wound it around the bundle of wheat in a fury, then stilled, struck by a sobering thought. Did her working alongside him bother Chad? Did it remind him of happier times?

She tossed the sheaf of wheat aside, her angst melting away. Twice, she'd misjudged the man. Was she making the same mistake again? Perhaps she should explain why she'd acted so foolish.

Yes. She owed him that.

The corner of her mouth lifted. Perhaps the more time she and Chad shared together, the richer their friendship would grow.

But then, budding relationships required talking.

At the far end of the field, Chad lifted his hat and raked a hand over his forehead. He reached for his canteen and raised it to his lips. Glancing her way, he held out the container.

Charlotte brushed chaff from her hands and started toward him, needing no further invitation. As she neared, his eyes met hers. She smiled and reached for the water jug. "Thank you."

With a nod, he peered up at the cloudless sky, the hot sun streaming overhead. "What say we break for lunch?"

She swallowed her mouthful of water, its coolness relieving her parched throat. "I'm afraid I've not much to offer other than some ham and bread for sandwiches."

"No bother. I've packed a lunch."

"Oh." Charlotte's mouth twisted. He certainly wasn't making this easy. How could they ever further their friendship if he continued to shut her out? She took a step back, pointing over her shoulder. "Then, I'll fetch a sandwich and come join you."

Not waiting for a response, Charlotte lifted her skirt and hiked to the cabin. Within minutes, she'd put together her packet of food, including an extra sandwich for Chad just in case, and started back. He'd taken shelter beneath the shade of a white oak. He looked so serene sitting beneath its outstretched boughs, sunlight shimmering through its plume of leaves. She drew in a breath. Lord willing, might there still be a chance for them?

She strode over and looked for a clean, level place to sit. As though reading her thoughts, he removed his bandanna and fanned it out on the ground.

"Thank you." A smile tugged at Charlotte's lips. Whatever their differences, he remained ever the gentleman.

She smoothed her skirt under her and sat beside him. A robin chirped in a branch above, breaking the stillness as she unwrapped one of the cloth-covered sandwiches. Venturing a glance his way, she gripped her sandwich and leaned against the tree. "How's your work for Mr. Brimmer going?"

"He's easy enough to please." Chad drew a knee to his chest, biting off a chunk of jerky.

Charlotte's gaze drifted to his near empty tin where all that remained were a couple of slices of jerky and a shriveled, boiled potato. She arched a brow. Just as she'd suspicioned. He'd brought little of substance. "Is that all you've brought to eat?"

He shrugged. "It's what I'm used to."

Charlotte shook her head. "It's a wonder you've energy to work at all." She picked up the extra sandwich of home-baked bread and smoked ham and held it out to him. "Here."

He hesitated, then reached for it. "Thanks."

As he clasped it, his hand brushed hers, sending a wave of warmth through her. She dropped her gaze to the grass between them, heart racing. "N-nice of Mr. Brimmer to give you time off for harvest."

"Yep." The tremor in Chad's voice hinted she wasn't alone in her awkwardness.

She brushed crumbs from her hands and folded them, determined not to let discomfort seep back in between them. "Would you say grace?"

The words seeped out before she'd given thought that he might have already prayed over his food. He certainly hadn't waited on her to begin eating. Was he so famished he couldn't wait or had he hoped to avoid her company altogether?

Chad paused in mid bite and bowed his head. "Thank you for the plentiful harvest, Lord, and for this good food and the hands that prepared it. In Jesus' name. Amen."

"Amen." Charlotte lifted her head, a light airiness working through her. Such a simple, God-honoring prayer. A smile tugged at her lips. "Perhaps you'd better taste it before you're too thankful."

"It's sure to beat what I brought." Raising the sandwich to his mouth, he took a large bite.

Charlotte searched his face, hoping to glean a response, but he merely bit off another mouthful. She'd baked the bread fresh just yesterday, the loaves having risen taller than usual. She pinched off a chunk of her own sandwich and dropped it onto her tongue, grateful for its pleasant flavor. Much better than some she'd made.

She brushed a strand of hair from her cheek. "How long will you work for Mr. Brimmer?"

Chad wiped a crumb from his lips. "A couple more weeks, or until he feels I've earned my wages."

Silence fell between them as they ate. Charlotte strained for something more to say, but nothing came, save the desire to clear the air between them. Perhaps the Lord was giving her the opportunity to set things right. She tucked her feet under her, eyes lifted heavenward. *Lord, grant me strength to speak the truth and to bear what follows.*

Chad brushed his hands together and started to rise. "Much obliged for the victuals."

She caught him by the arm. "Chad." The soft-spoken word hung in the air like morning mist.

He turned to her, eyes filled with question.

Heat rose in her cheeks as she loosened her hold. Now that she'd gained his attention, would she have the courage to continue? She eased back, in search of words. With a deep breath, she laced her fingers together in her lap. "I realize I haven't been pleasant to be around at times. For that, I apologize."

He twisted his hat in his hands. "No harm done."

Charlotte swallowed the unsteadiness in her voice. "I've treated you rudely and misjudged you for circumstances which weren't your fault."

Chad's stare intensified as though searching for the motive behind her words. "I figured I'd offended you in some way."

She drew a hand to her chest. "You've not offended *me*. I distrusted *you*."

"Because I didn't return when I said?"

She plucked a blade of grass and leaned against the tree, pricked by the confusion in his voice. "You were away so long. I was worried, so . . . I went to your cabin to check on things."

She wet her lips, her heartbeat drumming in her ears. It wasn't easy to admit her faults, especially to this man she'd come to admire. "I . . . I went inside and saw the picture of your wife and child on the mantel. I assumed things. The wrong things."

Chad hung his head and raked a hand through his hair.

"It was wrong of me. I'm sorry. I overheard you tell Johnny you'd lost your wife and child."

His cheek flinched and a pained expression spread over his face. Standing, he nodded toward the field of wheat. "Best get back to work."

Moisture pooled in Charlotte's eyes as she watched him walk away. Was he angry with her? Obviously, his wounds were still fresh. Would he forever keep his hurt locked inside, choosing to cling to the past rather than move forward?

Perhaps his tragic past left no room for a future, for joy. Or love.

Or was it merely something they'd have to fight to achieve?

One thing was certain, only God could provide the healing Chad needed.

CHAD TOOK up the cradle scythe, swinging it with more force than necessary. So that's why Charlotte had been so standoffish. She had him pegged as a louse for deserting his wife and child. Well, she had no right to go inside his cabin. No right to pry into his past.

He slowed his pace enough to hear the sound of Charlotte's gentle gathering and binding of sheaves. Pausing, he cast a glance over his shoulder. All the blame shouldn't fall to her. He'd been long overdue, enough so it had given her cause for worry, which only proved he'd let himself get too close. He'd known better, even given himself fair warning to keep his distance.

Yet, he found her company hard to resist.

She'd grown fond of him as well. He could see it in her eyes, sense it in her voice. She'd even blushed at his touch. He couldn't deny Charlotte owned a piece of his heart, but for both their sakes, he needed to curb those impulses to spare further heartache.

The Lord had seen fit to take Lauren home to be with Him. Why? Chad would never fully understand. He only knew he dare not risk such a love again.

Chapter Thirty-Two

CHARLOTTE FANNED herself with her hand, the July heat stifling inside the church building. She held back, waiting for the room to empty before taking her turn to greet the Brodys on her way out. As she edged forward, she caught a glimpse of Chad through the open window. A somber expression lined his jaw as he mounted his horse. What she wouldn't give to know his thoughts. After their mealtime conversation, he'd retreated even deeper inside himself. Had she been wrong to disclose her secret?

Confession was supposed to be good for the soul. In her case, it had made matters worse. At least the burden of guilt she'd been harboring had lifted. She needed someone she could confide in. With Pa gone and Ma and Esther away, the Lord seemed her only solace.

She clutched a hand to her upper arm, watching Chad ride out of sight. Would he shun her for the duration of harvest or allow her grace to make a mistake? She only knew she had to keep trying. She cared too much not to. He was hurting and, like her, had no one.

Becky's warm smile pulled her back to the present. "How are you, Charlotte? Have you heard from Esther and Aunt Clara?"

"I received a letter a couple days ago saying they'd made it safely to Cincinnati."

"Wonderful. When you write, tell them they're missed."

"I'll do that." Charlotte gave a slow nod. "Have you any news of Johnny?"

Her cousin's somber expression left no doubt as to her answer. "Nothing yet, I'm afraid."

Pastor Brody stretched his hand out to Charlotte. "I'll be making a trip to Palmer later in the week. If you wish, I'll stop by the Flynns and check on him."

"Would you?" Charlotte's voice lifted. She had half a mind to ride along, but with wheat harvest in full swing how could she? One day soon she'd make the trip, be it alone or with someone.

"Be glad to. I was sort of wondering about the boy myself. He looked none too happy when he left."

"Thank you." Even with their unusual ways, Mr. and Mrs. Flynn seemed a vast improvement over the Crowleys. At least they seemed the type who'd treat Johnny as one of their own and not some vagrant farm hand. Pastor Brody must have given Ian Crowley quite a stern talking to for him to give up Johnny. Gooseflesh dotted her arms at the thought of how he'd mistreated the boy. The fact that they'd not seen or heard from him since was truly a blessing.

A ruckus in the street outside stole her attention. Though the congregation had thinned, those who lingered swarmed to the approaching wagon. It took but an instant to understand why. At the reins sat the fiery-headed groom and beside him, his beaming bride. Norris pulled the team of horses to a stop outside the church building and immediately was swallowed by the flurry of people, first among them Lola's parents. Mr. and Mrs. Brimmer waited for Norris to help their daughter down, then wrapped their arms around her in a tearful hug. Rumbles of laughter and jubilant voices split the mid-day air. It seemed all one had to do was run off and marry to earn fame in these parts.

Charlotte downed the steps and stood on the outskirts, a blend of regret and satisfaction washing through her. That could have been her seated on the wagon seat next to Norris. Then, her livelihood would have been secured, her loneliness quenched, her troubles over.

But would it have been so blissful to be married to a man she didn't love?

As she made her way through the gathering of people, she felt someone slip something into her palm. Mrs. Chaney gave her a wink and a tap on the hand before moving on. Though plagued with curiosity, Charlotte waited until she was hidden beside Willow before opening the tiny slip of paper.

SHIVAREE TOMORROW NIGHT BRIMMER HOME

Charlotte peered over-top the saddle, watching Mrs. Chaney weave her way through the remaining congregation, distributing the same short message into the palms of others. Word was sure to spread and the whole countryside would gather at dusk outside the Brimmer cabin to give the new couple a rousing welcome. How she pitied the household when they were descended upon by banging pans and shotgun blasts.

Becky and Pastor Brody had escaped the raucous wedding tradition, most likely due to their position and their willingness to share their joy with the community. Norris and Lola wouldn't be so fortunate, it seemed. They'd robbed the townspeople of a time of celebration and would reap the consequences in the form of an intrusive, yet fun-loving shivaree. An event Charlotte didn't wish to miss.

Would Chad be willing to escort her? A flutter rippled through her at the thought. More than likely he'd not take to such nonsense.

But then, if she appealed to his sense of chivalry, she might stand a chance.

Such a venture could prove just the thing to lighten the mood between them.

CHARLOTTE FINGERED the slip of paper in her skirt pocket, noting the tightness in her shoulders as she pushed her empty lunch plate aside and leaned against the oak tree. Was it the constant motion from binding the sheaves or the thought of approaching Chad about the shivaree that had her muscles in knots? It had taken a lot of restraint not to mention the invitation sooner. But she'd wanted to wait until just the right moment. As he scraped together the remnants of his piece of blackberry pie, it seemed as good of time as any.

The thought of spending the evening with him in a more social manner both warmed her and made her stomach reel. Yet, there was no sense getting her hopes up when he hadn't yet agreed to accompany her. He'd remained quiet much of the morning, speaking only when spoken to. Was that to be their relationship from now on? A trickle of short, stifled conversations that led nowhere? At least he'd accepted her offer to feed him.

She cleared her throat. "Have they such a thing as a shivaree in Tennessee?"

Chad's chewing slowed, and he set his plate on the ground. "Heard tell of them. Never went to one."

Slipping the note from her pocket, she forced a nervous smile. "You left church yesterday before Mrs. Chaney passed these out. Seems there's to be a shivaree tonight in honor of Norris and Lola Pickford."

She pushed the note toward him, hoping to stir his interest.

He gave the paper a quick glance, then stared out over the wheat field, a shadow spilling over his face.

Charlotte drew an arm around her middle, trying to ignore

her growing angst. "I don't suppose you'd be willing to accompany me?"

Chad's cheeks flinched, and he wiped a palm over his trouser leg. "Sorry, but I've better things to do with my time than interrupt a couple's privacy."

"It's all in good fun. Surely you could afford yourself a couple hours of leisure."

He donned his hat and took up his gloves. "It's best I don't."

Charlotte leaned forward and placed a hand on his arm. His silvery eyes found hers, giving her courage to forge ahead. "Allowing yourself some joy doesn't mean you love your wife and son any less."

He bowed his head and his face became hidden beneath his hat. "They were my joy."

She loosened her grasp on his arm, sensing him slip away from her.

In more ways than one.

CHAD SLUMPED down in the chair before his fireplace, the photograph of Lauren and John clutched in his hands. He breathed a loud sigh, Charlotte's words still playing over in his mind. She had no idea what he'd been through.

How could she?

He leaned forward and rubbed a hand over his face. She'd been right in thinking him a louse who'd deserted his family. It was his fault they were gone. If he'd been home, he might have saved them. The guilt of it still crushed him. How could he entrust his love to someone else when he carried such a burden inside? It was sure to wedge a gap between them.

Standing, he set the picture back in its place. Maybe he'd been wrong in keeping his past a secret. If Charlotte knew the whole truth, she might not be so inclined to want his companionship. Or his love. Her request for him to accompany her to the shivaree had taken him off guard. The last thing he needed was to be alone with her under the cloak of darkness. Already he was struggling to keep his feelings in check.

His stomach clenched. She'd asked for his protection, and he'd declined it. Surely she wouldn't be so foolhardy as to go on her own.

Or would she?

As headstrong as she was, he wouldn't put it past her.

The waning sun deepened the shadows inside his cabin. He tapped his fingers on the doorframe, then snatched his hat from its peg by the door. Maybe it was time to let go of his fears and be honest with himself, as well as Charlotte.

Chapter Thirty-Three

AN AMBER GLOW flanked the western sky, illuminating Charlotte's way to the barn. Chad or no Chad, she was going to the shivaree. It was only a couple of miles to the Brimmers. Surely no harm would befall her in that short distance, though the trip home would be swathed in darkness, save the light of the moon and stars.

If Chad had been concerned for her safety, he would've agreed to join her. The verdant smell of ripened wheat seemed to taunt her with thoughts of him. She pursed her lips and tugged at her sleeves. Apparently she wasn't as important to him as she'd hoped.

Outside the barn, Rubie let out a low growl, followed by a threatening bark. A slight rustling sound over by the smoke shed gave Charlotte reason to pause and stare into the lengthening shadows of evening. Yet, the summer night air hummed with the songs of katydids and crickets. Dismissing the noise as some sort of varmint traipsing through the yard, she called Rubie to her side. The dog gave a reluctant glance back and then one final bark before trotting over.

Charlotte rubbed a hand down the Border collie's back.

She'd have to stay behind, lest her barking alert the Brimmer household and spoil the surprise. Too bad. Charlotte would've enjoyed the companionship. No doubt Rubie would have loved it too. She missed her romps hunting with Pa, not to mention the way he'd spoiled her.

Grasping Rubie by the scruff of her neck, Charlotte led her to the corner of the barn. She looped a rope around the dog's neck and tied the end to a post. The sorrowful look in Rubie's brown eyes pulled at Charlotte. She gave the dog a scratch under the chin. "Sorry, girl."

Willow nickered from her stall, and Charlotte walked over and patted her on the neck. She breathed in the scent of straw and horseflesh, her thoughts turning to Johnny. What fun he would have had on the nighttime outing. She longed to know how he was faring. It didn't seem fitting to receive word of him second-hand. Wheat harvest would likely be finished in another day or two. Perhaps she could catch Pastor Brody in time to ride along with him to Palmer.

Lifting the bridle from its peg, she slid the bar from the front of Willow's stall. At Rubie's sudden barrage of barks, Willow reared her head, letting out a high-pitched whinny, the whites of her eyes showing in the shadowy light.

"Whoa, now." Charlotte edged toward her, pressing a hand to her chest. "Hush, Rubie."

A scuffing noise sounded behind her. Before she could turn, a strong arm clutched her around the waist and a hairy hand muffled her screams. She struggled to pry herself free of the man's hold, gasping for air as she writhed back and forth.

Willow gave another sharp whinny and reared, her hoof grazing Charlotte's leg and ripping the hem of her dress in land-ing. She gave a loud moan, searing pain shooting through her shin. A little more and the blow might have broken it.

"Shush, you." The man's gruff voice held a familiar tone she couldn't place. He pulled her back, dragging her from the stall.

She quieted, heart pulsing in her ears. Who would come to her aid anyway? There was no one within miles.

The stench of sweat and foul breath filled her nostrils as the unknown assailant pressed his stubbled chin to her cheek. "Where's the boy?"

Her eyes darted to her left. She knew that voice. It belonged to Ian Crowley. She should have known he wouldn't let Johnny go without a fight. For the first time she was relieved Johnny wasn't with her.

With a sigh, she pointed at his fingers across her mouth.

He squeezed his hand tighter around her middle. "Don't try anything."

Charlotte nodded, attempting to catch her breath.

Gradually, he loosened his hold on her mouth. "That boy's around here somewheres. Now, where is he?"

Cringing, Charlotte rubbed a hand over her jaw. Johnny's battered body seared her mind. She would never betray his whereabouts to this monster. Never.

Crowley twisted her toward him and gave her shoulders a shake. "Answer me."

Charlotte lifted her chin, clutching her hands together to keep from trembling. "Somewhere safe. Somewhere you won't hurt him." The cockiness in her tone surprised her. Despite her tough exterior, her insides had melted to butter.

The corners of Crowley's eyes creased. He leaned toward her, his whiskered jaw growing taut. "I've every right to that boy. It was his pa's wish I have him."

"You gave up that right when you beat him." She shoved at his chest, her own anger flaring.

"Why, you . . ." The man's eyes spewed hatred as he drew back his arm. He swung the back of his hand at Charlotte's face. She flinched and jolted back, dodging the worst of the blow.

A burning sensation pulsed through her chin. Almost instantly, her face began to throb, and she staggered back, realizing too late she was at this man's mercy. Willow was her only means of escape. If she could distract Crowley long enough to mount her, she might have a chance. But with her injured leg, it seemed improbable.

Lord help me.

With a bear-like growl, Crowley lunged at her.

A cry escaped her as she limped away. Her eyes searched the dim barn. If only she had some way to defend herself.

A scuffling noise sounded behind her, and the door smacked shut, making the dim barn all the darker. A moment more, and he'd be on her. She drew a jagged breath and groped for the three-legged milking stool. If she was going down, she would go fighting.

Weapon raised, she wheeled to face him, bracing herself for the on-coming attack. Instead, two shadowy figures wrestled in the darkness.

Charlotte blinked hard, slowly lowering the stool. Where had the other man come from? Had the Lord sent an angel to defend her?

She squinted, straining to distinguish what was happening. The tall, slender figure planted a fist on the jaw of the larger man. He stumbled back, his guttural grunt identifying him as Crowley. The thinner man took a blow to his middle, but held his ground, landing another punch to Crowley's face.

Charlotte gulped shallow breaths, inwardly rooting for her unknown champion. She gnawed at her lower lip as Crowley backed in her direction. Taking the milk stool in both hands, she swung with all her might. It struck just below his knees, and he toppled down with a groan. The impact of the blow jolted Charlotte backwards, and she fell in a heap beside him. In an instant, the newcomer was on Crowley, bludgeoning him left and right until he ceased struggling.

Charlotte scurried out of the way, trying desperately to catch a glimpse of her defender.

Heavy breaths sounded from both men. The taller man leaned toward her, keeping Crowley penned to the floor. "You all right?"

She sucked in a breath. She'd know that smooth voice anywhere. "Chad?" Ignoring the throbbing in her leg, and the onslaught of emotions, she squeezed out the words, "I'll be fine."

"Did he hurt you?" The words spilled out in a low rush.

His obvious concern touched Charlotte's spirit. "No. He was after Johnny."

"Johnny?"

"Yes. He was using Johnny for labor."

Crowley groaned and stirred. Chad gripped the stunned man by the shirt, and pulled him to a standing position, holding him within inches of his face. "Go home, Crowley. Go home to your wife and kids while you still can. 'Cause if you ever bother Miss Stanton or Johnny again, I'll see to it you don't see your family for a good long while."

He gave Crowley a shove forward. The beaten man shuffled toward the door, shoulders hunched. Following him outside, Chad stood watch until Crowley's horse cantered away.

Charlotte picked herself up, brushed straw and dirt from her dress, hoping Chad's method of warning would prove more effective than Pastor Brody's. She limped to the doorway, a trickle of blood oozing down her leg.

Turning toward her, Chad's eyes trailed to her torn, blood-stained hem, his cheeks growing taut. "What happened?"

"Willow's hoof came down on me. It's nothing."

Chad gripped her elbow. "Sit down and let's have a look."

She nodded, sensing his concern.

He led her to a pile of straw and eased her down onto it. "Have you a lantern?"

"Over there, in the corner."

Rubie whined at his approach, the one-time stranger now a

noted friend. He bent to scratch her behind the ear, then slid the lantern from its peg on the wall. Lighting it, he turned the wick and carried it to Charlotte. He reached for the milk stool, only to discover one of its legs had broken off. Shoving it aside, he sat down beside her. "That was some wallop you gave that fella. Reckon you did him more harm that I did."

The corners of Charlotte's mouth tipped upward. "That was for Johnny."

Chad propped her boot up on his thigh. His fingers gripped the hem of her dress. Lantern light shone in his eyes as he gazed at her, turning them a dark slate. "May I?"

With a nod, Charlotte raised her skirt up over the wound, cringing at sight of the bloody scrape along her shin.

Chad's brow furrowed. "Nothing, huh?"

In the dim light, it was hard to tell where the cut ended and the trail of blood began. Shrugging, she forced a grin. "It's not bad. Really."

"Bad enough you won't be traipsing off to any shivaree. Let's get you inside and get you washed up."

She pulled back. "But I wanna go."

Chad's eyes narrowed. "Surely you're not that reckless?"

Charlotte tilted her head to the side, hope rising in her heart. "Is that why you came, to go with me?"

He shrugged. "You didn't leave much choice. I knew you'd be too bull-headed to stay home. I couldn't let you go alone."

Charlotte thrilled inwardly. He knew her better than most. This time it had worked to her favor.

He drew a handkerchief from his pocket and tied it around her leg. Heat rose in her cheeks at his tender touch. The pain seemed to melt away as she gazed at his sandy hair and handsome profile. Such quiet strength poured through this gentle man of honor. How could she help but be drawn to him? He was everything she'd ever hoped for in a man. God-fearing. Kind. Hardworking. Caring.

If only he could return her admiration.

But it could never be. Not while he clung so tightly to his past. To his dear wife and child.

He stood and reached to help her up. Charlotte placed her hand in his, drawn by the gentleness in his touch. She let her fingers linger, gazing up at him. And in that moment she knew.

He held her heart as well.

Chapter Thirty-Four

CHAD'S SADDLE creaked under him, breaking the stillness. He glanced back at Charlotte, troubled by the flurry of emotions her touch had stirred within him. He had no business accompanying her. The more time spent together, the harder it would be to sever ties.

Something he had to do. Before she wormed her way into his heart completely.

The large, full moon hung low in the east, casting a faint, orange glow over the landscape. He rubbed Tag's neck. The horse had filled out nicely in the weeks since his return. The once broken-down mount now held her head high, spryness in her step. Amazing what a bit of kindness could do.

Tag stumbled, and Chad pulled back on the reins, shifting in the saddle. He clenched his jaw. Foolhardy. That's what this venture was. Charlotte should be back in her cabin, leg propped, the wound cleaned and bandaged. Instead, here they were, fumbling around in near darkness with only the moon and stars to guide them.

Laughter rang in the distance, followed by a chorus of

singing. Chad pulled Tag to a stop. A string of lanterns danced ahead of them. Why hadn't he thought to bring one?

He craned his neck for a closer look. "Sounds like we're late for the party."

A huff sounded from Charlotte. "That Crowley. He's spoiled everything."

Chad dismounted and tied Tag's reins to a tree branch. Stepping over to Charlotte, he placed his hands around her waist and lifted her from her horse. As he set her on the ground, their eyes locked, the dim light seeming to accentuate her beauty. He fought back a grin at the memory of her whopping Crowley with the milk stool.

Charlotte's head tilted to one side. "What is it?"

"What you did back there took guts."

She lowered her gaze, a smile touching her lips. Had he embarrassed her? How different she seemed from the spiteful gal he'd happened upon a few months back. The Lord had done a work in her for certain. If he'd somehow played a part in it, he was grateful.

He nodded toward the spattering of lanterns ahead of them, then glanced at her leg. "Can you make it?"

"I think so." She limped forward and stumbled on something in the grass.

With a gasp, she reached out, and he caught her by the arm. "Here. Take my hand."

Without hesitation, she slid her palm into his.

Heat flooded his cheeks as he wrapped his fingers around hers. Had he lost his senses?

It had been well over a year since he'd held a woman's hand. Yet, Charlotte's felt strangely comfortable, natural even, tucked within his.

Together, they made their way toward the dimly lit cabin. A scuffling noise sounded at its front. Two lanterns broke away from the rest, setting off a rash of shouts from the onlookers.

"Let go of me," a man's frantic voice called in the distance.

"Bring him back. Norris!" The tearful voice no doubt belonged to the flustered bride.

Charlotte gave a slight giggle, gesturing toward the fleeing lanterns. "There goes Norris, barefoot and blindfolded. He'll not find his way back till morning light."

Chad flinched his cheeks. "They've no call to steal him away."

Charlotte stilled, her gaze drifting from the bobbing lanterns to the distraught bride. "I reckon it wouldn't be so funny to have your new husband whisked away like that your first night home."

The crowd began to disperse, singing *Stars of the Summer Night*. The lamp light dimmed as the serenaders filtered out across the prairie. Lola's brokenhearted sobs sounded near the cabin door. A shadowy figure moved toward her, and the two silhouettes blended into one. "There now. He'll be all right." Hank Brimmer's voice trailed out to them as he held his daughter.

Chad seethed inwardly as he took in the scene. If someone had tried that with him on his wedding night, he'd have fired off a few warning shots and sent the mischief-makers packing.

Norris was soft. Too soft to be left to his own defenses all night.

Taking Charlotte by the shoulders, he guided her onto a nearby log. "I need to leave you for a bit. Will you be all right?"

"Why? Where are you going?"

"Just stay put. I'll be back shortly."

Amid Charlotte's hushed protests, Chad stole silently away. Heading in the direction the captors had taken Norris, Chad maneuvered around the scattered shivareers, their snickers burrowing beneath his skin like the prick of thorns. Many would brand him a killjoy for undoing the merriment, but losing Lauren and John had unleashed a deep desire within him to ensure no one else suffered a severed relationship. Even for a night.

That is if he could find the misplaced groom.

As the sounds of song and laughter fanned out further into the prairie night, one sound grew steadily louder, steering Chad closer to his mark.

A man's frantic cry for help.

Chad's lips hinged upward. Norris wouldn't be hard to find. Not so long as he continued to beller like a weaning calf.

"Help!" Another call rang out, closer now. Chad worked his way through the jumble of trees, squinting into the night. The full moon had risen above the treetops, casting a bluish light over the prairie. One final cry brought Chad close enough to spot Norris up ahead, braced against a sturdy tree.

Making his way over, Chad squatted and touched him on the shoulder.

Norris startled. "Who's there?"

"Chad Avery. I've come to help." He kept his voice low, leery of any stragglers who might not take to him spoiling their fun.

"Praise be." Nightshirt raised over his knees, Norris scooted away from the tree, exposing his tied hands. "I feared I'd be forced to stay the night."

Unsheathing his knife, Chad cut through the ropes that held Norris's trembling wrists.

Norris removed his blindfold and rubbed his wrists, huffing as he tried to catch his breath. "I'm grateful to you, Mr. Avery. I'd have been raw-nerved by morning."

Chad cuffed him on the arm and peered into the night, catching an occasional glimpse of lantern light. "Stay till you're sure everyone's gone. You don't want to find yourself out here a second time."

"No, sir." Norris brushed his fingers through his hair, an adamant tone in his voice.

Chad gestured to the south. "You'll find your cabin through those trees. I need to go. Someone's waiting for me."

The slight hesitation in Charlotte's former suitor's response hinted he'd guessed who. If Norris held it against Chad, he was a big enough man not to let it show. With a nod, Norris extended a hand. "Thanks again. I won't forget this."

Chad gave his hand a firm shake. "My pleasure."

As he retraced his steps, Chad knew without a doubt he'd done the right thing. Norris would've been reduced to a puddle of nerves come morning. He belonged at home in the comfort of his new wife's arms.

A pleasure Chad no longer had to enjoy.

He weaved his way back toward Charlotte with only instinct and the white glow of the moon to aid him. Without the advantage of her voice to guide him, he kept his ears cocked for any sound or movement. The scenery began to blend together, moonlit shadows hindering his search. Would Charlotte grow uneasy? Would he even find her?

A familiar horse's nicker up ahead jolted him to a stop. Tag. He was in the vicinity.

"Charlotte?" he called, his voice soft and low.

"Over here," she answered up ahead, a bit of anxiety creeping into her voice.

He picked up his pace, striding toward her. Thank the Lord he hadn't freed one stranded person to abandon another. As he came into view, she rose to meet him, eyes filled with question. "Where'd you go?"

"To set Norris free." He tensed, awaiting her response. Would she think him a hero, or a cad for his unpopular deed?

A hint of a smile touched her lips. "Better hope the others don't find out."

Truly, he could care less if the others knew he'd spoiled their fun. A new husband and wife belonged together, not separated by some cruel prank. His stomach clenched. Life threw enough hardships a couple's way without the help of a mob of raucous townspeople.

He clasped Charlotte by the hand. "Come on. Let's head back."

Moments later, they were on the horses, trekking toward home, the only sane part of the whole venture. Chad sensed Charlotte's eyes upon him as they rode side-by-side over the open prairie. Her silence hinted her mind was filled with questions he would just as soon not answer.

As she drew a deep breath, he braced himself for the inevitable. "Tell me. What was she like? Your wife, I mean."

He stared into the dim path laid out by moon glow. How could he answer that? He'd kept Lauren locked so deep inside, his memories of her seemed almost larger than life. Charlotte deserved more than he'd given her. It was time to bare the truth. At least in part.

He cleared his throat. "She was the sort that could fend for herself. A lot like you, I reckon. Not in appearance, but the same fiery spirit."

"And your son, John? Was he spirited as well?"

Chad gave a curt grin, sensing himself relax. "A spit-fire, like his ma."

Charlotte fell silent, and he glanced her way, surprised at her stillness. Had he sated her curiosity so easily? Somehow he didn't think so. Best he divert her mind onto other topics before she asked more than he was willing to tell. "How's the leg?"

"Sore, but I'll manage."

"Soon as you're back, you'll need a poultice."

At that, she turned to face him, her voice little more than a whisper. "You're a kind man, Chad Avery."

He met her gaze, the sincerity of her words spilling over him. Even the darkness of night couldn't shield him from the poignant message underlying her tone and demeanor.

She loved him.

The thought should frighten him and yet instead, he had the uncanny urge to take her in his arms. And then he knew.

He loved her too.

BY THE TIME they rode into the yard, Charlotte's leg was throbbing. Chad was right. She'd been foolish in going. Still, she'd have done it all again for the time spent with him. His concern for her was touching, as was his willingness to go to Norris's aid. Best of all had been his willingness to take her into his confidence regarding his family. Be it ever so slightly, he'd opened up to her. She could only pray it was the first of many such intimate conversations.

There was so much more she wanted to know. How his wife and son had died. What had prompted him to come here? And why he kept his past so hidden? Was it out of pain? Regret?

Or something more?

And yet, this night she couldn't bring herself to ask him. The bond between them had deepened somehow. She refused to spoil it by probing too deeply.

Dismounting, Chad turned to her. "Stay put till I come back."

She gave a nod, her leg more stiff and sore than she cared to admit, enough so she didn't choose to argue. She shivered in the humid night air. Had she grown feverish?

Chad made his way into the barn and lit the lantern, his presence prompting a low "moo" from Nell. A moment later, he returned and took hold of the bridle. Charlotte ducked under the doorway as he led Willow to her stall. The yellow glow of the lantern spilled onto Chad's face, revealing a myriad of emotions as his strong hands encircled her waist. The moment his silvery eyes locked onto hers, Charlotte nearly forgot her throbbing leg. Had his feelings for her deepened as well?

A soft moan escaped her as her feet met the ground.

Chad tightened his hold on her waist. "You all right?"

"Yes." She let out a nervous chuckle, shifting her weight to her opposite leg. His nearness lit a fire inside her, and she leaned into him.

He brushed the back of his hand over her cheek. At the warmth of his touch, her heart beat faster.

He pulled her to him, his breath warm and sweet.

A gentle smile tugged at Charlotte's lips as she draped her arms around his neck. How she'd longed for this moment.

Chad wet his lips, drawing her closer. His lips brushed hers but an instant before he tensed and pulled away. Loosening his hold on her, he stared at the straw-covered barn floor. "I can't. I'm sorry."

Chapter Thirty-Five

WHAT DID CHAD MEAN, 'he can't'? He was deliberately holding back.

What was he afraid of?

Charlotte peeled back the poultice on her leg, the pain forcing her to be gentle, despite her frustration. With a sigh, she dipped the cooled cloth in a bowl of warm water and wrung it out. After their almost kiss, Chad had stayed just long enough to see her to the cabin and fix a warm compress for her leg. Then he'd left without a word, leaving her to ponder his sudden change of heart. His wife and child had such a hold on him. Did his hurt run so deep he couldn't rid himself of it?

She touched a tender spot on her leg and cringed. Drawing the lantern closer, for the first time, she saw the full extent of the wound — a six-inch trail of raw, severed flesh down her shin. Thankfully, it didn't appear deep, merely bruised and swollen. Much of the bleeding had stopped, yet a bandage would be needed to keep it from oozing onto her bed sheets.

She wrapped a clean cloth around her leg, and tied it in place. Chad's blood-stained handkerchief lay on the floor beside her. She clasped it between her fingertips, recalling his tender touch as he'd tied it around her leg. He cared for her. In her heart, she knew it to be true. But something tore at him inside so deeply it continually wedged a chasm between them. Chad had built an impenetrable wall around himself, one Charlotte wasn't sure she could topple.

The Lord alone had the power to heal a wounded heart. Charlotte could only pray He'd prompt Chad to let go of his past and find room for her in his heart. They could share so much together, have the happy life she'd always dreamed of.

Given time, would he come to his senses, or throw it all away?

Hobbling over to her bed, she set the lantern on the night-stand. A yawn escaped her as she eased down onto the feather mattress. Despite her turbulent thoughts, the warm room, coupled by the late hour, left her drowsy. Dousing the lantern flame, she lay back on her bed, and stared up at the darkened rafters. An hour earlier, she might have gone to sleep dreaming of Chad's pleasant smile and warm lips upon hers. Now, tired as she was, she seemed destined to a restless night, filled with uncertainty.

CHAD RAKED a hand through his hair, pacing back and forth before the dying embers of his fireplace. What had he been thinking? He was confusing himself. Worse yet, he was confusing Charlotte. With all his good intentions, he'd still loused things up.

And in doing so, exposed his growing affection for her.

He plopped down in his straight-back chair, releasing a frustrated groan. There was no getting around it. He needed to sever all ties with Charlotte. He'd glimpsed the longing in her eyes, sensed the depth of her true feelings for him. How could he have let things go this far?

How could he even face her again?

His chest tightened. One more day of wheat harvest and his obligation to the Hollisters would be ended. Then he could resume working for Mr. Brimmer and engross himself in his cattle farm.

Wasn't that what he'd been working toward?

Leaning forward in his chair, he dug his boot-heel into a crevice in the floorboard. With her injured leg, Charlotte needed his help now more than ever. As much as he'd like to spare himself the agony of seeing her again, he couldn't leave her in a bind. Nor could he leave her wondering why he'd held her in his embrace only to pull away. He owed her an explanation. Owed her the truth.

The question was, did he have the courage to tell her?

"If you need a break, I can finish."

"I'm fine," Charlotte snapped, her tone more agitated than reassuring. She stooped to gather another armload of wheat and limped her way to the wagon.

Chad shook his head, admiring her stamina. That leg had to be hurting. She'd worked alongside him much of the day without complaint, and for the most part without words. She was angry with him and had every right to be.

He finished loading the wheat sheaves onto the wagon, then brushed bits of chaff from his shirt. He cast Charlotte a sideways glance, wondering if her pained expression was more his fault than her leg's. Obviously, things wouldn't sit right between them until they'd cleared the air. Now just didn't seem the time.

Or was he simply avoiding the issue?

He tossed a rope over the tower of sheaves, tying first one end then the other to the wagon to secure the wheat for the ride into town. Lifting his hat, he raked a sleeve over his sweaty brow. He squinted up at the afternoon sun, its harsh rays hot against his skin despite the breeze.

He propped his foot on the wagon wheel and sank his hat back on his head. "Guess that about does it."

"Not entirely." Charlotte strode toward him, her tone unsettling.

Chad sensed her deeper meaning and shifted his gaze to the shaved field beyond. "Was a fair yield. Your uncle will be pleased."

"Chad."

The sound of his name, spoken so softly, assured him any further attempt to divert her attention would prove worthless. He tensed, eyes veering toward her.

She stepped closer, her fawn-like expression pleading. "I need to know."

He wet his lips, swallowing the tightness in his throat. The time for putting off was through. She wanted an explanation, and he couldn't deny her one. With a deep sigh, he leaned against the wagon wheel. Where to begin?

He stared at his dusty boots, his hidden past rushing back in a whirl. "It'll be two years this December. Lauren, my wi —" The word caught in his throat like a wad of jerky. Would the hurt ever lessen?

He sniffled. "She had her heart set on turkey for Christmas. I left at dawn that Wednesday morning, hoping to return with a big tom by nightfall. I walked all day without so much as a sign of one. So, I decided to camp for the night and try again at first light. The next morning, I came across a small flock in a clearing. Wasn't long before I was on my way home, my prize draped over the saddle."

Chad's stomach clenched, the memories flooding back more vividly. The cold, December morning. The plume of smoke. The charred cabin. He rubbed a hand over his face, the scene forever etched on his mind. He swallowed, sensing Charlotte's hand touch his arm. "I saw smoke in the direction of our cabin. Not the white smoke of a fireplace, but dark, billowy smoke that sent overwhelming dread surging through me. So long as I live, I'll never forget it."

His voice quieted to a whisper as he stared out over the prairie. "The fire claimed everything. My wife. My son. My home. Everything."

Charlotte squeezed his hand, drawing him back into the present. "I'm so sorry."

He nodded, working to ease the tension in his jaw. Her words weren't shallow ones. She, too, knew the pang of loss. He turned to her, her anguished expression mirroring his own. "I don't even know how the fire started or why they didn't make it out."

He slumped against the wagon. "If only I'd come home that night. I might have saved them."

"Or you might have died too." Charlotte edged closer. "You can't blame yourself for something you had no control over."

"They were my family. I should have protected them."

"You couldn't have known they were in danger, any more than I could have stopped my father from being killed."

He shook his head. "It isn't the same."

"Yes, it is." She wet her lips, forcing out the tension in her jaw. "You're putting yourself in place of God. He's the keeper of our souls, not us."

Chad tossed a stray piece of chaff into the breeze. "That may be so, but what sort of man lets his family die unprotected?"

Charlotte's hands flew to her hips, her once gentle voice escalating. She brushed a lock of hair from her face and let out a huff. "You may not have been able to save your wife and child, but just look how you protected me from Ian Crowley. He might have killed me if not for you."

The words sliced through him, stealing his voice. He couldn't deny the truth of her words. She'd have been in an awful fix if he hadn't arrived when he did. The Lord had stirred his heart at just the right moment.

This time. Why not for Lauren and John?

If he surrendered his heart to Charlotte, how could he be certain he'd not fail her at some point as well?

She stepped closer, her emerald eyes poised up at him. "You're a good man, Chad Avery. You'll not convince me otherwise. And I know you care for me."

Heat worked its way up the back of his neck into his cheeks. He wasn't fooling anyone, least of all Charlotte. "You're right, I do care. But it can't be. After I lost Lauren, I pledged not to love another."

Charlotte's cheeks paled. "Is that why you backed away?"

He gave a slow nod, forcing himself to meet her gaze.

Moisture pooled in her eyes. "Surely the Lord never intended you to close off your heart forever."

It sounded appalling to hear Charlotte speak it. He straightened, determined not to waver in his resolve. "It's the way it has to be. I can't risk another hurt. Another failure."

Even as he said the words, the pain in her eyes deepened. She bowed her head, the rim of her bonnet hiding her face. He'd not meant to be harsh, merely straightforward.

All at once, her head lifted, revealing a single tear trailing down her cheek. She swiped it away, regaining that air of determination he'd grown to recognize all too well. Crossing her arms in front of her, she tilted her head to the side. "You once made me take a much needed look inside myself, Chad Avery. Now it's your turn."

He tipped his hat back with a nod and drew a long breath, bracing himself to hear what she had to say. He owed her that.

Her emerald eyes deepened. "I imagine you favor yourself much like Job in the Bible, having lost home and family for no apparent reason."

Though he hadn't given it much thought, she had a point.

Even much of his life's savings had been snatched from him, leaving only a smidgen of his dream to cling to.

Charlotte stepped closer. "Was Job guilty of not protecting his family? Did he blame himself for what happened? No. Even when his friends claimed he'd done something to deserve it, he maintained his innocence. He knew he'd done nothing deserving of such loss, and neither have you."

"Yes, but…"

She pressed a finger to his lips to still him. "You seem to have forgotten how, in the end, the Lord blessed Job twice over with a new home and family. Maybe He has in mind to do the same for you."

If only he could believe that. How he longed to take Charlotte in his arms and claim her as his own.

Moisture glistened in her eyes, and her voice softened. "Are you willing to sacrifice what could be for the sake of what you lost?"

His heart drummed in his chest, that beseeching gaze of hers threatening to undo him. What she said made sense. Was he foolish to pass love by, to hold to the past and let fear keep him from surrendering his heart?

He cupped his hand atop hers, for a brief instant believing he could leave the pain and grief of his past behind. But in that same moment, the charred remains of his cabin and his lost loved ones resurrected in his mind, like an unrelenting nightmare bent on destroying him.

He couldn't. The risk was too great, the threat of loss too real.

Dropping his gaze, he slid his hand from hers. "I'm sorry."

Chapter Thirty-Six

THE MAN WAS INFURIATING. Here Charlotte had given him every reason to embrace the future, and he'd stubbornly insisted on clinging to the past.

She tapped her heels into Willow's sides, spurring her toward town. Hopefully she could catch Pastor Brody before he left for Palmer. Seeing Johnny would prove a welcome distraction after yesterday's disappointing encounter with Chad. Now that wheat harvest was complete, perhaps some time apart would do them both good.

She fingered the letter in her pocket, having channeled last night's disgruntled energies into penning a note to Ma and Esther. Nearly a month had passed since she'd written them. Far too long. Somehow Chad's refusal generated a longing for her displaced family. Both Johnny and Chad, two of the reasons she'd remained behind, had eluded her. Now the decision seemed ill-guided, impulsive.

Had she made the wrong choice?

A deep-seated notion tore at Charlotte. How Chad must have loved his wife to pine away for her all these months. If only he could love her half as much.

The town of Miller Creek lay sprawled out ahead of her, growing, thriving. Before long the Brodys' home on the outskirts of town would reside within its midst. As she passed their cabin, Charlotte watched for signs of life about the place, but no one stirred. Had she missed her chance? Had Pastor Brody already left?

The sound of laughter pulled her attention to the schoolhouse yard as she made her way into town. Johnny's absence forged a crevice across her heart. He should be among the group of frolicking boys. Instead, he was off in some unknown place. A place he'd not wished to go, with a family he didn't know. By now, had he settled in?

Her lips hinged downward. It seemed the boy's lot in life to be saddled with girls, first with the Crowleys and now the Flynns. How she ached for his company. Did Johnny miss her as much as she missed him?

Bringing Willow to a halt outside the post office, Charlotte dismounted, her leg tender as she shifted her weight onto it. More than likely, she should stop in and let Doc Pruitt have a look at the wound, but it would only delay her. A few more days with a warm poultice should clear it up.

But Ian Crowley dare not show his face again or this time she'd be ready.

Mrs. Chaney's welcoming grin faded as Charlotte hobbled in. "Why, Charlotte Stanton, what have you done to yourself?"

"Willow came down on my leg. It's nothing, really." The last thing Charlotte wanted was to have her personal affairs broadcast by the chatty postmistress. Best to leave out unnecessary details. She slid the letter from her pocket and placed it on the counter. "I wish to send this to Ma and Esther, but by now, I'm certain the direction is incorrect. I don't suppose you've a letter for me?"

Mrs. Chaney lifted a finger. "Why, yes. I believe one came for you just the other day." With that, she rummaged through the stack of mail on her desk, finally pulling a letter from the pile. "Here it is, and it looks as though they've listed a new direction."

The declaration was sweet balm for Charlotte's soul, soothing some of her heartbreak over Chad. Taking the note from Mrs. Chaney, Charlotte read over the directive. Perry Street. It was indeed a different street name. Was it along the outskirts of the city or nestled deep within?

She slid her finger beneath the wax seal, careful not to tear the parchment. As she unfolded the note, Esther's handwriting stared back at her like an old friend.

Dear Charlotte,

I hope this note finds you well. Over the weeks, Ma has grown more and more anxious to hear from you again. Perhaps you've written and your letter has not yet reached us, as we have relocated to an apartment on Perry Street.

Cincinnati is far different from the prairie, but has a splendor of its own with its sparkling river and grand places to see. The hardest to take are the crowds of people and buildings. I doubt I will ever grow accustomed to them. When Ma and I grow lonesome for the quietness of the prairie, we stroll to the banks of the river to drink in its beauty.

Do plan to come for a visit. There is much to see, and we miss you so. The Lord keep you safe and well until we are together again.

Fondly,

Esther

Charlotte pressed the letter to her chest, envisioning her sister and mother amid the throng of people and buildings. She could well imagine her worrisome ma was eager to hear from her. Even after only a short time in the city, Esther's wording seemed more refined. She was proving a suitable companion for Ma. Much better than Charlotte would have been.

"Good news?" Mrs. Chaney's voice interrupted Charlotte's thoughts.

"What? Oh, yes. They're well."

With a nod, the postmistress reached out her hand. "I can redirect that if you wish."

"Please do." Charlotte gave her the letters and watched as she folded a second piece of paper over the first.

Taking up her quill and ink bottle, Mrs. Chaney penned the new direction and then sealed the letter shut with wax. A grin lined her lips as she waved her hand to dry it. "I'll see to it this gets sent as soon as possible."

"Thank you." Charlotte lifted Esther's letter from the counter and turned to go, her thoughts returning to Johnny. If she delayed any longer, she'd miss her chance to catch Pastor Brody.

If she hadn't already.

Sliding her left foot into the stirrup, she swung her sore leg over Willow, thankful the wound was on the top side of her leg and not pressed against the saddle fender. As it was, she didn't relish enduring the five-mile ride home, let alone the even longer trip to Palmer. The constant motion aggravated her throbbing leg. But to see Johnny again, well and happy, would make it all worthwhile.

She approached the Brody cabin with not the slightest flicker of dread. Months ago, her insides would have coiled tighter than a rattlesnake. She had Chad to thank for the improvement. With a few riveting words, he'd exposed her spiteful ways, forcing her to realize how self-centered she'd become. How grateful she was he'd thought enough of her to incite her to change without wounding her spirit.

Yesterday's candid conversation came spiraling back at her. How could Chad have seen her flaws so clearly and yet couldn't grasp the darkness that had cloaked his own heart, robbing him of joy?

Was he so steeped in his past he had no room for a future?

As Charlotte halted Willow before the cabin, its door swung open, chasing away her uncertainties. Becky stepped onto the porch, a drying cloth in her hands and a smile on her lips. "What a surprise. Come in, and I'll warm some coffee. Pa will be pleased for the company. He's forever asking if I've heard how things are coming with wheat harvest."

Charlotte leaned back in the saddle. "Thanks, but maybe another time. I was hoping to catch Pastor Brody. Has he left yet for Palmer?"

Becky's smile faded. "I'm sorry. He left early this morning for a church meeting in Scottsdale and won't be back until late this evening. I believe he planned to swing by Palmer and visit Johnny on the way. I'm sure he'll let you know how he's faring."

Charlotte bit at her lip, doing her best to cloak her disappointment. Outside of Esther's letter, the thought of seeing Johnny was the only bright spot she had to cling to. Somehow hearing second-hand no longer seemed enough. Yet, without Pastor Brody to guide the way, how would she find the boy?

Palmer lay ten miles further south. Even if she knew where the Flynns lived, the long trip might prove more than her leg could withstand. Dare she try it alone?

She tightened her hold on the reins, confident she wouldn't rest until she'd seen Johnny. "Thank you, but I believe I'll ride over that way myself. Tell Uncle Joseph the wheat harvest looked to be more than a fair yield. I believe Chad — Mr. Avery — brought the last of it into town yesterday."

Becky gave a cheerful nod. "I'll do that."

With a wave goodbye, Charlotte headed back into town in route to Palmer. By midday, Lord willing, she and Johnny would be reunited. She only prayed their second parting would prove easier than the first.

THE SWISH OF the cradle scythe echoed through the stillness. Chad looked over his shoulder, half expecting Charlotte to be gathering up the downed stalks of wheat. His chest squeezed, remembering yesterday's ardent discussion. She'd offered him companionship, love, a future, only to have him turn away.

Was he right in refusing, or just plain thick-headed?

He cut another swath of wheat, determined to stay focused. Besides the wheat to harvest, he had cattle to tend, a cabin to mend, and his work for Mr. Brimmer to complete. So much to do, and yet emptiness pulled at him. Despite every attempt to squelch it, Charlotte had found a place in his heart. To deny it left him wanting, and yet Lauren's memory pricked at him mercilessly.

Would it ever let go?

He'd become a lonely soul, intent on shutting out any hope of a future, save his dream. The Lord's presence was all he had to cling to. Yet even that seemed to elude him at times. Dreams were meant to be shared. Yet, somehow he couldn't bring himself to open his heart again. He'd loved too deeply, been hurt too much to let it happen again. If it meant living life alone, so be it.

Charlotte was young and attractive. She'd find someone else to love. He had no doubt of that. Her beauty now infiltrated the depths of her soul. Best he step aside and let her have the freedom to move forward.

Something he himself could never do.

Chapter Thirty-Seven

"SORRY, MISS, NEVER HEARD OF 'EM."

Charlotte nodded her thanks and reined Willow further into Palmer, frustrated by yet another failed attempt to locate Mr. and Mrs. Flynn. Parched and fatigued, she was beginning to think she'd never find Johnny, or even the Flynns, for that matter. Though new to the region, surely someone had to know where they lived. Their Irish accent was certain to garner attention.

The heat of the sun only escalated the throbbing in her leg. Confined to one position for so long, it had grown stiff. If she didn't exercise it soon, most likely she'd not be able to bear weight on it at all. Though not as large as Miller Creek, the unfamiliar town of Palmer seemed to stretch for miles. The townspeople, intent on their own business, paid Charlotte little mind as she rode through town. Was she being overlooked or ignored?

Up ahead, lay the mercantile. Surely the Flynns had stopped in for supplies now and then. She dismounted, cringing as she landed on her sore leg. Not only had the stiffness intensified, but the pain as well. She'd be fortunate to make it home. Pushing aside her discomfort, she tied Willow to the hitching post, then started toward the mercantile.

The bell above the door jingled as she entered, drawing the attention of the apron-clad storekeeper. She made her way toward him, working to conceal her limp.

The lanky fellow combed a hand through his thinning, chestnut hair, his smile widening. "What can I do for you, miss?"

"I'm looking for someone. Do you know where I might find a Mr. and Mrs. Flynn?"

The man's forehead furrowed, and he glanced up at the log rafters. "Flynn. Flynn. Nope. I don't believe I know anyone by that name."

"They're quite distinctive and just recently moved to the area. Irish accent, red hair."

The storekeeper's mouth twisted, his eyes shifting to her own crimson locks. "Be they relatives of yours?"

"No sir. I just need to find them. Do you know them?"

He rubbed a hand over his chin. "Could be you mean Michael and Mattie."

Charlotte leaned against the counter, hope stirring within her. "I never learned their given names. Are they newcomers to the area?"

"First I recollect seeing Mike and Mattie was back in early spring. I remember because they had no inkling as to what they needed to grow wheat or corn. Said they'd only dealt in potatoes. Moved here from out east I believe."

It must be them. "Do you know where they live?"

Once again the storekeeper scratched at his chin. "Well now, that I can't help you with."

Charlotte's shoulders drooped. Would this all be for nothing?

"Now, wait a minute." He lifted a finger. "I recall Mike saying something about living a stone's throw west of Tyler Creek. If you go north out of town and head east, you're liable to land smack dab onto their property."

The corners of Charlotte's mouth tipped upward. "Thank you."

She swiveled and limped her way to the door. It wasn't much, but it was a lead. She envisioned the smile her surprise visit would bring Johnny. Lord willing, they'd soon be together, be it ever so short of time.

The man's directions led her to a cabin near a creek, a plume of smoke rising from its stone chimney. It didn't take long to recognize the woman tending the garden. Charlotte tapped her heels into Willows flanks, spurring her to a canter. The woman turned and squinted in Charlotte's direction, her complexion fading to ghostly white, a welcome reminiscent to the one Charlotte had received from Mrs. Crowley. The trio of young girls romping in the yard stopped their play and skittered over to their mother. Either they were shy of visitors or a suspicious lot. Charlotte panned the yard for Johnny, but to her dismay, he was nowhere.

She swallowed down her swelling angst as she stopped Willow at the garden's edge, praying nothing was amiss.

Mrs. Flynn set down her half-filled bucket of string beans, her smile cautious. "Why, Miss Stanton. Tis quite a surprise t' see ya here. Have ya ridden all this way in this heat?"

Charlotte returned a stiff grin, not certain if her surprise was a welcome one. "I'm afraid so. I admit it was the thought of seeing Johnny that spurred me on. Is he around?"

The woman took a handkerchief from her pocket and dabbed her dampened brow, her eyes trailing to the vegetation at her feet. "Well now, he's not to be had at the moment. I'm sorrowed if you've made the trip for nothin'. Perhaps you'd like to come inside for a cup of tea and sit awhile."

Charlotte couldn't deny the woman's hospitable nature, but neither could she shake the feeling Mattie Flynn was hiding something. "Is Johnny with Mr. Flynn?"

"Nnnn . . . not entirely. That is to say, he could be."

"What do you mean, he could be?" Charlotte's hands grew

cold and clammy despite the sweltering mid-day heat. Surely Johnny hadn't run off again.

Mrs. Flynn's expression softened. "Come inside, dear. I'll explain the whole situation over a cup of tea."

Charlotte bit at her cheek in attempt to still the anxious questions churning inside her. This couldn't be happening. Not again. The only person Johnny hadn't run out on was her. Had she been right all along, certain Johnny and she belonged together?

Urging Willow forward, she followed Mrs. Flynn to the cabin, bucket of beans in hand. The five-year-old twins darted back and forth around their mother, full of giggles as they pulled at her skirt. The oldest daughter prattled on about the heat and wanting to go for a swim in the creek. At last, Mrs. Flynn conceded and shooed them on. "Off with you, then, but Lindy, mind your sisters."

"Aye, Mam," the older child answered as she scurried away, the younger girls trailing behind amid a barrage of giggles.

Dismounting, Charlotte cringed as she landed on her sore leg.

Mrs. Flynn took her arm. "Have you injured yourself, Miss Stanton?"

"It's nothing. Just a scrape."

The stillness of the cabin came as a welcome relief to the clamor of the children. Charlotte held back her questions until she'd taken a seat at the table. "Has Johnny run off?"

Mrs. Flynn set a pot of water atop the hot embers in the fireplace, then turned toward Charlotte, her face apologetic. "Aye. I'm afraid so. Mr. Flynn is off now in search of him."

Charlotte hung her head. "When?"

"Just this mornin'. Soon after your pastor stopped by for a visit." With a shake of her head, she took a seat beside Charlotte. "He and the girls haven't taken to each other like we'd hoped. Be it for you or someone else, he seems to pine away his days wishing to be someplace he isn't."

Regret tore at Charlotte's middle. In trying to do right by Johnny, she'd only succeeded in making him miserable once again. "He can't be far. I need to find him." As she stood, Charlotte felt her leg give and braced herself against the table.

Mrs. Flynn caught her by the arm, brows knit. "It appears to me you're in need of some tending to rather than traipsing all over the countryside. Mr. Flynn will see to Johnny. You'll be goin' no place for the time bein'. Now sit yourself down."

Charlotte hesitated, then gave in to the woman's plea. She wouldn't have the first clue where to look. Besides that, the soreness in her leg was becoming unbearable. Easing back into the chair, she propped her leg up on the seat opposite her.

With a satisfied nod, Mrs. Flynn rested her hands on her hips. "Now then, let's have a look at that leg of yours."

Hiking her skirt, Charlotte peeled back the make-shift bandage, stained with a trail of dark drainage. A ring of redness now encircled the still-raw wound.

Mrs. Flynn's face pinched as she leaned over it. "'Tis infection that's set in. You'll be needin' a strong poultice. I'll have ya fixed up in a whip-stitch."

Much as Charlotte wanted to protest, she knew better. The pain had worsened considerably throughout the day. To continue to let it go untreated might prove devastating. She had no choice but to let the woman have her way and pray Mr. Flynn soon returned with Johnny.

The woman hummed a lively tune as she set to work grating a potato, along with a handful of herbs, into a bowl and then adding warm water to make a paste. Charlotte found herself taking frequent glances out the window, each time hoping to see Johnny and Mr. Flynn riding up. Instead, golden prairie grass and the timberline flanking Tyler Creek stared back at her, filling her with longing. She should be out searching for Johnny, calling his name. If he knew she'd come for him, more than likely, he'd return of his own accord. But as things were, he could be anywhere.

Mrs. Flynn tapped her wooden spoon on the side of the bowl. "Here we are. This should do the trick." Striding over, she pulled a chair up next to Charlotte. With a smile, she stuck two fingers in the glob of off-white paste and applied it to the wound.

Charlotte tensed at her touch, but soon relaxed, the warm goo instantly soothing some of the pain. "You're very kind, Mrs. Flynn. Thank you."

The woman waved her clean hand at her. "Tis nothing and, please, call me Mattie."

"I don't know that I could have made the ride home without your help, Mattie."

"I'm only sorry you've come all this way in this condition for naught."

"Perhaps it won't be, if Johnny is found."

"Aye. If anyone's able to find the lad, it's me Michael, God bless 'im."

Movement outside the window stirred Charlotte's hopes, but it was only the Flynn girls returning from their swim.

The giggly trio burst through the door just as Mattie started wrapping Charlotte's leg. Their smiles faded, wet pigtails clinging to their rounded faces, as they locked eyes with Charlotte. Had they forgotten she was there? Creek water trickled from their soggy shifts, pooling on the puncheon floorboards beneath them. With a wave of her hands, Mattie shooed them back outside. "You young'uns know better than to traipse in soppin' wet. Off with ya, till you've dried out."

Amid moans and groans, the three girls trekked outside, leaving Mattie with a rueful grin. "Sorry, miss. The girls get a bit rambunctious at times. I fear your Johnny didn't quite know what to make of them." Her expression sobered. "Perhaps that's why he took off on us. He didn't quite seem to fit in."

Heaviness pulled at Charlotte's chest. The one place he had

fit in — with her — he'd been sent away from. She couldn't be both a mother and father to him, but God had given her a heart to love him. Was that enough?

Would she have the chance to find out?

The door swung open, and Mr. Flynn tromped inside, his widening gaze taking in Charlotte before turning to his wife. His tortured expression gave clue to the answer to the question burning within Charlotte. There was no need to ask.

Johnny hadn't been found.

Chapter Thirty-Eight

CHARLOTTE HAD WAITED as long as she could before leaving Palmer, had scoured the town for some inkling of Johnny. But it was as if he'd vanished. Despite the Flynns' reassurances that they would let her know when Johnny was found, it was all Charlotte could do to force herself to leave. The one hope she'd clung to was that Pastor Brody had some knowledge of where Johnny might be. But he, too, knew nothing.

The soreness in Charlotte's leg paled in comparison to the ache in her heart as she reined Willow into the yard with nary a half-hour of daylight to spare. If not for Mattie's kindness in tending her wound, she never could have made the long journey home. The packet of excess poultice meal in her saddlebag would most likely see her through a couple of days.

The Flynns, though kinder and more well-to-do than the Crowleys, still lacked what Johnny needed most. Love and understanding. If and when he was found, she'd not have the heart to send him away again.

She and Johnny belonged together. Somehow she'd known it from the start. He'd made her look beyond herself to care for someone else.

So had Chad. For that she'd forever be grateful.

Tired of mind and body, she dismounted and led Willow inside the barn. Long hours of travel had allowed ample time to think and pray not only for Johnny but for her and Chad as well. The more she'd prayed, the more the Lord seemed to urge her to let go and trust Him to right things, whatever that entailed. Nothing she could say or do could persuade Chad. It was his decision whether to let go of his past or remain stagnant.

She could only pray the Lord would heal his wounded spirit.

The scent of fresh straw pulled her thoughts back to Johnny. Her eyes lifted to the loft above as she slid the saddle from Willow. Twice Johnny had taken refuge in the loft. Oh, that he would be hiding there now. But it wasn't possible. It was too far.

Wasn't it?

Her heart pounded in her chest. The youngster's resourcefulness had surprised her before. Was there a chance? She stepped to the bottom of the ladder and stared up at the floorboards. "Johnny? Are you there?"

The plea met with silence.

Unwilling to let the notion go, she climbed the ladder and peered into the shadowy loft. "If you're there, Johnny, please come to me."

No rustling noise. Nothing.

With a sigh, Charlotte eased her way down the rungs. How silly. No seven-year-old could travel fifteen miles over unfamiliar terrain. It was merely wishful thinking.

As she slipped Willow's bridle off and hung it on its peg, Rubie let out a string of barks. Thoughts of Ian Crowley's recent visit sent shivers down her, causing the pain in her leg to sharpen. After Chad's stern warning, would the lunatic accost her yet again? Determined not to be caught without some sort of defense, she pulled the pitchfork from a pile of straw along the far wall. Limping her way to the barn door, she craned her neck for a look around. Rubie stood ears cocked, staring into the shadowy twilight. With a high-pitched "yip", she trotted across the yard to the far side of the cabin. Charlotte relaxed a bit, certain Rubie would never respond so to anything threatening.

Whatever it was had won the Border collie over.

Tossing aside the pitchfork, Charlotte ventured outside and trailed Rubie. A horse's soft whinny sounded in the distance. She stepped around the corner of the cabin, shading her eyes against the glow of the sun, setting like a ball of fire on the western horizon. The shadowed image of a man on horseback stole her breath. Given Rubie's friendly welcome, it could only be one person.

Chad.

Charlotte moistened her lips, forcing herself to calm. Had he had a change of heart?

Please, Lord, let it be so.

As he neared, she took a step toward him, both eager and apprehensive. A small head peeked from behind him only to disappear just as quickly. Charlotte took a slow blink. Had her eyes deceived her?

She quickened her pace until she was close enough to read Chad's expression. His silvery eyes met hers and a hint of a grin lined his lips. Her gaze shifted to the short leg snugged up behind his, and her hand flew to her mouth.

It *was* Johnny.

Hiking her skirt, she hurried toward them as fast as her leg would allow, not knowing whether to laugh or cry. Uncertainty marred Johnny's features as she reached to offer him a hand down. He leaned toward her, and she gave him a tight squeeze before setting him on the ground. "Oh, Johnny. I was so worried. Thank the Lord you're safe."

The boy's face scrunched to one side. "You ain't mad?"

With a shake of her head, she stooped and brushed a hand over his blond hair. "I'm just relieved you've been found."

She peered up at Chad. "How did you come to find him?"

He nodded toward Johnny. "I'll let him tell you."

Johnny slid his hands in his pockets and scuffed his toe in the dirt. "I snuck a ride in the back of Pastor Brody's wagon back to Miller Creek, then lit out on foot t' find you."

Chad's saddle creaked under him. "Found him wandering around in the pasture with my cattle."

Johnny ventured a look up. "You was harder t' find than I thought."

"Well, you're here now. That's what matters, though you've caused me and the Flynns a world of worry."

His eyes widened. "Please don't make me go back, Miss Charlotte."

With a chuckle, she stood, resting her hands on her hips. "Was it so bad?"

"No, ma'am. It's just, well, they have all them girls. They don't need me, but . . . you and me, we're all alone. We need each other."

The words pierced Charlotte like a sharpened knife. How perceptive of the boy to know how much she needed him. She placed a hand on his shoulder. "You're right, Johnny. I do need you, and I promise, I'll never send you away again."

Moisture pooled in his eyes as he lunged forward, wrapping his arms around her waist. She held him close, her gaze drifting to Chad. She mouthed a "thank you," and he gave a slight nod and tipped his hat before reining his horse toward home.

Charlotte watched him ride away, relishing Johnny's embrace, and yet aching for Chad to realize how much she needed him as well.

WE'RE ALL ALONE. *We need each other.*

Each rhythmic beat of Buck's hooves seemed to pound Johnny's words in deeper. Chad brushed a hand over his face, trying to rid his mind of them. He'd forgotten how to need anyone . . . or at least how to allow himself to need anyone. He was a loner bent on staying that way. Was that the future God intended for him, or had it become some sort of self-imposed punishment he'd chosen for himself?

The look of gratitude in Charlotte's eyes had nearly undone him. He'd rather she'd snubbed him and sent him on his way. He wouldn't have blamed her, not after the way he'd left the night of the shivaree. Why was it every time he tried to walk away from her, something always pulled him back?

It was good she and Johnny had each other. Maybe he could help ease the sting of her father's death and her family's absence. She and the boy understood each other. Together they'd find strength and comfort. Somehow that brought Chad some semblance of peace. What he was unwilling to risk, they had achieved.

The thought both warmed him and left him wanting.

"I CAN HARDLY WAIT to see the chicks. Have they grown much?"

"You'd be surprised." A soft breeze tousled the stray wisp of hair at Charlotte's cheek as she followed Johnny to the chicken coop, a smile tugging at her lips. How soul satisfying it was to see his joy and enthusiasm return. After the night's rest, he was his old self again.

Tugging open the hen house door, she stepped aside to let the small cluster of chickens flutter out. The two-week-old chicks filed out behind the mother hen, their downy fluff giving way to stiff wing feathers. Johnny's eyes widened. "They're all feathered out."

Charlotte took a handful of wheat from her pouch and gave it to Johnny. With a wide swing, he tossed it to the awaiting chickens, giggling as they scurried after it and scratched in the dirt.

Reaching in her bag, Charlotte took out another handful of grain and nodded to Johnny. "Cup your hands together on the ground."

Johnny squatted and made a small bowl with his hands. As Charlotte poured the seeds into his palms the chicks rushed over to pluck the grains of wheat. Johnny smiled down at the growing chicks. "They're sure hungry. Jus' look at 'em go."

"I see." Charlotte brushed grain dust from her hands, suddenly aware of her own empty stomach. "How about I go get us some breakfast while you finish feeding?"

The question garnered only a slight nod from Johnny, his attention still trained on the bobbing chicks. Charlotte slipped the pouch from around her neck and looped it around Johnny. "Not too much grain now."

With a backward glance, she trekked toward the cabin, a sudden thought clouding her joy. Last night she'd pledged Johnny a home, with the promise she'd never send him away. Had she spoken in haste? Would the Flynns raise a fuss at her not returning him? At the very least, she needed to let them know Johnny'd been found. The decreased pain in her leg was a vivid reminder of her indebtedness.

And what of Ian Crowley? Would he heed Chad's warning to stay away or forcibly rend Johnny from her a second time? The very thought left her cold.

Then there was schooling. In a matter of weeks, classes would begin in town. So far out, there'd be no choice but for her to teach Johnny herself. Her stomach churned. She was no teacher. Was taking in a child more responsibility than she alone could manage? The uncertainty of it left her homesick for her family. Pa had always known the right way to tame her worries and bring a smile to her lips. How she ached to hear his voice and feel his calming presence. No one else even came close.

Except Chad.

Her stomach clenched. But he'd made it clear he wanted no part of her.

Ma and Esther were so far away it seemed they were in another world. Just to see them would bring such comfort. What would they think of her taking in a youngster? Perhaps tonight she'd write and tell them. Yes. She needed someone's advice and approval.

She turned, eyes panning the yard and the vast golden prairie beyond. So many uncertainties. The Lord alone knew what the future held.

She squared her shoulders. Tomorrow, she and Johnny would make the trip into town to telegram the Flynns he'd been found and that he planned to stay.

But today belonged to her and Johnny.

CHAD DUCKED LOWER in the prairie grass, the volley of giggles and barks from the far side of Charlotte's cabin growing louder. He ventured another peek, suppressing a grin as he watched Johnny and Charlotte's Border collie romping around the yard in a game of chase. What a fine cattle dog she would make with her speed and agility.

Skirt hiked, Charlotte was doing her best to join in, though her leg obviously still pained her. How he longed to be a part of the fun, though he'd come out of a sense of protection, not child's play.

It seemed intrusive to spy on them, but with the boy back, there was every chance Ian Crowley might catch wind of it and try something, despite Chad's warning. He may not be able to watch over them every minute of the day. He'd have to rely on the Lord for that. But it would put his mind at ease to stop by each evening to ensure all was well.

The amber glow deepened in the western sky as the sun kissed the horizon, signaling it was time for Chad to head home. He lingered another moment, long enough to catch a glimpse of

Charlotte throwing her arms around Johnny and giving his sides a tickle. Laughter echoed over the prairie as the boy squirmed beneath her touch. Chad hung his head, trying to shut out the deep yearning inside him, a longing to be a part of their special bond. It was as if a bountiful feast had been laid out before him, and he was unwilling to partake of it.

With a sigh, he backed away, keeping low to the ground and wondering if he'd ever know true happiness again.

Chapter Thirty-Nine

"Why do we gotta tell the Flynns I'm here?"

Charlotte snugged her arms around Johnny in the saddle, pondering how to answer. She shifted Willow's reins to her right hand and reached to give his leg a reassuring pat with the other. "Wouldn't be right not to let them know you've been found and have them searching for no reason, would it?"

He heaved a sigh, leaning into her. "I reckon not. But what if they come and try to take me?"

The question was one she'd asked herself a dozen times throughout the long night, but one she wasn't fully prepared to answer. She'd spent half the night finding just the right way to explain to the Flynns that she and Johnny wished to be together. "We'll not worry about that. Let's just send word and trust the Lord to work it out."

The response seemed to satisfy him for he quieted. They rode in silence, the gentle rolling motion of Willow's gait soothing away the uncertainties. As they passed Chad's property, Charlotte's eyes pulled in the direction of the cabin. How she longed for him to take notice and ride out to greet them. And yet, she saw no sign of him, only his small herd grazing in the distance, their red-and white coats standing out against the golden prairie grass.

Johnny straightened, veering his head toward them. "There's Mr. Avery's place. Can we stop by and see him?"

Charlotte tensed and shifted her gaze from the homestead. "You just saw him day before yesterday. Besides, it doesn't appear Mr. Avery's about."

Johnny seemed undeterred. "He said he'd get his new bull the end of the week. Can we come then?"

A soft sigh escaped Charlotte. The way Johnny doted on Chad and his cattle it was going to be difficult to curb the boy's notion to visit him. "We mustn't pester Mr. Avery. I don't take him as the kind to cotton to many visitors."

"Oh, he wouldn't mind us. He likes us, I can tell."

Tension oozed its way into her tone. "Well, if he wants to see us, he'll have to be the one to come calling."

Charlotte felt a tug on her dress sleeve. Johnny peered back at her, blue eyes full of question. "Don't you like Mr. Avery?"

"'Course I do."

"Then why don't ya wanna see him?"

Heat rushed to Charlotte's cheeks as she fastened her gaze on the path ahead of them. Not only did she want to see him, she longed for him to take her in his arms and never leave. But then, she couldn't express that to Johnny.

Nor Chad.

She smoothed Willow's mane with her fingers. "Why don't we just wait and see if Mr. Avery extends an invitation?"

"All right," came Johnny's less than enthusiastic response.

Charlotte breathed easier as he turned back around. His inquisitive nature, especially where Chad was concerned, would prove her undoing. Of course, she could understand the young boy's fascination with the handsome cattleman. She shared that fascination, for different reasons, though it did her little good.

Would that Chad could rid himself of his past and embrace a future with her and Johnny.

It was the one hope she had to cling to.

THE VIEW of the grist mill nestled along Miller Creek was a picturesque one, and possibly much of the reason the town was thriving. Chad helped the mill workers unload the last of his sheaves of wheat onto a cart, then waved as he headed into town. At last he'd finished with harvest and could start back to work for Mr. Brimmer. By the week's end, he'd have his new bull. Yet, somehow the luster of it had dulled. Young Johnny had seemed plenty excited for the both of them. But as things were, he'd have little opportunity to enjoy the new purchase. Much as Chad would like to accommodate the boy, it had grown too painful to be around him and Charlotte. It was difficult enough to view them from a distance. Another face-to-face encounter would only worsen the sting.

He tapped the reins down on Buck and Tag's rumps, guiding them toward the mercantile. As he did, he caught a glimpse of Charlotte and Johnny riding into town. Another moment and they'd spot him. He steered the team to an empty spot outside Dottie's Restaurant and hopped from the wagon. He darted inside and made his way to an empty table by a window facing the street. He'd just caught a glimpse of them when a waitress approached.

"What can I get you?"

The question drew his attention from the window to the sturdy blond waitress poised over him. Too late for breakfast and too early for lunch, the mid-morning dash inside had seemed an apt means for hiding out, rather than a way to alleviate hunger. "Coffee, please."

The waitress gave a quick nod and strolled toward the

kitchen. Chad took another tentative glance out the window. Charlotte and Johnny had dismounted and were headed inside the post office. More than likely Charlotte was letting the Flynns know Johnny had been found, that or hoping for a letter from her kinfolk. Keeping a careful eye on the post office door, he nodded to the waitress as she poured him a steaming cup of coffee. "Thanks."

He took a sip of the hot brew, then set it in its saucer and waited. Moments later, the pair emerged and strolled onto the boardwalk. Charlotte cast a long glance toward the restaurant, causing Chad to slink back behind the blue-and-white checkered curtain. Had she recognized his horses and rig?

Worse yet, had she seen him dart inside like a coward?

At last, she took Johnny's hand and started toward the mercantile. Chad breathed a sigh of relief and leaned back in his seat. Hungry or not, it appeared he'd either need to order something or sip at his coffee until they'd finished.

He cupped his hands around the warm mug. He'd face Ian Crowley or thieving Rusty Duran without a moment's hesitation. But Charlotte?

Charlotte terrified him.

He peered into the murky blackness of the coffee. Or was it his own fears that had him running scared?

Whichever, it was fast becoming more work to avoid than face her.

CHARLOTTE PURSED HER LIPS, glaring over at the restaurant where Chad's wagon still remained. It most certainly wasn't her imagination. Chad was avoiding them. She'd seen the way he'd skittered off like a swarm of bees was after him. He couldn't possibly have reason to stay so long in the restaurant this time of morning.

She helped Johnny into the saddle and then heaved herself up, jaw clenched. She was losing patience with Chad.

Worse yet. She was losing hope.

Obviously, he wanted nothing to do with her and Johnny. She kicked her heels into Willow's flanks a bit too hard, and the horse lunged into a quick trot. Johnny's grip on the saddle horn tightened, reminding her she had more than herself to consider. She couldn't let Chad's inability to move forward hurt her any longer.

Charlotte was grateful they'd stopped by the Brodys to borrow a McGuffey reader on their way into town rather than wait until now. The further from Chad she could get the better.

"Are we headin' home now?" Johnny's question pierced through her solemn mood.

She pulled her thoughts back to Johnny. The challenge to teach him might just prove a welcome distraction. "Yes."

"You ain't gonna start schoolin' me just yet are ya?"

Charlotte arched a brow, convinced his grammar needed some schooling. "Not yet, but soon."

Johnny's soft moan hinted he was less enthused about learning than she was teaching.

They fell silent, with only the squeak of the saddle and the song of insects to fill their senses. In the quiet, Charlotte brought her thoughts back into focus. She'd lost her peace again, taken her worries and concerns about a future with Chad back from the Lord. It was so hard to give up what she wanted so deeply.

Forgive me, Lord. Help me to entrust Chad to You. You alone have the power to change hearts. Show him how to love again, whether that includes Johnny and me or not.

Chapter Forty

A CHORUS of bawls sounded from inside the corral. Chad propped his boot on the fence rail, gazing over the discontented group of calves. What a fine looking bunch. They'd doubled in size since he'd brought them home. Their mothers answered from the pasture beyond. Weaning was never a fun task, but a necessary one, if his herd was to grow.

Chad's gaze trailed to the bulky, red bull lurking at the back of the small herd. Big Red was everything Mr. Brimmer had claimed and more. The young bull's attentiveness to the cows was encouraging. He'd taken to them like a fly to molasses. By this time next year, Lord willing, the herd would have multiplied to near twenty head. A fraction of what he'd hoped to have, but a good start.

The cows ambled toward the creek, leaving their restless calves behind. A while longer and the bond between cow and calf would be severed, and they could roam together once again. Big Red followed behind the row of cows, his white head swaying with each stride.

Chad sank his hands in his pockets, widening his stance. Something about the scene made him heart-sore. Was it the air of contentment? The sense of belonging he wished for but didn't own that ate at him? He'd chosen this life of solitude. After what he'd been through, he couldn't stomach anything else.

Could he?

Emptiness washed over him as he turned toward the cabin, its lifeless frame resting cold and silent against the prairie. He envisioned Charlotte's slender form greeting him in the doorway, her face alight with gladness to see him. Weeks had passed since he'd allowed himself the pleasure of gazing into her emerald eyes.

His chest tightened. He was tired of this tug-of-war raging in his heart. He'd made his choice. It wouldn't do either of them any good to turn back now.

As the invitation song came to a close, Chad saw Johnny point in his direction. Charlotte's gaze flickered downward, her face having lost its smile. Chad knew it was his doing. He had to get away. It pained him too much to see. With a few courteous nods and greetings, he shouldered his way to the door. He'd barely downed the steps when he heard Johnny's boyish voice hail, "Mr. Avery, wait!"

The youngster's plea stopped him in his tracks. To continue on would be beyond rude. It would be downright hurtful. As he pivoted, the boy's smile returned.

Johnny ran to him, a glimmer in his eyes. "Did you get him?"

The tension in Chad's shoulders lessened, knowing at once the boy referred to his new bull. "Sure did. Had Big Red a couple of weeks now."

Johnny's eyes widened. "Is he a whopper? When can I see him?"

Soft footsteps came to a stop behind Johnny. Chad's gaze trained upward, taking in Charlotte's beige dress and womanly form, but stopped short of meeting her gaze. He swallowed down the lump choking off his words. How was he to answer? To invite Johnny and Charlotte over would go against everything he'd worked to undo. But to refuse was unthinkable. It would crush the boy. Best to answer his first question and ignore the second. "Yes. He's a big fella, a welcome addition to my herd."

"Can we come by and see him?"

"Johnny." It was hard to decipher if Charlotte's scolding was due to the boy's eagerness or her own apprehension.

Chad cleared his throat. "Maybe after he gets settled in a while."

Johnny's shoulders slumped in obvious disappointment.

Charlotte placed an arm around him, her tone a blend of hurt and angst. "Sorry to detain you, Mr. Avery. Come, Johnny."

With a final disheartened glance, Johnny gave into Charlotte's pull.

Chad watched them go, heaviness weighing on his chest. Their shattered expressions sealed his fate. He'd put them off one too many times. Now, he was destined to live out life alone.

Light rain pattered on the windowpane, rendering the darkened cabin even drearier. Unable to sleep, Charlotte rose from her bed and lit a lantern, doing her best not to awaken Johnny. Lightning flashed, followed by a distant rumble of thunder. The welcome rain was the first moisture they'd received in weeks, but did little to bolster her sullen mood.

Since their almost kiss the night of the shivaree, Chad had retreated deeper inside himself like an injured animal who'd given up hope. How could such a kind and caring man lose all will to interact with others?

Obviously his loss was too great. He'd loved too deeply to

surrender his heart a second time. The thought no longer angered her. Now, she pitied Chad.

Worse yet, she loved him. The pain of seeing him eaten away inside was more than she could bear. Why, just when she'd learned to give of herself, to truly love others, was Johnny the only one who was going to benefit?

Esther's letters called to her from the fireplace mantel. Taking them in hand, Charlotte eased into a chair before the dying embers cradled in the stone fireplace. She curled her feet up under her and leaned close to the lantern flame to read her sister's words yet again.

Please do come for a visit.

Though Charlotte had read the words dozens of times, now they seemed to leap out at her like a lost treasure. She held the letter to her chest. How wonderful it would be to see Ma and Esther and to experience the grandness of a large city. She'd been content to stay behind when she'd had hopes of settling down and sharing Chad's dream. But now, that hope had ended. There was nothing for her here, save Johnny.

What would he think of the idea?

She smiled, envisioning him with eyes glued to the surroundings, each new sight an adventure. Now that harvest had ended and the Flynns had sent word Johnny was hers to keep, what was to stop them from going?

A nervous twinge pricked her middle. In fact, what was to keep them from leaving for good? Autumn had all but arrived, with the harshness of winter soon to follow. Already there was a chill in the air each evening. She and Johnny would be hard pressed to survive out here alone. Chad being their closest neighbor, the thought of begging him for assistance didn't set well. In Cincinnati, Johnny would have every advantage. Proper schooling. Friends. The means to make something of his life.

Here all he had was her love.

The rain slowed to a trickle, the rumbles of thunder growing fainter. Charlotte smothered a yawn, too muddleheaded to think clearly. This was too important of decision to make hastily. Tomorrow, she'd give it more consideration and a great deal of prayer before broaching the idea further.

Standing, she refolded the letters and placed them on the mantel. She leaned against it, blinking back the sudden moisture pooling in her eyes. She didn't wish to leave, but somehow staying now seemed more grievous than going.

Chapter Forty-One

"A-MEN!" Johnny's head snapped up, his enthusiastic end to Charlotte's prayer followed by a reach for a biscuit.

"Can we read from that there Bible again tonight, Miss Charlotte?" He chomped on his biscuit, peering up at her with pale, blue eyes.

"If you like."

With a nod, he wiped a crumb from his cheek.

Warmth settled over her. She'd had little success interesting him in the McGuffey reader, but the boy had taken to the brave antics of Daniel and David as though starved for adventure and heroes. How much better if some of God's truths seeped into his heart in the process?

She toyed at her plateful of stew with her fork. For a time, Chad had been Johnny's hero. But now, a shadow fell over his face whenever he mentioned Mr. Avery, which had become less frequent of late. Their neighbor's disappointing lack of interest had wounded them both.

For two days now, she'd teetered back and forth about leaving, finally convincing herself it was as much Johnny's decision as her own. Now seemed as good of time as any to probe the topic. She wet her lips and stabbed at a chunk of potato. "Are you happy here with me, Johnny? I mean, do you ever get lonely?"

He shrugged and finished chewing his mouthful of food. "Not much. I like being with you."

The corners of Charlotte's mouth tipped upward slightly, then fell. "Do you ever wish you could be with other children your age?"

Johnny paused mid-bite and straightened. "You ain't thinkin' of sendin' me away again, are ya?"

She cradled his chin in her palm. "I'll never send you away. I only wondered if you'd be happier if it were more than just the two of us."

His eyes widened. "You gettin' married?"

With a shake of her head, Charlotte sat back. Somehow this subtle approach wasn't working. Time to be more direct. "No, Johnny. I mean I'm homesick for my ma and sister. Winters can be harsh here in Illinois. It may be difficult for us to manage. What would you think of joining them in Cincinnati?"

Understanding settled in his eyes. "You mean leave here and go to live in the city?"

"Yes. We've nothing to hold us here. You'd have other children to be with, new places to explore, and every advantage a boy could wish for." Charlotte pasted on a smile, trying to convince herself as much as Johnny.

"For how long?"

"Mmm. I don't know. For a while. If we like it well enough, maybe for good."

He poked at his biscuit. "Ain't never been to a big city, have you?"

"No, I haven't. It would be a new experience for us both."

"What about the chickens and Rubie and Mister . . . this place?" The slip of his tongue hinted it was more than the animals and homestead he would miss. Even considering Chad's negligence of them, the thought of never seeing him again was devastating.

"This place is my uncle's to do with as he sees fit, and I'm certain the Brodys would give the animals a good home or find someone to take them in."

Johnny's bottom lip jutted out, and he squinted up at her. "Is it what you want?"

"I think so, yes." Even as she spoke the words, her stomach clenched. In truth, she did miss her mother and sister, but the thought of leaving her prairie home and the man she'd come to love was akin to being gored by a bull.

He gave a soft huff. "Then I reckon so long as we're together, it don't matter where we are."

With a weak smile, Charlotte brushed a hand over his blond hair as he returned to eating, uncertain whether to be pleased or disappointed by his response. "Well, all right then. Tomorrow I'll wire Ma and Esther we're coming and make our travel plans. If all goes well, by week's end, we'll be on our way."

Johnny's half-hearted nod did little to reassure her she'd made the right decision. She could only pray she had.

"You're sure of this?"

Becky's question sliced through Charlotte like a well-sharpened knife. No, she wasn't sure. She only knew staying was no longer an option. Not with how she and Johnny felt about Chad. Maybe in the city, away from the constant reminders each time they passed by his place or saw him at church, they could forget. She was merely trying to do what she couldn't persuade Chad to do. Move forward.

She slipped an arm around Johnny's shoulders, knowing any reason she gave would be an excuse. "I really think it's for the best. With winter coming on, things will go much easier for us in the city with Ma and Esther."

By the Brodys' shared look, she'd not convinced them. Did they see through her? Did they sense she was running away?

She turned her attention to her uncle. "I'm grateful to you, Uncle Joseph, for letting me stay at your place these past few months. I don't know how to ever repay you."

He sat forward in his chair. "My pleasure. You did us a service in keepin' it up. I hate the thought of it sittin' empty again."

It did seem a shame. It was such a cozy cabin, one like she'd always dreamed of living in. She'd never hoped to live in some crowded apartment in a big city. Esther never complained in her letters, but there was always an underlying longing for home.

"If you need a ride north, I'll be happy to oblige." Pastor Brody's deep voice broke through her thoughts.

Johnny leaned into her, and she forced a smile. "Thank you. I was hoping you would."

"When will you leave?" A spark of sadness sounded in Becky's tone. The two of them had come a long way. Thanks in large part to Chad's poignant words.

Charlotte cringed inwardly. Oh, that her words had had a similar effect on him.

She worked to control the tremor in her voice. "Is day after tomorrow too soon?"

Pastor Brody glanced at Becky and then gave a quick nod. "I'll be by for you first thing."

"Thank you. We'll be ready."

Johnny's head lifted. "What about the animals?"

Uncle Joseph crossed his arms, his unseeing eyes turned downward. "Don't you worry none. Becky and I'll see to them."

Following a few hugs and tears, Charlotte and Johnny turned to leave. All that remained was to send the telegram alerting Esther and Ma they were coming.

Charlotte clasped Johnny's hand in hers, tightness gripping her throat at the thought of springing the news of him. Though she'd mentioned Johnny in her last letter, she wasn't certain how Ma would respond to taking in the youngster. Perhaps it was best to break the news to her in person. In her telegram, she'd say that she was bringing along a surprise. Otherwise, Ma would work herself into a frenzy before they arrived.

She squeezed Johnny's hand and gave him a wink. Once her mother met him, how could she refuse?

Something wasn't right.

Chad cocked his ear, eyes trained on the small cabin to the east. No matter how long he watched or listened, the only activity he witnessed from Charlotte or Johnny was a quick trip to the barn or chicken coop. No laughter. No chattering. As if the life had gone out of them. Had they received troubling news? Were they ill or fretting over some unknown concern? As far as he knew, Crowley hadn't caused a ruckus.

How Chad longed to go make certain all was well. Instead, he lay low in the grass until dusk blanketed the prairie. At last, he slipped away to Buck and headed home a bit unsettled in spirit. The entire mood of the place had shifted from one of contentment to one of terse silence.

Why?

The uncertainty of it ate at him like a disease. Worse yet, there wasn't a blessed thing he could do about it. Except pray.

The western sky flamed red as the sun dipped below the horizon. Chad leaned back in his saddle, drinking in its beauty. What better time to talk things over with the Creator than now, when He seemed so near?

Chapter Forty-Two

"READY?"

Dampness lined Charlotte's palms as she nodded to the pastor. "Yes. We're ready."

Her eyes panned the homestead, taking to memory its simple, rustic charm. In the few months she'd been here, the place had become almost as dear to her as her own home. Odd how precious a thing became when you were about to leave it. She glanced at Johnny, who looked as miserable as she felt. Managing a weak grin, she clasped his hand in hers. Surely in time, things would get easier.

Taking her satchel, Pastor Brody placed it in the back of the wagon. They would leave with the few possessions they'd come with, her father's worn hat and pocket watch among them.

Rubie pawed at Charlotte's feet, her soft whine signaling she knew something was amiss. Johnny pulled loose of Charlotte's grasp and threw his arms around the dog's neck. "Can't Rubie go with us?"

Charlotte bent down and gave the dog's face a rub. "I'm afraid we'd have no place to keep her in the city. She'll be happier here."

Pastor Brody stepped up beside them. "Don't you worry. She and our dog, Nugget, will have a big ol' time. Becky and Joseph will be by later to take the animals to our place."

Johnny loosened his hold on Rubie. "The chicks too?"

"Every last one." The pastor's warm tone was reassuring.

At Willow's high-pitched whinny, Charlotte's gaze fled to the barn. She gnawed at her lip to still its trembling. She hadn't expected leaving to be so difficult. For either of them. All they needed now was for Chad to come parading by. She squared her shoulders, determined not to be swayed by her swelling emotions. Placing a hand on Johnny's shoulder, she forced a smile. "You just wait. We'll have a lot of grand adventures ahead. There'll be so much to see and do. And we'll have Ma and Esther for company."

With a slow nod, he gave Rubie one last pet and turned toward the wagon.

Charlotte cast a final glance over her shoulder, heaviness pulling at her chest. Yes. There'd be many new adventures in the weeks and months ahead. But would they be the kind she and Johnny needed?

She closed her eyes, envisioning Chad smiling at her atop his horse, his handsome face full of life and vigor. The way it was meant to be. The way it had been the night of the shivaree, before he'd backed away. That night, she'd caught a glimpse of what life could be for them.

But it wasn't to be.

Opening her eyes, she swallowed down the hurt. Had she given up on him too soon? If there was even an inkling of a chance he could love her and Johnny, she would stay. But he was too steeped in his past for that. Too afraid of hurt.

With a deep breath, she took her place on the wagon seat next to Johnny, one prayer coursing through her.

Thy will be done, Lord.

CHAD HEAVED the ax over his head and then brought it down hard on the chunk of wood. The crack of the wood splitting vibrated across the prairie, loud against the stillness. He tossed the two halves in his growing pile. Placing another block of wood on the tree stump, he took up his ax. There'd been a chill in the air the past couple of mornings, a sure sign he needed to replenish his depleted supply of wood. His cabin, too, was still badly in need of repair before winter. There never seemed enough hours in the day to do what was needed.

Or was it that his priorities were a bit skewed? Somehow chinking cabin walls didn't appeal to him. But now that he'd finished work for Hank Brimmer, he had little excuse not to get to it. Cold weather would soon catch up with him.

He tapped the ax against the log's center, his thoughts turning to Charlotte and Johnny. They had a snug cabin to stay in, but would they have the sawn logs to heat it? Stocking a homestead with wood was a challenging task. Proud as Charlotte was, she most likely wouldn't accept an offer of help. But maybe he could sneak a few logs over in his saddlebags of an evening from time to time. The threat of Ian Crowley harming them seemed slimmer as time passed, but until the weather turned for the worse, he'd do his best to continue his nightly checks.

The rattle of a wagon drew his attention southward. Turning, he recognized Mrs. Brody at the reins, her father, Joseph, beside her. At their approach, Chad leaned his ax against the tree stump and turned to greet them. More than likely they'd come to settle up his earnings for the work he'd done.

Mrs. Brody brought the team to a halt beside him, a pleasant smile lining her lips. "Good day to you, Mr. Avery."

He tipped his hat. "Ma'am."

"Pa and I want to thank you for your help with harvest. You did us a great service."

"Glad to help."

Joseph reached in his pocket and brought out a sum of money. "Here you go, son, your well-deserved share of the crop."

"Much obliged." Chad strode over and took it from him, grateful. The income would help see him through until his bull calves were ready to sell. But more than that, he'd enjoyed the time spent with Charlotte.

With a nod, Joseph sat back on the seat. "We've another proposition for you if you're interested."

He propped his boot on the wagon wheel. "What might that be?"

"Your property being joined with ours, we wondered if you'd be interested in buying our place off us. Except the plot where my wife and daughter are buried. We'll not part with that portion."

Chad flinched, the question far from what he'd expected. What a proposal — more acreage for his herd to expand, a ready-made homestead, a new cabin that wouldn't need fixing. If only he could afford it.

And what of Charlotte? Did they intend to kick her out or force her to become his tenant?

He shifted his gaze from Joseph to his daughter and back again. Both appeared in earnest. Chad cleared his throat. "It's a grand offer, but I'm afraid I haven't the means to buy it."

Joseph pursed his lips. "We'd offer a fair price and not expect full payment all at once. Just as you're able."

"Truth is, we've no longer need of it and would rather see it go to someone like yourself who'd put it to use." Mrs. Brody's gentle encouragement had Chad's thoughts whirling.

But one thought rose above the rest. "What about Charlotte? What would she do?"

The pastor's wife seemed almost apologetic in her response.

"Charlotte's gone. She and Johnny are on their way to join her mother and sister in Cincinnati."

"What?" The word tumbled out before he could stop it. His breaths shallowed. "When?"

"Early this morning. Two, maybe three hours ago. We're on our way to our place now to collect the livestock."

Chad removed his hat and raked a hand through his hair. Had that been why Charlotte and Johnny seemed so sullen of late? By shutting them out had he unwittingly forced them into leaving?

A hint of curiosity flickered in Mrs. Brody's eyes. "They came by a couple of days ago and asked Matthew to take them to catch the canal boat in Peru. Neither seemed very eager to go."

Chad met her gaze. Did she guess the reason for his struggle? That he was somehow to blame for them leaving?

He swallowed the dryness in his throat, unable to shake the feeling something precious was being rent from him. Stepping away from the wagon, he donned his hat. "I thank you for telling me and for your kind offer. Can I get back to you once I've had time to sort things through?"

Joseph gave a slight nod. "Sure. Just let us know what you decide."

Mrs. Brody took up the reins, her gaze still fastened on him. A faint smile touched her lips. "Charlotte's a different person than she used to be, Mr. Avery. I give God the glory for that. But I like to think you had a part in it too."

With that, she tapped the reins and the horses plodded off, leaving Chad to ponder her words.

"Are you willing to sacrifice what could be for the sake of what you lost?"

Chad leaned against the fireplace mantel, staring at the

copper-plated picture of Lauren and young John, Charlotte's poignant question mulling around in his head.

Nearly two years had passed since his loved ones had perished in the fire. He'd determined then and there not to love again. Never thought he could. But he could no longer deny that he loved Charlotte and the boy. The thought of their leaving wrenched him apart.

Maybe he'd had an impact on Charlotte's change of heart, like Mrs. Brody alluded. But Charlotte had had a similar influence on him. As iron sharpens iron, the Lord had used them to refine each other, to spur each other to forgive past grievances and forget hidden hurts.

Charlotte had once likened him to Job, pining away for all he'd lost when the Lord had great blessings in store for him that he'd not yet experienced. Chad brushed a finger over the faces in the photograph. Could the same be true of him? If he had the courage to let go of his fears was the Lord ready to bless him?

Was he willing to sacrifice what could be for the sake of what he'd lost?

His mind cleared. For the first time it made sense to risk love again. If he allowed Charlotte to leave, he'd most certainly have lost her. But if she stayed, they stood every chance of happiness.

But was he too late?

Lifting the photo, he pressed it to his lips then set it face down on the mantel. Lauren and John would always have a place in his heart, but it was time to press forward, to give love room to grow.

And the Lord a chance to work His will.

WITH EACH TURN of the wheels, the pang of regret dug deeper into Charlotte. No matter how hard she tried, she couldn't convince herself or Johnny leaving was a good thing. She forced a smile, giving the boy a pat on the leg. He leaned against her, his head jogging up and down with each bump in the road. "How much longer?"

Pastor Brody kept his eyes on the path ahead. "I'd say another hour or so till we reach Peru. Then we'll get you on that canal boat to Chicago, and you'll be on your way."

Whether from the constant jostle of the wagon or the pastor's words, nausea tore at Charlotte's middle. The only thing spurring her on was the thought of seeing Ma and Esther. She could only hope they'd be receptive of her "surprise".

A faint shout stirred her to listen closer. Had it merely been the rattle of the wagon?

There it came again, louder, a man's voice calling to them from behind.

With a backward glance, Pastor Brody tightened his hold on the reins, slowing the team.

Johnny's head lifted. "What is it?"

"Thought I heard someone."

Then it hadn't been Charlotte's imagination. Turning, she craned her neck for a look. A cloud of dust trailed in the distance, and in its midst, a horseman. "There is someone."

Johnny whirled around, knees on the bench, straining to see. His eyes widened. "It's Mr. Avery!"

The enthusiasm in his voice sent Charlotte's heart pounding. "It can't be. The horse isn't a buckskin."

Johnny refused to be deterred. "He has another horse, Tag. She's fast. Just look at her go!"

It was true. Chad had come home with a second horse from his cattle venture, a scrawny chestnut mare that he'd restored to health. Charlotte dug her fingernails into the back of the wooden bench. Johnny was right. It did look like Chad. "Stop the wagon!"

At Charlotte's command, Pastor Brody pulled back on the reins, nearly sending her and Johnny tumbling from the wagon seat. Charlotte bit her lower lip. What could have spurred Chad to follow them all this way?

With bated breath, she waited for him to come alongside them, his horse coated with sweat and dust. His silvery eyes met hers, and she tried to decipher the depth of emotion streaming from them.

He dismounted and strode toward them. Stepping on the wagon hub, he brought himself to eye level. Charlotte met his gaze, her legs and arms atremble. She opened her mouth to speak, but no words came. He lifted his hat and held it to his chest, his sandy hair a shade darker where it wasn't tainted with dust. Charlotte leaned closer, drawn by his presence. Anxious. Hopeful. Confused. Almost forgetting Johnny and Pastor Brody sat behind her.

"You were right." His words were soft, airy, meant for her alone. "I'd be a fool to sacrifice what could be for what once was. I love you, Charlotte."

Moisture pooled in her eyes, blurring her vision. He loved her? How she'd longed to hear those words.

He touched a hand to her cheek. "I don't want to lose you. Stay with me."

The warmth of his hand on her face nearly stole her breath. Was she dreaming? Had it taken the thought of losing her to bring him around? Then her decision to leave hadn't been for nothing, but part of the Lord's grand design.

A slow blink sent tears streaming down her cheeks. "And I love you."

A gentle smile edged out the intensity of his gaze as he wiped away her tears.

Charlotte felt a tug on her sleeve and turned to find Johnny at her elbow. "Does this mean we can stay? That you're gonna get hitched?"

With a chuckle, Chad gave the boy's hair a tousle. "If she'll have me."

Warmth flooded over Charlotte at his words. She laced her hand in his. "Of course, I'll have you."

Lifting her from the wagon, Chad swung her to her feet, then turned to Pastor Brody. "I hope you brought your wedding sermon, preacher."

Pastor Brody gave a hardy laugh and patted his vest. "Right here in my Bible."

Charlotte swiped a stray strand of hair from her forehead, trying to catch her breath. "What? Now?"

"Why not? We've a preacher, haven't we? All we need are witnesses. Surely we can find a couple willing in the next town."

Charlotte stared up at him, dizzy from his nearness. "Next town?"

His chin lifted. "You promised your Ma and sister a visit, didn't you? Well, let's not disappoint. We'll make it our wedding trip."

Charlotte's lips parted in a wide smile. She'd be bringing Ma and Esther a surprise all right, though a different one than intended.

She gazed into the eyes of this man she'd grown to love, a prayer of gratitude to the Lord not enough. With a gleeful sigh, she wrapped her arms around his neck, never to let go.

Epilogue

One Year Later ~ September, 1856

CHAD GAZED out over the pastureland, his swelling herd of cattle dotting the acres of prairie. The Circle J Ranch was fast becoming all he'd hoped and dreamed it would be.

He sidled up behind Charlotte and slid his arms around her rounded belly, feeling the movement within. She turned to him, more beautiful than the day he'd married her, a sweet smile lining her lips. She leaned into him, giggling to herself as she watched Rubie chase Johnny through the golden tall-grass prairie.

How the Lord had blessed them. First with Joseph's generous wedding gift of the cabin and land for a mere half-share of the crop, and then with the abundance of calves born to grow their herd. Chad was truly beginning to feel like Job. Blessed beyond measure.

He kissed the nape of Charlotte's neck, her crimson hair tickling his forehead. Indeed his greatest gift, the one most precious to him, was his family — Charlotte, Johnny, and the child yet to be born.

God was a God of second chances, and Chad was so grateful he'd found his.

"As iron sharpens iron, so one person sharpens another."
(Proverbs 27:17)

Author's Notes

Dear Reader,

Thank you so much for investing your valuable time into reading Chad and Charlotte's story. I pray their journey touched your heart in some small way. I'm honored you've chosen to read *Under Prairie Skies*, and pray you've sensed the Lord's presence and healing within these words.

If you enjoyed *Under Prairie Skies*, I'd be honored if you would post a review on www.amazon.com www.barnesandnoble.com and/or www.goodreads.com. Reviews are so important to writers. Thank you very much!

If you missed Book One in the series, *Under This Same Sky*, I encourage you to read it to gain a richer understanding of what transpired prior to this second book. Also, be on the lookout for Book Three in my Prairie Sky Series, *Under Moonlit Skies*, which will feature Charlotte's younger sister, Esther as the heroine.

To be among the first to receive updates on my upcoming novels, event highlights, and giveaways, I invite you to sign up for my Author Newsletter by visiting my website: http://cynthiaroemer.com or my FB Author Page: https://www.facebook.com/AuthorCynthiaRoemer/

Thank you so much! God bless you all!

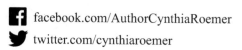

facebook.com/AuthorCynthiaRoemer

twitter.com/cynthiaroemer

About the Author

Cynthia Roemer is an Inspirational Historical Romance author from rural Illinois. She and her husband, Marvin, have been married for twenty-four years and have two college-aged sons. They enjoy quiet living and God's wondrous creation on their 300 acre farm.

Cynthia's thirst for writing began her junior year in high school when her short-story won first place in a local college writing contest. She went on to pursue a career in writing by earning a B.A. in English/Creative Writing from U of I of Springfield (IL). Since then, Cynthia has had over 100 articles/short-stories printed in various Christian teen and adult publications. She has been a finalist in both the ACFW Genesis Contest and the Olympia Contest and was named Historical/Historical Romance Category Winner in the Writers of the West (Rattler) Contest.

Her debut inspirational historical romance novel, *Under This Same Sky*, released in April, 2017. *Under Prairie Skies* is Book Two in her Prairie Sky Series. She is currently working on Book Three in the series, *Under Moonlit Skies*.

When she isn't writing, Cynthia enjoys spending time with her family, taking walks in the country, 4-wheeling, biking, gardening, and reading. To learn more about Cynthia and her writing, visit her website: http://cynthiaroemer.com and Face-

book Author Page: https://www.
facebook.com/AuthorCynthiaRoemer/

Also by Cynthia Roemer

She thought she'd lost everything ~

Instead she found what she needed most.

Illinois prairie - 1854

When a deadly tornado destroys Becky Hollister's farm, she must leave
the only home she's ever known, and the man she's begun to love to
accompany her injured father to St. Louis. Catapulted into a world of
unknowns, Becky finds solace in corresponding with the handsome
pastor back home. But when word comes that he is all but engaged to
someone else, she must call upon her faith to decipher her future.

Matthew Brody didn't intend on falling for Becky, but the unexpected
relationship, along with the Lord's gentle nudging, incite him to give
up his circuit riding and seek full-time ministry in the town of Miller
Creek, with the hope of one day making Becky his bride. But when his
old sweetheart comes to town, intent on winning him back—with the
entire town pulling for her—Matthew must choose between doing
what's expected and what his heart tells him is right.

She had her life planned out ~ until he rode in

Illinois prairie ~ 1859

After four long years away, Esther Stanton returns to the prairie to care for her sister Charlotte's family following the birth of her second child. The month-long stay seems much too short as Esther becomes acquainted with her brother-in-law's new ranch hand, Stewart Brant. When obligations compel her to return to Cincinnati and to the man her overbearing mother intends her to wed, she loses hope of ever knowing true happiness.

Still reeling from a hurtful relationship, Stew is reluctant to open his heart to Esther. But when he faces a life-threatening injury with Esther tending him, their bond deepens. Heartbroken when she leaves, he sets out after her and inadvertently stumbles across an illegal slave-trade operation, the knowledge of which puts him, as well as Esther and her family, in jeopardy.

Under Moonlit Skies is a <u>2020 Selah Awards</u> finalist the Western category.

Made in the USA
Coppell, TX
02 July 2021